PENGUIN BOOKS

DEAREST DOROTHY,
MERRY EVERYTHING!

Charlene Ann Baumbich is a popular speaker, journalist and author. Her stories, essays and columns have appeared in numerous magazines and newspapers, including the *Chicago Tribune,* the *Chicago Sun-Times* and *Today's Christian Woman.* She is also the author of the first four books in the Partonville series, *Dearest Dorothy, Are We There Yet?; Dearest Dorothy, Slow Down, You're Wearing Us Out!; Dearest Dorothy, Help! I've Lost Myself!; Dearest Dorothy, Who Would Have Ever Thought?!;* and six books of nonfiction. She lives in Glen Ellyn, Illinois. Learn more about Charlene at www.welcometopartonville.com.

Praise for Charlene Ann Baumbich's
Dearest Dorothy Series

Dearest Dorothy, Who Would Have Ever Thought?!

"In a sea of CBA heroines who are unfailingly young and beautiful, readers identify with Dorothy, the plucky 80-something grandma who's a demon at the wheel. Baby, you can drive our car."
   —*Publishers Weekly* (Picks for Funny Faith Series)

"With the down-home spiritual wisdom and small-town-living laughs that made the first few books of the series so successful, author Charlene Ann Baumbich has served up another entertaining slice of Partonville life for longtime Dearest Dorothy fans and new readers alike."   —*Boomer Times & Senior Life*

"Charming."   —*Albuquerque Journal*

"There's something for everyone here: love, laughter, inspiration, mystery and hysterical mayhem caused by a hacksaw wielding madwoman. . . . I recommend taking frequent trips to Partonville."
   —*Everything! Naperville* (FL)

"Another fantastic chapter in the continuing saga of Partonville, Crooked Creek Farm, the Happy Hookers and Dearest Dorothy. One of the most phenomenal aspects of Charlene's writing is her ability to create developing characters that are both unbelievable and wholly believable at the same time, and, in this book, she employs that talent to the max. . . . You can't read one of Charlene's Dearest Dorothy books without recognizing the characters, empathizing with the characters and gaining new insight into your own heart. Thank You Charlene!"   —*Epitaph-News*

Dearest Dorothy, Help! I've Lost Myself!

"Fans of Jan Karon's Mitford or Philip Gulley's Harmony will revel in the antics of the residents of Partonville . . . the characters are quirky and charming; there are several laugh-out-loud moments; and Baumbich offers gentle inspiration without hammering readers over the head with God, whom Dorothy delightfully calls 'The Big Guy.'"   —*Publishers Weekly*

"Every small town needs a resident like Dorothy Jean Wetstra."
                                                              —*The Hartford Courant*

Dearest Dorothy, Slow Down, You're Wearing Us Out!

"Be warned—this series is addictive. You'll soon be hooked on the small town of Partonville and its cast of assorted characters."
                                                              —*Bookreporter.com*

"For readers who enjoy books that celebrate life's simple pleasures, 87-year-old Dorothy Jean Wetstra and her beloved town of Partonville, Ill., are sure to become instant favorites . . . hilarious and touching."   —*Evening Star* (Hanover, PA)

"Baumbich has created a town readers will want to visit and people they'll want to meet . . . engaging, believable, real, funny, and poignant."   —*Church Libraries*

Dearest Dorothy, Are We There Yet?

"All of the other crazy wonderful characters in these books make the pages come alive. The whole town has a life, an energy to it. From Harry's Grill to the Happy Hookers meetings, you just know that something exciting's going to be happening. If you enjoyed Jan Karon's Mitford series, I think you'll love the Dearest Dorothy series."
                                                              —*Christian Fiction Reviewer*

"[Baumbich] has crafted a story using humor and Christian values to follow the issues facing everyday people."
                                                              —*Northwest DuPage Press*

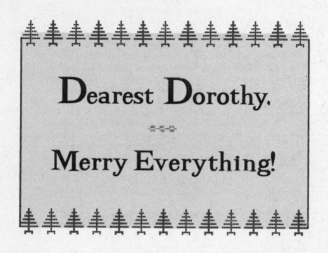

Dearest Dorothy,

Merry Everything!

Charlene Ann Baumbich

PENGUIN BOOKS

PENGUIN BOOKS
Published by the Penguin Group
Penguin Group (USA) Inc.,
375 Hudson Street, New York, New York 10014, U.S.A.
Penguin Group (Canada), 90 Eglinton Avenue East, Suite 700, Toronto,
Ontario, Canada M4P 2Y3 (a division of Pearson Penguin Canada Inc.)
Penguin Books Ltd, 80 Strand, London WC2R 0RL, England
Penguin Ireland, 25 St Stephen's Green, Dublin 2, Ireland (a division of Penguin Books Ltd)
Penguin Group (Australia), 250 Camberwell Road, Camberwell,
Victoria 3124, Australia (a division of Pearson Australia Group Pty Ltd)
Penguin Books India Pvt Ltd, 11 Community Centre, Panchsheel Park, New Delhi - 110 017, India
Penguin Group (NZ), cnr Airborne and Rosedale Roads, Albany,
Auckland 1310, New Zealand (a division of Pearson New Zealand Ltd)
Penguin Books (South Africa) (Pty) Ltd, 24 Sturdee Avenue,
Rosebank, Johannesburg 2196, South Africa

Penguin Books Ltd, Registered Offices:
80 Strand, London WC2R 0RL, England

First published in Penguin Books 2006

1 3 5 7 9 10 8 6 4 2

Copyright © Charlene Ann Baumbich, 2006
All rights reserved

Publisher's Note
This is a work of fiction. Names, characters, places, and incidents either are the product
of the authors' imagination or are used fictitiously, and any resemblance to actual persons,
living or dead, business establishments, events, or locales is entirely coincidental.

LIBRARY OF CONGRESS CATALOGING-IN-PUBLICATION DATA
Baumbich, Charlene Ann, 1945–
Dearest Dorothy, merry everything / Charlene Ann Baumbich.
p. cm. – (Dearest Dorothy ; bk. 5)
ISBN 0-14-303791-9
1. Older women–Fiction. 2. Illinois–Fiction. I. Title.
II. Series: Baumbich, Charlene Ann, 1945– Dearest Dorothy ; bk. 5.
PS3602.A963D427 2006
813'.54–dc22   2006045176

Printed in the United States of America
Set in Berthold Garamond
Designed by Sabrina Bowers

＊＊＊

Acknowledgments

The older I get, the more amazed I am by the HUGE wad of stuff I don't know. That in and of itself wouldn't be such an issue (HA!) if the fine folks in Partonville (from those who do the planning and building, to the guy who does the burying) didn't have to know what *they* were talking about. So in order to help *them* wax knowledgeable, I called on the expertise of a fine batch of gentlemen in Winona, Minnesota, the beautiful place I "hide" to write. Thank you, Jim Carlson (see if you can spot his "secretly coded" character's name so you can detect what *he* helped me with), Howard Keller (who will probably be hearing from me again as the mini-mall renovations continue), Nick Doenes (Realtor Extraordinaire) and Tim Hansen, who is a licensed funeral director, not an "undertaker," like Eugene insists on being. I also send a sincere thanks to Croft Waddington, another fine gentleman, but one who lives in Illinois and who therefore understands what needs to happen in a law office in Partonville.

Lest you think I don't seek the company of women for guidance, thank you Shirley Johnson (back to Winona) for helping this old lady learn that things HAVE changed in driving school. Kudos to Katherine Carlson for your careful editorial eye and for teaching me how to spell D'oh! Carolyn Carlson, bless your Executive Editorial Heart for con-

tinuing to believe in my circle-the-square town and for so
gracefully helping me bring it to life. To the rest of the crew
at Penguin Books, especially Maggie Payette, bless your hardworking hearts. Now hear me SHOUT from the rooftops
that Danielle Egan-Miller, my sterling agent, has not only
guided me, but steered, dragged, drop-kicked, cheered and
carried me through a wild year in the cyclonic waters of
publishing. She is a patient saint.

George John Baumbich, thank YOU (XOXOXOXOXO)
for allowing me to circle the square for months on end.
There would be no Partonville without your freedom, your
anchor, your love.

Introduction

⨯ ⨯ ⨯

And now, welcome to Partonville, a circle-the-square town in the northern part of southern Illinois, where oldsters are young, trees have names and chickens sometimes do odd–very odd–things.

Dearest Dorothy,
Merry Everything!

1

⧫ ⧫ ⧫

Josh flipped the interior light on and looked in the rear-view mirror, not to check on the traffic traveling seventy miles per hour behind him but to take note of the arch of his eyebrows. After a quick study he realized his stepmom had been right: same as his dad's. He flipped off the light and drew his attention back to the road in front of him, to the darkness made darker by what looked to be an impending storm making its way across the flat farmlands. He could barely make out the silhouette of a barn maybe a half mile off to his right. *Looks like a giant down on its haunches sneaking through the storm. Eerie.* His eyes darted back to the mirror for one more quick peek, especially at that left eyebrow, the only one he could raise independently of the other—same as his dad. He flipped on the light and watched himself give the inherited brow a quick up-and-down salute, which is what had first caused his stepmom to notice the similarity.

Keep your eyes on the road, Joshmeister! He turned off the light and faced forward, assuming a posture of one who'd been scolded. Although the keep-your-eyes-on-the-road thought came in the form of a self-inflicted reprimand, he knew it was just the type of thing his friend Dorothy would say to him if she caught him looking at his eyebrows in the mirror rather than the road. Although she was one of the few people to call him Joshmeister, especially in their e-mails, she'd never be as harsh on him as he was on himself. He knew the feisty eighty-eight-year-old well enough to know she'd have said the words *kindly*, but she would have made her point. His mom, now *she* would have YELLED it. Nonetheless, he was over four hours into the last leg of his first solo road trip and getting careless with his driving only fifty miles from home would not be smart. He needed a stern word, even if he was the only one present to deliver it. He stiffened his spine and snapped his full attention back to the task at hand. Of course, his mind wandered. . . .

Before Josh left Partonville, Dorothy was reveling in the joy of having her sons and grandsons in town to take part in the Thanksgiving festivities. The only time Josh had gotten to spend with them was a brief hello the night before he left. Their lively company made him sorrier than ever that he had to go. *All in all, I've only been gone less than . . . let's see . . . fifty-five hours.* But he missed Dorothy and wondered how things had gone for her, how the community Thanksgiving dinner at the church had turned out—really. During a brief phone conversation with his mom, all she'd told him was that there had been some kind of a "wrestling match" with a turkey. Said he wouldn't *believe* it. Said she'd give him details when he got home. He was also anxious to get the recap on Dorothy's birthday party yesterday. Although her birthday was actually on Thanksgiving this year, May Belle had invited everyone, including his mom, the day after Thanksgiving for a birthday celebration complete with turkey leftovers. He hated to miss all the fun. Well, not that he hadn't had *any* fun in Chicago, but it was not the same as spending time with a whole pack of people he'd grown to care about, which reminded him of his beautiful Shelby. He wondered how her holiday had gone and hoped she'd missed him as much as he'd missed her. She had so many cousins and nieces and nephews that she'd probably been too busy to even give him a second thought. He guessed that's why she hadn't answered the e-mail he sent from his dad's. Maybe she could go with him to deliver Dorothy's birthday gift which he had wrapped and ready in his bedroom. He could hardly *wait* for Dorothy to see it. When would he give it to her? *Tomorrow at church? Nah, Shelby won't be there.* Or maybe later in the day. He inhaled, imagining he could already smell the clean scent of her silky blond hair.

He sat up straight again and repositioned his hands on the steering wheel to nine and three o'clock, just the way he'd been taught in drivers' education not that long ago. He remembered how his mom had said, "When I learned to drive, it was ten and two o'clock. Are you sure you heard your instructor correctly?" "Yes, Mom. Sometimes things change after a billion years." And sometimes she made him nuts, he thought.

He'd spent his Thanksgiving weekend in Chicago at his dad and stepmom's and ended up way behind on sleep. Their daybed was like a brick, but it was either that or the floor since his two half-siblings and his stepmom's extended family members filled all the real beds. Between getting to sleep late the night before his journey to Chicago, spending the full day after Thanksgiving in downtown Chicago looking at Christmas store windows followed by another restless night of sleep, he'd awakened tired. Then a late brunch with "the family" (his dad had insisted) and a few too-brief hours this afternoon with his best friend, Alex, he was not only exhausted, but distracted and—he never thought he would admit this—wishing his mom, no matter how annoying she could be, were in the car with him, if for no other reason

than the conversation and/or yelling to help keep him
awake.

Air! I need some fresh air! Despite a falling mixture of rain
and snow he decided to crack the two front windows, at least
that had been his intention. He pushed the electronic buttons hard, causing the windows to automatically open *all* the
way as he fumbled to readjust them. Since he wasn't wearing
his coat, which made him feel crowded when he drove, he
cranked up the heater to compensate for the sudden cool-
down. But even with the windows cracked it soon became so
hot that his windows started to fog over, so he lowered the
climate control again and fumbled to find the defogger button. When he finally got the defogger activated, he looked
up and discovered that the car had drifted across the center
line of I-57. Without thinking to check his sideview mirror, he
veered back into his lane. His heart began pounding as he realized the disasters he'd mindlessly and miraculously missed.
Good thing nobody was passing me—on either *side!*

When he spotted the road sign for the next exit, he
flipped on the blinker. *Time to mainline some caffeine and pull
myself together.* Although he hated to stop so close to home,
it felt too dangerous not to. If he only stopped for a few
minutes that should still get him home by 9:30 P.M. He'd
use his cell phone to call his mom and tell her he was running a little behind. *But not until you are off the road and
parked! No more distractions!*

⚏⚏⚏

Dorothy was seated in the middle of her couch, her teen
grandsons, Steven and Bradley, flanking her, with Sheba,
Dorothy's wiry-haired, brown-and-black, eight-year-old mutt
dog, curled up in her lap. They'd made a big deal out of

tucking their grandma in with an old quilt she kept tossed over the back of the couch. They'd placed a throw pillow behind her head, scooted the footstool over from the side chair and propped her feet up on it, lifting her legs as though they belonged to a pink (her trademark color and today she wore a pink sweat suit) rag doll rather than a five-foot ten-inch woman with an ample body. A little too ample, she'd mused lately, but nonetheless a mostly working body, one for which she gave thanks—even though she did take a heart medication and pop an occasional nitroglycerine.

Jacob, her older son, handed her a mug of hot tea with a dollop of honey stirred in. Vinnie, his younger brother and the father of Steven and Bradley, followed close behind with a TV table in one hand, and in the other a plate piled with the last piece of lemon chiffon cake left over from her birthday party the day before. "You boys are spoiling me! I tell you, I won't know how to take care of myself after you're all gone!" A shadow flickered across her face just thinking about the void their absence would leave. *Less than eighteen hours until Vinnie and the boys depart for Denver!* she noticed with a quick peek at the old Register wall clock. Jacob was scheduled to leave for Philadelphia on Monday, just one short day after that.

"I doubt you can *be* spoiled, Mom," Vinnie said, handing Steven the cake while he set up the table. "You've been taking care of yourself for decades now, and none the worse for wear, I might add. Better let us wait on you while you've got the chance." When he reached to retrieve the cake from Steven, he caught his son sliding his finger around the edge of the bountiful icing. "HEY! That's Grandma's!"

"Who do you think I learned this from?" Steven said, dipping his icing-smeared finger into his mouth. Dorothy took the plate and with one slick move swiped the entire edge of the frosting off the cake and onto her pinky. She'd scalped it clean as a whistle. She held up her stealth conquest and pointed it at Vinnie. "Yeah! Where do you think he learned that?" The giant wad of icing started to slide off her finger and she rushed it into her mouth in the nick of time. They all cracked up laughing, Dorothy laughing so hard she had to struggle to keep from spewing the entire mouthful. Sheba was already lapping up the remaining smear of icing from her owner's hand.

"Mom," Jacob said sternly, trying to sound reprimand-ing, "look what you're teaching my nephews!" He scruffed Steven on the head, then stepped over his mother's ex-tended legs to bonk Bradley who launched off the couch and grabbed his uncle's right hand before it could land on the crown of his head.

"Think I'm old and strong enough to take you yet, Uncle Jacob? Huh? *Huh*?" No need to explain the implication; some Wetstra traditions needed no words. In a wink they were both sprawled head-to-head on the floor on their bel-lies, left forearms supporting their upper bodies, right elbows on the floor, right hands linked in an arm-wrestling lock. Vin-nie settled into Bradley's vacated spot on the couch to watch the competition. Sheba jumped off Dorothy's lap assuming the boys were on the floor to play with her and they had to tell her to get back in Grandma's lap, which she did.

"Sheba," Dorothy said, "first they tuck me in so tightly I can't move, then they sequester you. I bet they're afraid we could whip 'em if we had the chance! Or are they worried we might turn their challenge into tag-team wrestling like we saw on the television the other night?"

"Oh, like *that* would ever happen," Steven said with a laugh.

"You think not?" Dorothy asked, wearing a devilish grin. "Well then, you haven't seen The Dreaded Dorothy and Sheba the Wonderlick in action! Let's sick 'em, Wonderlick!" she said, launching a surprised Sheba toward her son. "You get Vinnie and I'll take Steven!" As if Sheba understood English, and most in Partonville thought she did, she began licking Vinnie on the chin while Dorothy started tickling Steven under the arms.

"All right, you three . . . four," Jacob added when Sheba started barking. "*We're* the show here."

"On the count, Uncle Jacob," Bradley said. "Ready, set . . ."

"GO!" Jacob shouted before the count was over. In one swift move he'd pinned Bradley's hand to the floor at the same moment Steven yelped "I GIVE!" so his grandmother would stop the tickling. Since he was a baby, he'd been rendered powerless by her tickling attacks.

"No fair! No *fair!*" Bradley protested to his Uncle Jacob.

"You see, Bradley, it doesn't matter if you're old and strong enough, it only matters if I'm still *smart* enough," Jacob retorted.

"Out of the way, son," Vinnie said as he set Sheba back in Dorothy's lap. None too gracefully (he definitely wasn't in his brother's hard-body shape), he lowered himself to the floor and positioned himself in front of Jacob as Bradley rolled aside. "Let me show you what Mr. Smarter *Than* looks like when pitted against He Who Thinks He's Smart *Enough*."

"Now boys," Dorothy said trying to stifle a grin and sound commanding, "no roughhousing inside." She wondered how many times throughout their youth she'd uttered those words. *Funny, Lord, how a thing you most want to end eventually does, and then you miss it. Thank You for these memories, both the oldies and the ones being formed right this second.*

Jacob and Vinnie locked arms and rocked their stretched bodies until they were balanced and settled on their bracing forearms. Jacob looked over his shoulder at his mom. "I assure you, our dear mother, you were heard but shall be completely ignored. Besides, this will not be roughhousing; this will be another swift defeat." Sheba let out one loud bark as though to reprimand him. Jacob turned back toward his brother, whose face wasn't more than a foot from his own. They locked eyes. "Somebody give us the count." But before the last word was out of Jacob's mouth, Vinnie had made his move. After fifty-plus years of brotherhood, Jacob had anticipated just that and was prepared for the challenge. What Vinnie perceived to be his jump, Jacob—who spent hours in the gym every week—quickly made up for in reflexes and conditioning.

But Vinnie wouldn't go down as easily as Jacob thought. After all, his sons were watching and he didn't want to get shown up in front of them, especially by his own brother. Although the wrestlers continued to smile, their fun game soon turned For Real, as they used to call it in their "dare you, double-dare you" days. It wasn't long before Vinnie's face was red and Jacob's chiding voice revealed a tad of shortness in his breath, which made Vinnie smile through his gritted teeth.

"Don't you boys hurt yourselves now," Dorothy said. She'd moved the footstool aside and leaned forward to watch, half-eaten piece of cake still on the plate in her hands, Sheba keeping a close eye on it. "You'll like to give yourselves hernias!" The boys now flanked their dad on the floor, as though their presence could infuse him with their youthful strength. "If you all knock yourselves silly down there, then what? The new doctor in town doesn't make house calls, and old Doc Nielson sure couldn't get you up off the floor. I'll have to call 911 for the whole lot of you!"

"Don't worry, Grandma," Bradley said, "this'll be over in a minute. Dad's about to take him."

"Come on, Dad!" Steven shouted, slapping his palm on the carpet. "Show him what you got!" Vinnie's only response was to grunt. Jacob smiled. He knew Vinnie was running out of gas, and yet, the cheers of his sons spurred him on to fight the fight with all his might.

Three against one, Jacob thought, all three whom he loved. *Strength in numbers,* he mused just before the pang arrived: with no family of *his* own, who was there to root for *him*? Such an odd thought out of nowhere, and in the middle of a *game.* The residue of the emotion drove straight into his forearm (he'd long ago learned to disperse hard emotions into physicality) and he unquestionably knew the moment had arrived when he could take his brother, no matter how many people were on his team.

But he didn't.

In the midst of "COME ON, DAD! HE'S FADING! YOU GOT HIM!" Jacob started to grunt and groan. In a sudden shudder of surrender, he allowed Vinnie to crash his hand to the floor. The boys went wild cheering as they piled on their dad in a victory tumble. Jacob rolled onto his back and huffed and puffed, partly for real.

Vinnie raised his arm high in the air, fist balled. "Oh, Victory! How *sweet* your rewards!"

"I'll take you next time, bro," Jacob said, his momentary pang of hollowness quickly lost in the triumphant joy of his brother and nephews. "Just wait and see."

Dorothy laughed at the sight of them. Here were her two men-children nearly head-to-head down on their backs, talking to each other while they faced the ceiling, her grandsons' gangly limbs flailing here and there as they punched the air and touted their father's "Victory!"

After the celebration ended, the boys crawled up off the floor and reclaimed their seats on the couch, but not before tucking Dorothy back in and once again propping her feet up on the footstool.

"Who were you rooting for, Grandma?" Bradley, the younger of the two, asked as he threw his arm over her shoulder.

"Now, how could I pick one of my own sons over the other, huh? It would be like having to choose one of *you*!" She looked from Bradley to Steven, then back again.

"Yeah, but wasn't Dad something?" Steven asked, gently elbowing her.

"He certainly was. He certainly was."

"He was too much for me," Jacob said as he sat up with a groan and caught his mother's eye.

She winked at him, and he knew she knew he'd thrown the match. His entire life she'd been able to detect when he was telling a whopper, when he was sad even though he was laughing, when he was tenderhearted even when he often sounded so gruff. She'd always been able to read him, his "hidden" feelings revealing themselves to her as though he were a neon sign.

2

⧫ ⧫ ⧫

Even though Katie was bone tired, she was restless, fidgeting up and down out of her cushy chair to get a drink of water, find another magazine, retrieve a slice of lemon for her water, jot a few more notes about her new business venture, look out the front window again *(Come on, Josh! You should be home by now!),* check the clock again (9:05 P.M.), plop back down and begin the cycle—again. It had been a long day.

When she'd phoned her friend Jessica at noon to see how she was feeling—early pregnancy playing havoc with her stomach and energy—Jessica had sounded like she was holding tight to her last drop of sanity. Sarah Sue was cranking at the top of her five-month-old lungs in the background. Paul was torn between trying to help Jessica clean the rooms at their little motel and calming their teething daughter. Katie, happy for something to do, decided to offer her assistance (not that she had ever in her life stooped to anything like cleaning hotel rooms—nor was she about to do that now) by coming over and entertaining Sarah Sue so her parents could finish their tasks and maybe have a moment to rest, regain their sanity. Then for the umpteenth time that weekend she'd remembered she didn't have a car; Josh had taken it to Chicago. Just like when your electricity is out and you keep mindlessly flipping on the light switches, she thought. She was stranded out in the country several miles from being able to help anyone. "Let me phone Dorothy's," she'd said, after having vocalized her *DUH* of a moment. "Maybe one of her sons or grandsons can come get me, bring me over."

"That's a really sweet offer, Katie, and I thank you for it," Jessica said, "but we'll make it. We always do. Besides, Dorothy doesn't get to visit with her family very often; let's not tear any of them away over a few unmade beds."

"You're probably right. But this *really* has me thinking. Josh has been bugging me for a car and I've been holding strong against it, but I'm beginning to wonder if it's maybe time. Single parenting has so many drawbacks, and I guess making solo decisions and being stranded alone are just a couple more on the long list. Now I know how Josh feels out here on the farm when I'm gone with the SUV for the evening. You'd think after all these years of the two of us being on our own, I'd be better at this."

"Well, owning a car is a big responsibility, Katie. Don't beat yourself up. I think you're right to move slowly with that decision. Plus I can't even imagine how much the insurance must cost you for a teen driver, let alone doubling that with another car! Isn't it more for boys, too?"

"Let me assure you, I am paying a bundle." In the background Katie heard a motel guest asking Paul a question and realized she was holding up the Joys' progress. "I'm hanging up now, Jessica. I'm sorry for taking this much of your time. The longer I keep you on the phone listening to me whine, whine, whine, the less you're getting done."

"I really do have to go, Katie. But now I feel like I'm abandoning *you* in your hour of need."

"You know what Dorothy would say about my hour of need, don't you?"

"What?"

"Pish-posh." Their chuckling helped lighten their spirits, even if only the slightest bit. After their quick good-byes, without another thought Katie dialed Dorothy's number. Couldn't hurt to just *ask* Dorothy if she'd mind if someone gave her a ride.

"Wetstras," the male voice said.

Katie had been expecting Dorothy to answer and she had no idea which of her sons or grandsons might be on the other end of the line. Although Jacob's voice was somewhat lower than Vinnie's, they were similar. And boys, well, at their ages of development, they could sometimes sound like anyone from the father to the baby sister. "This is Katie Durbin. Who am I speaking with, please?"

"Katie Durbin, I recognized your voice. This is Jacob."

"Hello, Jacob. Is your mother there?"

"Nice chatting with you, too," he said dryly. But she neither heard him calling his mother nor the clunky sounds one usually hears when someone's passing off the phone.

Katie didn't know Jacob very well. She had a hard time telling when or even if he was kidding, that is unless she could see his bright, warm smile which didn't seem to appear very often, at least when she was around. He was a high-powered attorney and pretty much sounded like one at all times. They'd gotten off on the wrong foot when they'd first met, Jacob not trusting Katie and Katie resenting him for it. They'd ultimately settled into a wary truce before he headed back to Philadelphia after coming to Partonville to help his mother with her auction. A couple months later she'd enjoyed the company of both the Wetstra brothers at the Thanksgiving dinner at United Methodist Church, and she and Jacob had gotten along fine during Dorothy's birthday party yesterday. He'd seemed a little different to her from that last visit, less edgy. But today, here he was on the other end of the phone line somehow making her feel guilty for not chatting it up with him.

"Has everyone recuperated from Thanksgiving and the big birthday party yesterday?" she asked, attempting to engage in polite conversation.

"I think so. But we're just taking it easy anyway. Josh home yet?"

"No, he's not due until this evening. I'll be glad when he arrives."

"Yes, I bet you will."

Silence. Katie heard what sounded like dice rolling in the background, then she heard Dorothy laugh, one of the guys counting, "three," more rolling dice, "four . . ."

"Bunco?" Katie asked.

"How'd you guess?"

Flat. His tone of voice was absolutely flat. Was he kidding? Being sarcastic? Just asking?

"The counting. I heard the counting and the sound of the dice bouncing on the table."

"Oh, that's right. You're a Happy Hooker now, too, aren't you?"

"I can tell you I never thought I'd hear myself answering yes to *that* question!" He didn't exactly laugh, but she heard his muffled chuckle.

"No, I don't imagine you did. And you also can't imagine how odd it is to say your *mother* is a Happy Hooker and be . . . *happy* about it." Katie burst into laughter. "But sometimes it's just more fun *not* to explain the whole 'they used to hook rugs and thus the name' story. Gives folks something to fret about. Everybody needs more to fret about these days, don't you think?"

"Hey, I've got my hands full waiting for Joshua to return from Chicago, thank you very much. Sometimes I wonder what I was thinking, letting him set out alone at sixteen."

"Right."

Is he affirming my worry or my stupidity?

More silence.

"So, you want to talk to my mom. I'll see if I can tear her away from the action. Since I'm not playing—it's Mom and Vinnie against the boys—I guess I could offer to sit in for her turn while you ladies catch up on whatever might have happened since . . . yesterday."

Just when she'd conclude he had a dry sense of humor, he didn't sound funny at all. Sarcastically rude was more like it. What was *up* with him!

"Actually, I was going to ask her a favor. But now . . . You know, don't bother her."

"Nonsense. Mom," Jacob said without covering the mouthpiece, "it's Katie. I'll roll for you." Just like that, he had neither honored her request to not bother his mother, nor had he said good-bye. It flicked through her mind that Dorothy'd once told her he'd never married. She said he'd come close a couple times, but just when everyone thought he'd be popping the question he'd either find something wrong with the woman or things just seemed to fall apart. *Maybe the women got tired of trying to figure him out.*

"Katie! I'm glad to hear from you! Did Josh make it home okay?"

"No, he's not due back until this evening."

"In that case, how'd you like to come over and play a few rounds of bunco with us while you wait? We were just about to make popcorn."

Katie heard a male voice counting in the background, a tone of high-pitched exaggeration lacing the words. "One-sy! Two-sy!" She heard the sound of shaking then rolling dice. "Three-sy . . ."

"Uncle Jacob!" one of the boys yelped. "Do you think *you're* a Happy Hooker now?" Everyone including Dorothy was now laughing at his antics.

Jessica was right, Katie thought. She shouldn't interrupt their family time. "Thank you for the invite, but I don't have a car."

"For goodness sakes, of course you don't! What's wrong with me?" Someone shouted BUNCO! in the background. Dorothy laughed again. "How about I send a runner to come get you?"

After a brief argument with herself as to whether or not to even bring up Jessica, Katie plowed ahead and explained the situation. She knew Dorothy adored Jessica, too.

"I'll tell you what," Dorothy said, "I'll send Jacob Henry right over to pick you up and run you over to the Lamp Post. Maybe he can give the Joys a hand, too. To be honest, bunco isn't really his thing, or so he tells us. Nonetheless, he just rolled one!"

"That's not necessary, Dorothy!" Katie said, more emphatically than she intended.

"Don't be silly. He's been antsy today anyway. Besides, I don't need him here stealing my bunco thunder. Nobody will want me for a partner again if he sticks around with those hot rolling fingers! Get your coat on, he'll be right over. Good-bye, dear."

Dorothy set the receiver in the cradle and turned to look at Jacob, who was giving her his squinty evil eye, the same look he used to give her as an obstinate five-year-old. Obviously he'd overheard her conversation.

≜ ≜ ≜

Sarah Sue stopped squawking the moment Paul released her into Katie's open arms. What was it about fresh arms that so often quieted a baby's cranking?

Katie and Jacob had pulled up just when Paul, Jessica and Sarah Sue were exiting unit number nine, bundles of sheets and towels in Paul's arms and a wailing, flailing baby in his wife's. Although he and Jessica both insisted Katie and Jacob, who Jessica would later confess to Paul seemed a little awkward with each other, shouldn't have gone to all the trouble, it was obvious their arrival and offer to help was quite welcome. They only had three more units to go, and working together without the distraction of a hysterical baby, they'd be done in a flash.

"Oh, Sarah Sue, you have no idea how exhausting you'll *really* become to your parents when you get to be sixteen and are off on your first road trip," Katie said, rubbing her cheek against Sarah Sue's. "They think you're physically tiring *now!* They have no idea of the mental exhaustion that awaits them."

"Oh, THANKS!" Jessica responded. "Just what I need to hear with a new one on the way!"

"Any time," Katie said, tapping Sarah Sue on the nose and brushing a tear off her cheek.

"Hey! I thought you came by to help us, not torment us!" Paul said with a grin, rolling the room-cleaning cart down the sidewalk in front of room number ten. "I assume your presence means Josh isn't home yet?" Paul directed his eyes to Jacob, feeling like they were all talking around him. Jacob looked toward Katie figuring the question was hers to answer. Sarah Sue was occupied with one of Katie's earrings.

"No. Otherwise I swear I'd send him over here to clean rooms just so I'd know where he was. I'm expecting him around eight tonight. Until then, I'll be holding my breath. Right, Sarah Sue?" Katie said, plucking at Sarah Sue's chunky cheeks, then disengaging her busy fingers from her earring. Jacob watched Katie handle Sarah Sue. This was a side of her he hadn't seen before. She appeared softer, less guarded than usual.

Katie and Jacob took Sarah Sue to Paul and Jessica's living room while the parents went back to work. To Katie's surprise, Jacob had offered to help with the cleaning but they vehemently declined, saying he'd already done more than enough.

♣ ♣ ♣

Within an hour and a half Jacob had picked Katie up, dropped her back off and returned to his mom's. Katie had insisted on getting right home, saying Josh might have left a message on the answering machine.

"How'd it go?" Dorothy asked, pinning her eyes on Jacob. "I thought you might invite her back with you."

"Me too," Vinnie said. Jacob noticed his brother's voice sounded disappointed. He shrugged his shoulders as though to shake off any further questions. "Went fine," he said, diverting his eyes toward the abandoned scorecards, picking them up and giving them a quick study. "So, the young bucks took you old fogies, huh?" Again, he didn't look at his mom but walked to the refrigerator and opened the door. "What are we doing about dinner tonight? I could use a change from turkey. Partonville got any good pizza joints yet?"

⚹⚹⚹

After Jacob dropped Katie off she spent the rest of her evening tidying up, then resting (she was surprised to rediscover how tiring entertaining a baby can make you feel), then clock-watching, which had made her a nervous wreck, but she looked at the clock again anyway. This time it was 9:11 P.M. Still no Josh. No Josh, no phone call, no headlights coming up the driveway. She went to the kitchen and picked up the phone receiver just to make sure there wasn't something wrong with the phone lines. Dial tone. She retrieved her cell phone from the kitchen table and checked it for messages—as though she hadn't been on high alert just waiting for it to ring. Nothing. She sighed, went to the fridge and rustled a couple baby carrots out of the bag, chomping down on one as though decapitating it.

She decided to break down and phone her ex to make sure Josh had gotten out of town when he'd first predicted; maybe she was needlessly fretting. A quick call let her know Bruce had no idea what time Josh had actually headed for Partonville. "He ate a noonish brunch here with the family and then was off to see his friend." Bruce's use of the words "the family" prickled Katie, a reaction that made her feel small. After all, Bruce was Josh's dad, and extended family— no matter *how* extended, via half-siblings and step-relatives— was Josh's family, too. She just wished Bruce would take more sincere interest in his son who felt like he played second fiddle to Bruce's "daily kids," as Josh often referred to his half-siblings. Then again, she was still striving to get better at parenting herself so she decided to cut Bruce some slack—as usual.

Last Katie had heard, Josh's plans were to have a late breakfast with Alex, not Bruce and company, and hit the road by early to mid afternoon. She now knew he'd hooked up with Alex later in the day than he'd anticipated. *You should have called me, Joshua Matthew!* She'd assumed no word from him had meant that he was on his original schedule. She'd staved off calling his cell phone so as not to look like an overanxious mother, but now she couldn't wait any longer. After four rings she got his voice mail. Either he didn't have his phone turned on, he was out of a service range or. . . .

No, I am not going there! She decided that in this case, no news *was* good news—until it applied to Josh who, when he got home, was going to find himself grounded for being so inconsiderate.

3

⧾⧾⧾

At 9:55 P.M. Eugene Casey's phone startled him out of a sound sleep. Eugene was Partonville's only undertaker and sole owner of Casey's Funeral Home where the slogan on the sign out front read FINAL RESTING PLACE PREPARATIONS. Back in Eugene's schooling days students became undertakers, not morticians like his younger colleagues now called themselves. "If becoming an undertaker was good enough for me then, it's good enough for me to remain," he'd told his wife. He saw no need to give himself a fancy new label just because some whippersnappers had decided to split a hair.

After a lifetime in the business, one might think Eugene would be used to the phone ringing in the middle of the night, but the older he got (and he was plenty old), the earlier "the middle of the night" felt. Plus, since that fateful day thirty years ago when he'd received news of his own father's death via a 2 A.M. phone call, being awakened by a ringing phone still set his heart to hammering. He was glad his wife was in bed beside him—although instant fears for his children, his grandchildren and now one great-grandchild raced through his mind. He pushed the covers aside and swung his legs around, his toes finally locating his worn leather slippers he always left bedside. He groped until he located the light switch on the small bedside lamp, flicked it on and looked at the wind-up alarm clock sitting next to the light. He'd only been asleep thirty-five minutes. He cleared his throat and said, "Casey's Funeral Home. Eugene Casey speaking."

His wife rolled onto her side facing him, mostly to roll off the better of her two ears so she could hear the news. Shortly after he answered he gave her a slight wave of his fingers and shake of his head to let her know everything was okay with *their* family. Between silent gaps she heard her husband saying, "Is that right?" "I can't believe it!" "What a shame." "How's his mother? I can't even imagine how she'll handle this." "Does anyone know what he was doing out on the highway at that hour of the night?" "Yes, I'll be right down to collect him." "You got that right."

"Such a tragic accident," he said after he hung up. Even though he still didn't know the details, he shared what he'd learned with his wife as he rummaged around their bedroom getting dressed.

"Bundle up," she said. "The temperature's been dropping all day. *You* be careful on the roads, hear me? I know the hospital and the funeral home aren't that far away, but if the roads had enough black ice to send one car careening. . . . "

"Don't you worry, sweet pea. You know I always bundle up, especially during flu season. I promise I won't go over twenty miles per hour." He needn't have said that; everybody in Partonville doubted one of his vehicles had ever, rain or shine, gone over twenty-five.

⁂

10:20 P.M. Katie was now officially beside herself and on the verge of phoning the state police when she saw headlights coming down the gravel road, then turning up their lane. She couldn't tell what type of vehicle it was through the glare of the headlights. Visions of finding a pair of state troopers on her doorstep constricted her throat and brought instant tears to her eyes. If the pulsating fear in a worried mother-heart had the ability to stop blood from flowing, that would explain why Katie suddenly turned ash white. Fear froze her in place as she squinted, trying to catch a glimpse of the vehicle's size and color, fog and a light drizzle doing nothing to enhance her view.

Then she saw it: a flash of off-white, the shape of a large SUV, the assurance it was her Lexus—and her son! By the time the SUV was under the scrutiny of the farm's floodlight mounted high on a pole near the back door, Katie was standing beside its driver's-side door. No coat, no hat, just happy tears rushing down her cheeks. Josh turned off the ignition and slumped back in the seat. He hadn't realized how tightly he'd been wound sitting behind the wheel like a ramrod soldier. Katie opened the door and threw her arms around his neck.

"Joshua!" she said through a sob. The impact of her raw and bold emotions coupled with the release of his tensions caused his eyes to fill, too. Although he had often observed that some women (like Alex's mom) could burst into tears during sappy television commercials, his mom was always buttoned up. This unadulterated show of emotions not only surprised him, but at the end of the world's longest day, his mom's clinging hug touched and comforted his needy, weary soul.

"Oh, *Mom*! I'm so glad to see you, too. You have no idea how long this day has been."

"Oh, yes I do," she whispered into his ear.

After they held on to each other for several more seconds, Katie backed off to get a look at her son's face. That's when he noticed she was damp and shivering. "Come on, let's get inside, Mom. I'll bring my stuff in tomorrow. Right now I just want to get out from behind the wheel and crawl into my own bed."

The two of them entered the farmhouse in silence. Katie was exhausted and relieved and yet, now that she knew he was safe, she couldn't help wanting to grill him. Josh plunked down in a kitchen chair and Katie sat across from him. Before she could open her mouth Josh said, "Here's the short version. I promise to tell you every little detail tomorrow, but for right now, please, *please,* Mom, just accept this and let me go to bed, okay?" She hesitated before nodding her head.

"I was supposed to have breakfast with Alex this morning but Dad insisted I have breakfast at his house, which ended up to be really late."

"I know. He told me."

"You talked to Dad today?"

"Some time after nine this evening I just couldn't take it anymore, Joshua. I was worried sick. I also talked to Alex, and he said you got out of town after four. At least I knew not to expect you at eight anymore." She had to bite her tongue to keep from launching into a lecture about why he hadn't called.

"Things went well until about four hours into my drive home. I never knew how mind-numbing a long-distance drive by yourself can be. And I hadn't slept well at Dad's so I was tired before I started, and after hours of driving I got *so* tired I knew I needed to pull over and get some air, walk around, down some caffeine."

"Oh, Josh! I shouldn't have let you go a. . . ."

"Mom! Just *listen.*" It was an exhausted, desperate command. Normally Katie would have taken offense at his tone of voice, which he saw in her eyes, but before giving her a chance to crank up, he added, "Be happy I knew enough to pull over, okay?" She reluctantly nodded. "So I stopped at the first exit I saw, which is where I planned to phone you. I can't remember exactly what time it was, probably around eight-thirty or so. I went to the john, bought a Snicker's bar and a can of Coke, and when I got back to the car, a giant tanker truck had parked partially behind me and no matter how hard I tried, I couldn't maneuver my way out. So I waited. After fifteen minutes I finally went into the restaurant side of the place to scout down the driver who was busy flirting with the waitress half his age." Josh shook his head in disgust, stretched his arms back over his head and yawned. "Finally he moved his truck and I headed back to the highway. Then I remembered I hadn't called you." Katie opened her mouth but Josh put his fingers to his lips, signaling her to keep it zipped. "Rather than stop again, I figured I'd just get on home. And Mom, how many times have you warned me not to drive and talk on the cell phone? Huh?" She shrugged her shoulders. "Right. Then I thought I saw deer eyes near the side of the road so I tapped the brakes and realized it had gotten slick." Katie's eyebrows shot up in the air. "No, I didn't lose control, I just fishtailed a little bit. But I slowed my driving *way* down.

"Then probably about five miles from our exit I saw all these flashing lights up ahead, I mean like fifty zillion of them. Both lanes came to a complete stop for like thirty minutes." He yawned, rubbed his eyes. "I finally got out my cell phone to call you, only to discover I had a dead battery. The charger was in my bag in the back but I didn't want to get out and look for it since it didn't seem safe. I swear, Mom," he said, "I just kept thinking, *safety* first."

Katie bit her lip. "I'm going to make myself a cup of chamomile tea. Would you like one?" He shook his head. She filled the teapot with water, set it on the stove and turned the knob, then sat back down across the table from him. "Go on."

He leaned back in his chair and stretched, then slumped forward again. "Eventually they opened up one lane of traffic. But man, what a mess! There was an old car upside down in the ditch and another car spun out backwards on the shoulder, a bunch of tow trucks, an ambulance. . . . Hard to tell what happened." He brushed his fingers back through his hair. "Anyway, I made it." He rose, stepped around to her side of the table and gave her another quick squeeze. "It was a long trip home and I'm sorry I worried you, Mom. Thank you for not yelling. I tried my best."

Katie gently pinched his cheek, the same way she had pinched Sarah Sue's earlier in the day. How quickly the years passed. She then kissed him where she'd pinched him and said, "Good night, Josh. You look exhausted. If you wake up in time for church tomorrow we'll go, but if you don't, just get your rest. You've got school Monday. Thank you for telling me everything."

But, of course, he hadn't.

"I was sure glad to see that WELCOME TO PARTONVILLE sign, as glad as I'm going to be to see my own bed. Any real bed, for that matter." *And to wake up in it tomorrow, alive.*

⚜ ⚜ ⚜

"I'm sorry to call this late, Chloe," Katie said into the receiver, talking to her ex-husband's wife in a hushed tone so as not to awaken Josh, "but I knew Bruce would want to know Josh made it home okay."

"He figured as much." Chloe chuckled. "When he went to bed he wasn't worried. He said Josh and Alex probably just lost track of the time. But thanks anyway for letting us know. I'll tell him in the morning."

Katie was angry. How could they just brush this off so casually? How could Bruce have gone to bed not knowing if his son had made it home safely? "Well, when Bruce wakes up tomorrow, tell him the reason Josh was late was because of an accident. But he'll be fine. Good night." And she hung up. *Good.* She sat up waiting for the call from Bruce, sure Chloe would wake her husband to mention an *accident.* She wanted to catch the phone before it rang twice so it didn't awaken Josh. But the call never came. *Go figure,* Katie thought.

No wonder he's my ex! The whole experience washed up a laundry list of why she *still* didn't trust men, beginning with the fact Bruce had left her for a younger woman, the woman who answered while Bruce was sleeping, the woman who'd borne him two children—whom he knew to be safely tucked in *their* beds. She lathered herself into a tizzy just thinking about it. But by the time she'd settled herself down enough to crawl into bed, she'd begun to question her own responses. Maybe Bruce was right not to worry so much. Maybe she *had* overreacted. *Then again, maybe he's just too dumb to know better. Then again, maybe* I'm *too dumb to know better.*

Once in bed she felt guilted into a short prayer. "God, thank You for bringing my son home safely. Thank You for friends who love him. Thank You for . . . (sigh) . . . his father, since . . . without him I wouldn't have my son. And I'm only a *little* sorry I might have intentionally misled Chloe. Amen."

Okay, so it wasn't much of a prayer, but it was all she had

in her at this late hour. Besides, saying clever prayers wasn't her strong point since she hadn't been praying that long to begin with. And if Dorothy was right about God, He already knew everything she'd just told Him anyway. But Dorothy said God didn't care about how *fancy* prayers were, He just liked to hear them. *Whatever!* she thought as she thwacked her pillow, rolled into the fetal position and pulled the covers up around her neck. Eventually she began to drift off, one final prayer springing from her deepest self, ushering forth a tear from her deepest well. *Thank You. My son is home. Thank You.*

4

‡‡‡

Typically word of a death—especially the death of a life-time resident—would have spread throughout Partonville well before church convened on Sunday. But since the accident happened late Saturday night after most of the townsfolk were tucked in, Pastor Delbert Carol Jr.—who had been summoned to the hospital at 10 P.M. last night to pray for, and with, the victim's mother, who'd been in the car as well—had the unpleasant duty that morning to let his United Methodist Church parishioners know about the passing of a faithful congregant: Richard (Rick) Lawson, Partonville's only Attorney at Law.

‡‡‡

Rick Lawson was known by nearly everyone in Partonville, population 1,400 plus. He was the sole attorney for most of their legalities, including all the town's business establishments and the United Methodist Church. If you hadn't met him through his services, anyone circling the square would have nonetheless known exactly where he did business since RICK LAWSON, ATTORNEY AT LAW was printed in large block letters on his first-floor door, which was right next to Hornsby's Shoe Emporium on the square. The door opened to a narrow and steep stairway to his second-floor offices, the ascent causing him to huff and puff every working day of his life. He'd often joked that one day his final step on this earth would probably be one of those top three stairs. Who could have guessed he'd instead be sitting down and seatbelted in when he drew his last breath?

Perhaps more than anyone else in town, he was recognizable from a distance: no matter what the season, he wore worn, pin-striped, shiny wool pants a couple sizes too big held up by suspenders that were too long and sagged across a blue-and-white striped shirt with frayed cuffs. When the temperature dropped below forty degrees, he donned an ancient London Fog raincoat sans the lining which was too warm for his portly, hot-blooded self. Many speculated he only owned one set of clothes, but the truth was he owned several sets exactly the same. "Lowers my stress level," he'd once told his secretary. "Got enough stress without tormenting myself over what to wear every morning." His secretary had often thought about the sense in his theory as she stood in front of her closet rifling coat hangers from left to right and right to left again, peeking at the clock, promising herself that today she would not be her usual five minutes late—a promise she could never quite seem to keep.

Rick's office was even more of a mess than his appearance: papers stacked two feet high, dust on his green vinyl chairs, chaos everywhere. And yet he was remarkable at his job, never missing a detail. It was magic, the way he could pull just the right paper out of just the right stack. He always strived his hardest to make sure folks' legal affairs were in order. He was a dedicated, enthusiastic saxophone player in the Partonville Community Band; a robust fan of the Wild Musketeers, Partonville's mostly senior citizens softball team; and a supporter of any other event, sporting or otherwise, that took place in and around the community. When Earl Justice, a mentally challenged dear man in his forties, delivered a phone-in order from Harry's Grill to Rick's office (which was often), Rick always tipped him a dollar, even though most in town gave him a quarter. It's just the way Rick was.

How had the accident happened? How is his mother doing, poor thing? Who could have guessed, and so close to home for such a terrible tragedy! Since he was the only attorney in town, who would handle *his* estate? Who would now handle theirs? Where were their wills physically located? What if they couldn't find them in his big mess of an office and who could they trust to look through it? Would his secretary surely have a nervous breakdown just trying to help whoever sort through whatever?

Most in town had either seen firsthand or heard about his chaotic place of business, including Katie Durbin, who'd had to deal with Rick when she first came to Partonville from Chicago to settle her Aunt Tess's estate, Rick having handled Tess's trust. He'd also helped Dorothy draw up the papers to sell Crooked Creek Farm to Katie, and he'd handled the documents to donate twenty acres of the farm to the conservation district for what would one day become Crooked Creek Park. Although Katie, an upper-crust "city slicker," was at first repelled by the sight of the slovenly man and his ramshackle office, she was surprised to learn how dedicated, knowledgeable and thoroughly he handled any issue thrown his way (yes, she'd seen him work his magic when retrieving Tess's papers from one of his giant piles), and with kindness to boot. She had grown to respect him as a businessman, and one thing was for certain: you didn't earn Katie Durbin's respect easily.

⁂

May Belle Justice's hands were shaking as she measured the fragrant ground coffee into the filter and once again fired up the church's giant coffee pot. The usual Meet and Greet gathering following church had gone into overtime following Pastor's shocking announcement about the death of Rick Lawson. This was one of those rare two-pot mornings, May Belle thought. As she collected abandoned coffee mugs and paper napkins from here and there and refilled cups, she couldn't help but overhear snippets of everyone's conversations about the awful news. One thing was constant, she observed: they just couldn't believe it, and neither could she.

Rick's death rocked May Belle's world in an unsuspecting way, and it set her hands to shaking. She could hardly remember a time she'd spoken with him throughout the decades when he hadn't encouraged her to "come on up, May Belle, honey" and get some papers in order concerning her beloved son, Earl. "What will happen to him, May Belle, if something happens to you? We never know when our number's up," he'd said, shaking his head. "Now you know we all love that boy of yours and would look out for him best we could, May Belle, but I doubt he could stay at your house alone, could he? Where would he go? What will he do? He's still your dependent, May Belle, and it's possible he'd become a ward of the state if you don't have a plan on paper. Please think about it, May Belle. *Please.*"

Rick had started lobbying for her legal instructions regarding Earl soon after her husband died so many years ago. He didn't ask because he wanted her business—goodness, everyone knew May Belle didn't have an ounce of extra cash for anything, let alone legal matters. But rather than bring it up to her in a way that made her feel poorly about her lack of funds, he'd say, "I'd gladly trade you one little official document for a few batches of your award-winning double chocolate brownies me and Mom love so much. You'll feel better knowing something is in place, May Belle." And so she would. But what? What *could* be put in place for her now forty-four-year-old son?

She'd heard people talk about group homes for "special needs" adults, but the closest of those types of facilities was in Hethrow and she knew Earl would have a hard time adjusting to living in what he would undoubtedly perceive to be commotion compared to their simple, quiet life together. Commotion was hard on Earl, even among those he knew well. Besides, who would deliver the noontime call-in meals from Harry's if Earl wasn't around? Who would bring Earl to UMC on Sundays where folks knew him? How would their best friend Dorothy—the one person whom Earl loved and *trusted* as much as his own mother—visit him now that Dorothy no longer drove? No, a group home far away from the Partonville square, where everything and everyone was familiar to her Earl, would not be right. But where *would* he go?

Why hadn't she once thought to ask Rick what he would suggest? And now it was too late. What was there to do but to make another pot of coffee, rub her tired back and continue to pray for God to grant her breath.

⚜ ⚜ ⚜

Maggie Malone plucked the handset to her Cinderella-shaped telephone from its billowing-dress cradle. The phone had been presented to her last Mother's Day by her grandchildren and great-grandchildren. Shelby'd spotted it in a mail order catalog and said to her mother, "Well, *that's* got Grannie M written all over it!" Ben, Maggie's husband of fifty-plus years, grumbled within himself every time he tried to wrap his strong meaty hand around the handset, Cinderella's head quite the obstacle. But he never once mentioned it to Maggie, since every ounce of torment was worth it just to watch his enthusiastic wife clap her hands in delight every time Cinderella's gown lit up when the phone rang.

Maggie's shop, La Feminique Hair Salon & Day Spa, was closed on Mondays, so Eugene knew to call her at home. Eugene had been visiting Sadie Lawson in the hospital that morning to talk about funeral arrangements for her son, and she'd asked him to please give Maggie a call. She said the new doctor in town, Doctor Nielson, thought she'd be released by Thursday at the absolute latest, but when "good old Doc Streator" had stopped by to pay her a visit, he thought Sadie should plan on a Friday release, just in case. "You're still gonna be plenty sore," Doc had told her. "And goodness, Sadie, you've lost your *son*." Doc could tell she was still in severe shock. "Give yourself at least a day of leeway in there between getting out of the hospital and dealing with a funeral." Although Sadie thought the new doc had done a good job of running tests and diagnosing her cracked ribs, sewing up her cuts, bandaging her leg and putting a sling on her arm, Doc Streator did a better job when it came to broken hearts.

Aside from her medical concerns and issues of the heart, there were other things to be considered, like the fact that Eugene Casey was colorblind and Sadie wanted Maggie to make sure her son's clothes matched for the viewing. Poor Eugene. He'd never been able to live down "that one time."

That one time two families had each dropped off clothing and accessories for their beloveds to wear and through an un-believable series of accidental mishaps, Eugene had mixed up the pieces to the outfits. Oh, that terrible one time when, to the shock of the onlookers, he had one woman wearing a red blouse, an orange vest and a green necklace. Maggie Malone never got over the fact that "anybody with a lick of color sense would have known that no woman in her right mind would be caught dead *or* alive in a getup like that. And that other poor soul!" she'd raved in her shop for a week after the funeral. "Could you even *believe* the color of that lipstick up against her skin tone!"

The calamity, as Maggie referred to it, had left everyone feeling sorry for Eugene's affliction, and yet to this day they still had to swallow down peals of laughter (almost never suc-cessfully) when they discussed it. Truth be known, while one of the families chose to ignore the mishap the best they could, the other believed the incident to be pure grace since it brought a much-needed dose of laughter into their heartache. "Gracie would have laughed harder than any of us!" Gracie's husband said. "Her laughter is one of the things I love . . . loved . . . most about her. I wonder if she didn't orchestrate the whole thing from heaven just to get us going!" When Arthur Landers had passed by for the viewing and said, "I ain't never seen Gracie look perkier!" the entire family had busted out in belly laughs right there in the greeting line. They'd laughed until they'd cried again, both avenues of ex-pression and release helping them bear their grief.

And so Sadie asked Eugene to find out if Maggie could help him dress and prepare her son because Maggie, a mother many times over as well as a woman with a careful eye for detail, would take tender care with her son's cowlick—oh, how she remembered studying that sweet little swirl on the top of his precious newborn head—and give his wooly eyebrows, such a defining part of her son's face, a nice trim. Sadie also asked Maggie if she might be able to come to her home when she got released to do *her* hair since she was sure she would not be up for a shop appointment. There were times, in fact, when Sadie didn't feel up to drawing her next breath, so deep was her despairing grief. And yet, there was an odd grace in the preoccupation of details since it meant for at least a moment, there was something to think about other than the truth that her precious child was gone.

Eugene had, of course, obliged Sadie's wishes and given Maggie a call. "Eugene, you know I'll do anything I can," Maggie said into Cinderella's left hand. "Tell Sadie not to worry, I'll take care of all those details for her. I am a little confused that she'd worry about Rick's clothes matching, though. That man only has one set of clothes and if we dressed him in anything else, folks wouldn't know who they were viewing!"

"You got that right," Eugene said with a sigh, a sorrowful heart and a swallowed down smile that comes with knowing a buddy well, a true buddy he was already missing. "I'll leave that to you to bring up with Sadie, though."

"Ask her if she wants her roots done or just needs a trim, Eugene. Never mind. I'll stop by and visit her myself. She can have visitors, right?"

"I reckon they let me in because I'm the undertaker. Don't rightly know. Can't see any reason why she can't, though. Better check with the hospital just to make sure. And be prepared, Maggie. Poor Sadie isn't quite herself."

"How could she be, Eugene? She's lost her son." A chill ran down Maggie's spine, the smiles and scent of each of her own nine children springing to mind. "Has Sadie set the funeral arrangements then?" Maggie was preparing to start spreading the word. Some "news" spread in a beauty shop was indeed idle gossip, but other times La Feminique Hair Salon & Day Spa was one of the best places to help dispense a piece of information everyone *needed* to know.

"Funeral is on for this Saturday. Doc thought she should wait until at least Monday, but Sadie said waiting a couple extra days wouldn't make burying her son any easier. She's got that right." When they hung up, Eugene shuddered at how closely death lurks. All he could think about was that even after a lifetime in the business, he'd *never* get used to the constant reminder.

5

⁂

"**M**om, I've got some news I hope you'll like," Jacob said, flipping his cell phone closed as he entered the kitchen where Dorothy was cleaning up their lunch dishes. She was keeping herself busy, trying not to reveal the depth of her sorrow over the fact that the last of her visiting family would be leaving within the next two hours—Vinnie and the boys had left yesterday before church. The weight of her family's departure was extra heavy this morning since she could not stop thinking about poor Sadie. Caroline Ann, Dorothy's daughter, had lost her battle with breast cancer a little over a decade ago and Dorothy knew you *never* get over the loss of a child.

"I hope I'll like your news, too, son. Yesterday brought all the bad news I can stand for a spell. Did you know when Rick was a freshman in high school I taught that boy how to play the saxophone? I couldn't believe he'd never had a lesson; he was a natural. The band is scheduled to play for the church Christmas service and he had the lead solo in the prelude to 'Oh Come All Ye Faithful.' I bet Raymond just has us skip the prelude now since it would be too sad for us to hear someone else playing his part." She stuffed her dish towel down into the glass she was holding and gave it a good twist, then carefully set the glass in her cabinet, wiping a tear from her cheek.

Just when Jacob was about to stand and put his arms around her, she surprised him by chuckling. "It's too bad you weren't here for the Centennial Plus Thirty. You'd have laughed yourself silly at Rick's rendition of 'Put on Your Old Blue Bonnet,' during which he actually wore one! I'll tell you, he had *everyone* in stitches. And now. . . . I could barely get to sleep after Josh left last night thinking about how close *he* came to being involved in that accident! When he told us after church how he'd actually seen the wreck, it just took my breath away. A few minutes earlier and. . . . Well, I was sure glad when Vinnie called to say he and the boys had arrived safely home. As much as I hate to see you go, I'll be glad to know you've made it to your home, too." She shook her head and swiped her dish towel around the edge of the last sandwich plate, then dabbed at her eyes before stowing the plate away. She hung the dish towel over the cabinet door beneath the sink and plopped down in a kitchen chair across from Jacob.

"Okay then. Enough already with my fretting. And Lord, keep me from any more of it!" she said rolling her eyes toward the heavens. "Give me the *good* news, son. You've got my undivided attention."

"That was my secretary. Looks like you won't be receiving a phone call from me tonight since I'm not going anywhere. You've got company for another week, maybe even a little longer, depending upon a few other loose ends."

"What?" She'd been so busy trying to let go of him, it wasn't sinking in she didn't have to just yet.

"To be honest, I was hoping for a better reaction," he said in that flat tone that often stumped Katie but which Jacob's mother, who adored his wry humor, understood.

"But I thought your plane leaves at six-thirty tonight."

"It does, but I don't have to be on it. I knew before I left Philly that there was an outside chance I'd be able to stay longer, but I didn't tell you because I didn't want to get your hopes up. Colleen just let me know it's a done deal."

Dorothy's eyes misted over as she sprang out of her chair and threw her arms around Jacob. "Oh, honey! That's just *wonderful*! I am *e-la-ted*!"

"That's more like it," he said, patting his mother on the back.

She sat back down in her chair, then clicked her tongue and rapped her knuckles on the table. "You know, there's probably not a whole lot I'll have to do for Rick's wake and funeral, but there'll be some. Other than that, I'm yours! And like your grandpa used to say, 'Life is for the living!' He sure was right. You remember him saying that?"

"No, but I wish I did. I wish I remembered a lot more about him."

"Me too. He was a dandy. But back to the living! What would you like to do while you're here? Let's live it up, get high on the hog!"

"Do? *Do?* I'm looking forward to doing nothing but visiting with you. In fact, I might just lock my briefcase in the trunk and give you the keys. It's too tempting to see it sitting over there." He stared at the worn butternut-colored leather for a moment, noticed the two papers sticking out the top and thought about the upcoming brief, then forced himself to look away. Yes, life—and there *was* a life apart from the courtroom, he kept reminding himself—*was* for the living.

Dorothy smiled at her son, then sighed. "Too bad Vinnie and the boys couldn't have stayed longer. I bet you fellows could have found a grand adventure or two."

"What? But what about us? You're not telling me you've

lost your sense of adventure, are you? I know you're getting old, Mom, but you're not decrepit yet! Are you?" Of course he was teasing her. But nonetheless, he'd noticed a few slightly slower things about her and. . . .

With her left hand she began rubbing the first knuckle of her right index finger (which he'd noticed her doing on more than one occasion), taking note how the cool weather always made her arthritis bumps act up. "Well, not decrepit. I'd say a good bit slowed down and a tad more achy. But you know me, I'm always up for a road trip! Now. You hide that briefcase in your trunk and give *me* those car keys." She stretched her leg out and waggled her foot. "My right foot is already itching for the gas pedal! Where could we go?"

"Sorry. Rental's only insured for me." Frankly he was thrilled when The Tank had died and she announced she wasn't going to replace it. He imagined the town breathed a collective sigh of relief, too. "Do you even *have* a driver's license anymore, Mom?"

"Yes sirree! I'm going to keep it in my wallet until it expires, and then I'm going to keep it there until I expire just in case my mind goes and I can't remember who I am."

They both laughed, but the joke struck Jacob in a raw place. He'd just represented a multimillionaire corporate client whose wife suffered from Alzheimer's. "I'd give everything I own to have her back, to trade in some of the time I spent in the office for just one more vacation with her," he'd told Jacob. "All this wealth and what good does it do? I can't buy her memory back. Can you even imagine?" Jacob had sat across from him in the gentleman's plush office. "My wife of fifty-four years looked right at me and said, 'I used to have a husband like you.' I'll tell you, I'm a damn tough guy, but I bawled like a baby after I tucked her in that night."

Jacob shook his head as if to knock the memory of the conversation from his mind and set to work pondering where he might take his mom while he was here. He knew she missed "gallivanting around," as she used to call it. He stuck his tongue into the side of his cheek far enough that it protruded outward like a jawbreaker might be rolling around in there, something he'd done since he was a kid— but only when his wheels were really turning. He'd had to train himself to leave the habit behind when he sat in a tense courtroom.

Dorothy took note of his cheek. "What are you thinking about, Jacob Henry?"

"I'm thinking about where we could go for a night or two. My bags are already packed and you could just throw a few things in that new hot pink backpack Josh gave you for your birthday—and by the way, *now* I see why you like that kid so much," he said, staring at the backpack she'd left on the kitchen counter. "I think a short road trip together might be good for both of us. You must be sick of being stranded here in Pardon-Me-Ville."

She tilted her head as she considered his statement. "As odd as this sounds, perhaps even to me, I'm content here for the most part. Oh," she said, pausing a moment while tapping her fingertips together, "I'd still like to be able to fire up The Tank to drive May Belle to La Feminique the way I used to, or run to Hethrow to do *whatever,* or stop in at the Landerses and torment Arthur for a spell." Arthur's old garage was on the Landerses' property. She smiled at the memory of The Tank's hood in the air, Arthur's body folded over the front end, his head stuck down in the engine while the two of them engaged in lively bantering. "Or check out that new restaurant in Yorkville Nellie Ruth raves about, see if they got a New York dish on the menu yet." Jacob raised his eyebrows. "Long story for another time," she said. "But mostly when I get a hankerin' to run away it's just to head to the farm, have me a good long walk down by the creek or spend an hour or two in the barn. Other than that, though, I'm mostly happy in my little house in my little town with all my friends around. Of course, I wish my family lived closer, but . . ." she stopped and pursed her lips, "no, I wouldn't move to Denver or Philadelphia either. You boys would be the only people I'd know and it wouldn't take you long to get plum sick of trying to entertain me. Besides, how would the Happy Hookers ever get along without me!" She winked at her handsome son.

"It makes me feel good to know you're content here, Mom. I know leaving the farm and giving up driving were really hard for you. I don't know if I've said this or not, but I'm proud of the way you've adjusted." She folded her hands together, gave an upward nod to acknowledge the One who'd seen her through.

"You know, I don't know about going somewhere for a night or two," she said, shifting the subject, "let's table that idea for the moment. But maybe while you're here you could help me put up a few Christmas decorations. That would be just dandy! I let most of them go in the auction, but I believe I've got me a few in a box or three somewhere. I think maybe that kind of stuff ended up in the closet in the back bedroom where you're staying since the boys left. I don't know where else I could have possibly put it. This little house doesn't exactly abound with storage space." Jacob scooted his chair back. "Oh, not right this minute, son! Just some time before you go and only if you feel like it."

"Speaking of Christmas, what's going to happen with

the Hookers' Christmas party now that you're not at the farm?" He cast his eyes around her tiny place. "You used to get quite the mob every year."

"Mob indeed. That party grew to about sixty or seventy people the last few years. Biggest holiday shindig around." She screwed up her face. "Don't know what's gonna happen now, though. I'd been kind of hoping Katie might let me host it out at the farm. Or co-host it . . . or. . . ."

"Did she turn you down?"

"Haven't brought it up. Timing never seemed right."

"Maybe you could hold it at the park district building or something. Besides, you sure people would want to gather out at the farm now that she owns it? From what I could tell at the auction, she was pretty much considered an outsider. 'That City Slicker,' I believe it was."

Dorothy smiled, paused a moment before she answered. "They *still* call her the City Slicker. But oh, she's a smart one all right! She sometimes calls *herself* that now, and right to people's faces, which really gets 'em good. Our very own Acting Mayor Gladys McKern used to be one of her biggest opponents, but I think Gladys was just jealous of Katie. By now, I think she has all but won Gladys over with her new mini-mall venture."

"Mini mall?" he said, shaking his head. He pictured a tacky strip mall sprouting up along the highway near the edge of town.

"Katie bought the old Taninger building—you remember Les and Irene and their big old furniture store on the square, don't you?—and she's going to convert it into a mini mall. I'll tell you, everybody is so excited about the possibilities! She's going to maybe bring in an antiques place and a repairman, a tea room. . . . She said she wants to try to breathe new life into our old Pardon-Me-Ville of a square."

Jacob's mood seemed to darken. "Interesting. Of course, anything she does to add value to Partonville certainly ups the price of the farm, now doesn't it." He'd sounded nearly surly by the end of his sentence.

"Yes. And it would up the price of my little house here, too, and the Landerses' farm and Harry's Grill and . . . well, nothing wrong with *that*! The types of stores she wants to bring in would give a few folks the chance to make some extra dollars, too, whether they'd be working in them or maybe putting crafts on consignment—she's talking about a consignment store or. . . . Even May Belle is hopeful about the chance to make some extra money with her baking since there's talk of that tea room. Times have been hard around here, Jacob, what with the mine layoffs. There's even a rumor they might close down the Number Nine, which could be devastating. And as far as business, aside from Swappin' Sam's, Partonville doesn't have a single drawing card right now." She gave a strong nod of approval. "I for one am excited about the whole mini mall. And I'll tell you, when that woman puts her mind to something, she's got the courage, determination and financial resources to make it happen. She's hoping to get the renovations on the building started before Christmas."

Jacob didn't want to squelch his mother's optimism, but the whole idea of Katie's infiltrating every aspect of Partonville fed his wariness about her. He just didn't know *what* to think about that woman, so he decided not to. "Let's go find those decorations, Mom," he said, launching himself out of his chair and rolling up his sleeves.

6

⨞ ⨞ ⨞

"I can't wait for Christmas vacation. After four days off for Thanksgiving, being back at school stinks," Kevin said, right before shoving a fork twirled with spaghetti into his mouth, two-inch wild strands hanging from it this way and that. He chomped, swallowed and made a face. "For one thing, even my mom's leftover turkey casserole—with *peas* in it—tastes better than this slop."

Josh, sitting across the lunchroom table from his buddy Kevin Mooney, sucked the end of a noodle until it reeled up into his mouth (his mother would ground him for a month if she saw that), the final inch breaking off and dropping down onto his plate. "Doesn't even slurp right," he said, grabbing his fork and knife and proceeding to cut his entire pile into little squares.

Deborah Arnold sat next to Kevin, so close to him there was barely room for her to lift her hand to her mouth. They'd been quite the item since the Pumpkin Festival dance, not to mention the hot-buzz couple around school, what with Kevin being Mr. Jock and she a former prom queen. With perfect etiquette, she used her spoon as a receptacle to swirl her spaghetti into a tidy loop-de-loop around the end of her fork. She opened her mouth just so and slid the orange little ball in while observing Josh's completely inappropriate cutting procedure, then she crinkled up her nose. Josh glanced up and noticed her expression. "See, it *is* awful!" he said. "Trust us, men know these things."

"You know, I've never seen anyone," she paused and wrinkled her nose again, "*cut* their spaghetti before," she said, daintily wiping her mouth with the corner of her paper napkin before folding it and placing it atop her spaghetti, then peeling the orange she'd selected for dessert.

"The Manners Gestapo strikes again!" Kevin said, opening wide his eyes, throwing up his hands and trembling his head as though he were terrified, clearly making fun of both of them.

Josh grinned at his buddy, scooped up one of his perfectly square bites, shoveled it in, chomped and grimaced. "Squares don't taste any better. I hope I see Shelby coming in for her lunch hour when we leave. I gotta warn her." He took another bite, swallowed it whole and washed it down with a gulp of milk. "I don't remember the cafeteria spaghetti ever tasting this putrid. Makes me wanna hurl."

Deb was still peeling her orange, carefully digging her polished nails into the rind, trying to peel it in one length, occasionally inspecting her fingertips to see if she was ruining her manicure. "Josh, how's your mom's mini mall coming? I can hardly wait! I've heard buzz about an upscale fashion boutique, a spa, a diamond store," she stopped talking while she removed the last bit of peel, smiling at her perfect one-piece conquest, "a rare book store, designer home decorations, imported rugs. . . ."

"Last I heard, she was talking about a pet store that sold exotic monkeys," he said, grinning at Kevin.

"You two! Can you *ever* be serious about *anything?*"

"Well, I can only speak for myself," Kevin said, "but here's serious for ya: the Lakers are fourteen and six! How about that, Josh?" Even though Josh didn't really follow. basketball, or any professional sports, for that matter, he said, "Now that *is* serious, my man." He and Kevin wrapped knuckles across the table. Deb shook her head in disgust, gathered her books, gave Kevin a quick peck on the cheek and said she needed to visit the ladies room before the next class began. She noticed Anita and Becky staring at her, or rather at Josh. *Give it up, you two,* she thought. *He's taken.* They'd had hopeless crushes on Josh since the first day of school when he'd arrived as the mysterious new hunk from the big city. Now they were smiling and waving at him. *At least it* better *be Josh they're batting their eyes at!* She flashed a look back toward the table. Those two "boys," she thought, were so busy entertaining themselves that neither one noticed the girls anyway. Kevin and Josh had both been acting like constant goof-offs lately, which was really starting to get tiring. To be honest, she'd always thought Kevin was more mature than was turning out to be true. *Maybe they deserve those bimbos' batting eyes. Oh, look! There's Kirk Webster from the debate team. Nice plaid shirt. I heard they won last week, too. Hm.*

"Diamond store?" Josh asked Kevin incredulously after Deb was out of earshot. "Man, how does this kind of gossip get started? I might not be a whiz at economics, but even I know a diamond store doesn't make sense in Partonville."

"Heard your mom mention anything about a sporting goods store or a climbing wall?" Kevin asked, pretty sure that would never happen, but a guy could dream.

"To be honest, I haven't heard many specifics about her project lately. All I know is every once in awhile she gets out this plastic green filing box with a lock-down lid, shuffles files and papers around, bangs on her calculator, scribbles notes, puts it all away and says she's got to start collecting bids." He didn't mention how much he secretly wished the whole project would just go away. He worried she'd never be around anymore, like back before they'd moved to Partonville. Things were definitely better between them now, but would it last?

And poor Mr. Lawson. Try as he might, Josh couldn't keep the images of that old upside down car from resurfacing, especially after Pastor Delbert had made the announcement in church Sunday morning. Thank goodness his mom hadn't plied him for more details—yet—about his trip home from Chicago. He wasn't ready to share his own carelessness. Never would be, for that matter.

He'd had some terrible nightmares last night, strange images of heads floating in a fog, lines of eyebrows pasted on mirrors. He was *still* tired in school today and he was having trouble concentrating. He remembered the first time he'd met Rick Lawson, right after he and his mom arrived in Partonville to handle his great aunt's funeral and stuff. He'd never seen such a mess of an office in his life. But much to Josh's surprise, the guy had turned out to be interesting, somebody he enjoyed chatting with.

It's not that Josh ran into Mr. Lawson that often, but when he did, Mr. Lawson always remembered his name, asked about his mom, about Shelby (the Partonville grapevine in action, Josh would think), how things were going in his new school. In fact, one day Josh had stopped by Harry's for some fries while his mom ran errands. He'd sat down on a stool next to Mr. Lawson and the guy ended up picking up his tab, said he'd appreciated his mother's business, looked forward to working with her in the future. And now, now Rick Lawson *had* no future, Josh thought. He wondered if he'd been dead in his car when he'd driven by. The thought of it sent a shiver down his spine.

"Josh-o! Where'd ya go, space cadet? Somebody walk over your grave?" Kevin was just teasing him by repeating some old superstition about shivering and graves, but it gave Josh the ultimate creeps since he'd just been thinking about . . . death.

Josh took a final gulp of milk from his carton, tossed it on the lunch tray, retrieved his backpack from under his feet, slung it over his shoulder and picked up his tray. "I'll catch you later, dude. Gotta warn Shelby about the spaghetti." With that, he was gone, completely unaware of the sing-songy chorus of "Hi, Josh!" that came his way from the two girls still batting their eyes at him.

⁂

The mood at Harry's Grill was solemn. Monday morning usually found folks chattering a mile a minute: teasing, harassing, catching each other up on their weekend doings. This morning, however, all anyone could think or talk about was the sudden death of Rick Lawson and his poor mother. Such a shame!

"Welp, I tell ya, Lester," Arthur Landers, who was seated at his usual spot at the U-shaped counter, said to Lester's back as he fried bacon, "the Good Lord giveth and the Good Lord taketh awayeth. Sometimes I do wonder 'bout His timin', though. Never once did we think 'bout what would happen if Rick up and died, him being the only legal-eagle in this here town—and apparently he didn't think about it either. I'd say we's all up legal creek without our Rick Lawson paddle."

Lester K. Biggs, owner and the only employee of Harry's Grill, slowly turned to face Arthur. He held a bacon press in one hand and a long-handled metal spatula in the other. "Honest to *Pete*, Arthur Landers! Sometimes you say the dumbest things." He looked like he might be fixing to clock Arthur with his spatula, but instead he drew a deep breath and turned back to the grill with a loud sigh.

"Now Lester, ya know everybody's a-thinkin' the same gol' dern thing. Right, Doc? Somebody might jist as well say it and git it over with."

Acting Mayor Gladys McKern, seated to Arthur's right on her usual stool, yanked at the bottom of her blazer which always rode up on her ample bosom, and swiveled toward Arthur. "I quite agree with Lester, Arthur. This is *not* the time to be thinking of ourselves. This is a sad time for all of us who have lost such a dear resident of my fine town. *Our* fine town, of course," she blustered, darting her eyes away from Arthur and back to the butter she was smearing on her toast she always ordered dry, due to her cholesterol—which she always reminded everyone about. However, since death was on everyone's minds, she limited herself to smearing one pat this morning. It was time to start taking better care of herself, if she could believe the ongoing evening news' patter about cholesterol and women and heart attacks. "Death," Pastor had said one Sunday years ago, "demands we contemplate how we're living."

"I can't stop thinking about his poor mother," Doc said. "I dropped by the hospital to see Sadie again last evening and she's not only bruised from head to toe, but she's still in a *terrible* state of shock, I'll tell you. I'm glad she's got Eugene and Maggie helping her, not to mention everyone at the church. And I hear Roscoe and Sherri and their family are arriving tomorrow, thank goodness. I don't know how she's gonna get through this funeral, let alone make it without all the help Rick gave her every single day of his life. And you know, I never once heard him complain about a thing he did for his mom—or anything at all for that matter. I kinda wonder if she won't move to Des Moines to live with Roscoe now, although I know she and Sherri don't always get along." A couple heads nodded. In a small town such as Partonville, grievances seemed to maintain their own life.

"And another thing, as much as this shocks me to admit it, you *are* right, Arthur," he said, winking at Arthur. "I'm sure glad I've brought in someone to begin taking over for me." Doc picked up a spoon and stirred his coffee, which was black. "I guess none of us ever knows when our number's up, do we," he said rather than asked. He took a sip of his coffee and held the cup an inch from his lips as his eyes studied the brew. He hoped Rick hadn't seen it coming, or that he hadn't suffered. Although he hadn't read the autopsy report (young Doctor Neilson handled the call), he'd heard Rick's death was instantaneous. Dr. Neilson had reported that fact to Sadie, but it was Doc she'd asked about the suffering. "When you're drifting into the arms of the Lord, Sadie, I can't imagine you'd feel anything but awe." She'd whispered a much relieved yet gut-wrenching "Thank you!" before her body was racked with sobs. He'd wiped her tears with his hanky, then dabbed at his own eyes. Doc had lost his wife years ago, but the wound suddenly felt fresh. Funny how new death could so quickly resurrect old pains.

"You got that right," Eugene said in response to Doc's statement about the randomness of death. "What with Rick so busy being our only lawyer and all, I just hope he took the time to get his own papers in order before . . ." Lester slid his usual saucer of poached eggs in front of Eugene, cutting off his sentence. Eugene looked up and thanked him, put his napkin in his lap and reached for the salt, even though he'd all but lost his appetite. "I do know one thing Rick had in order," he said as he slid his fork tines through one of the eggs.

"Well, ya gonna tell us or jist think 'bout it?" Arthur asked.

Eugene swiveled and looked Arthur right in the eyes. "He had his *priorities* in order, Arthur. He loved his God, his mother and the people of this town more than anything else. I can't think of a time that man didn't go out of his way to answer a legal question, or work late, if he had to. Due to my line of business, over the years I surely did impose on him more times than I'd care to remember, often at the close of a business day, and never once did Rick complain about it. He just did his job. Every day that man got up and did his job, and every night he went home and took care of his mother."

He swiveled and looked toward the cash register. "You know how you've usually got that collection jar out on your counter, Lester?" Lester took note of its absence, then nodded. "I was sitting right here at this counter one day when I saw Rick passing by on his way to work. You know what he did? He walked in, looked at the name on the jar, nodded his head, opened his wallet, peeled out a few bills, stuck them in the jar and went on to work. I saw it with my own eyes."

While Lester flipped the bacon, he glanced at Doc. "It's who the man was." Lester was far from the mushy type, but it sounded like his voice cracked. The grill was silent for a few moments.

"I need a warm-up, Lester," Arthur said, raising his half-filled cup in the air. "And speakin' of *pri-orities*, Lester, what do ya think is gonna happen ta this grill one day when yer gone? Huh? Who's gonna git us our breakfast and serve us liver and onions on Wednesdays?" Gladys harrumphed. Arthur was tactless. The two men had barely gotten over their last flare-up, and now Arthur seemed to be poking another of poor Lester's sore spots, Lester having no extended family.

Lester picked up the coffee pot, glared at Arthur and began topping off cups—at the farthest end of the U from where Arthur sat—slowly, ever so slowly, working his way toward Arthur. He made sure he'd poured the very last drop out of the pot, which had caused him to all but overflow Gladys's cup, before he got to Arthur. Still, he moved in front of Arthur and held the empty pot in the pour position for quite some time over Arthur's raised, and by now completely empty receptacle, since he'd been waiting so long.

"I do believe, Arthur, I'm going to leave the grill to that magician from Champaign we had here in town one time." Questioning eyes turned in unison toward the slender man who continued pouring from a now empty pot.

Arthur, whose arm was tired from holding his cup in the air, moved it toward his mouth and took a pretend sip. "Because?"

"Because, Arthur," Lester said, turning to grab a mug and pouring himself an imaginary cup of coffee, then clinking it with Arthur's cup as though proposing a grand toast, "because I always admired the magician who could make someone disappear."

Everyone busted out laughing. It was a joke that had been used at the grill before, but this time Arthur'd walked right into it. When Arthur realized he'd been bested, again he raised his cup toward Lester in a "good one" gesture and even he couldn't help but to laugh.

"I'll tell you," Doc said after they'd finally collected themselves, "laughter is *indeed* one of life's great healing balms."

🌲🌲🌲

After the morning crowd was gone, Lester got out the big collection jar. "Sadie Lawson," he wrote on the piece of paper he had taped around the jar. He reached in his wallet and tossed in a twenty, then phoned the Floral Fling and ordered cut flowers for the funeral, plus a living plant to be sent to Sadie. He wished he'd long-ago thought to spend the twenty on a new pair of suspenders for Rick. But then, Rick probably wouldn't have worn them anyway. He'd been satisfied with the good old suspenders—with the very life—he'd had.

7

⚞⚞⚞

Wednesday evening newly retired Bob Del Vechia folded Sunday's *Partonville Press*, set it down on the end table and sighed. What a shock, to read about the sudden passing of an old college roommate, one of the few people with whom he'd kept in contact after graduation from law school, aside, of course, from the one he'd married. Back in their strenuous days at The University of Chicago Law School, before he and Louise got married and Rick returned to the hometown he'd spent so much time talking about to anyone who would listen, Louise had enjoyed hanging around with Rick as much as Bob had. Rick was funny, smart as a whip, quirky as they come and the most loyal friend they'd ever met. Yes, the trio had shared three years of some of their longest study days and wildest party nights.

For months before graduation, Bob and Louise had tried to talk Rick into coming back to Atlanta and opening a law practice with them. The closer graduation got, the more they pressed Rick to please reconsider, but he would hear none of it. As much as he adored both of them and knew they'd make a dynamic *legal* trio, he couldn't imagine living his life anywhere else but in his little town and with the people who had helped make him who he was. "They need somebody looking out for them who they can trust," he'd told Bob over a brew one evening. "It's hard for a small town of people like that to warm up to strangers, and besides, I hear they still need a saxophone player in the community band," he said with a grin.

Throughout law school Bob had heard Rick play in more than a few pickup bands, knew how good he was, how much he loved the instrument, and in particular jazz. Bob had laughed, feeling pretty assured jazz would not be a community band's forte, but he envied Rick's strong sense of belonging, his kind heart, his earnest quest to not only serve the people, but to return and be a part of them.

Hardly a phone conversation had passed (they'd taken turns calling each other at least every couple months all these forty-odd years) when "that night at Billiards and Beverages" didn't come up. "Oh, it was the merriest of times!" Louise would say. How many games of 8-Ball had they played? Wonder whatever happened to that cute shrimp boat (Lordy, *Lordy* she was tiny!) of a redhead who kept grabbing the cue ball right off the table and not giving it back until Rick gave her a smile, for which she'd kiss his cheek? If Rick actually ever did call that sassy little redhead, he never told a soul about it, not even Bob or Louise—although most speculated he'd at least tried, maybe was even engaged in a "secret" relationship so as not to endure questions, since he'd always been pretty private about his personal life.

About a year after their graduation, Rick flew to Atlanta to serve as Bob's best man. The next time they saw each other, Bob and Louise had ventured an extended weekend to Partonville for their first wedding anniversary. "We just had to see the place," they'd said. After the dime tour—Rick called it that because, he'd said with a grin, "it only takes ten minutes to see everything from my office to the cemetery, which is as high and as low as you can get in these parts"—they'd dined at the new (but ill-fated, short-lived and now long-gone) Partonville Country Club.

A surprise to almost nobody but the St. Louis Investors, the club went bankrupt a little more than a year after its opening. It was then purchased in its entirety by Challie Carter, the area's largest land-holding and leasing farmer—the very same guy who had sold the investors this chunk of his property to begin with. (Challie swore the first two years after he replanted the rest of that acreage that the corn was always at least two inches shorter in the circles where the greens had been. "Looks like a band of aliens stopped by and swirlygigged two inches right off the stalks," he used to say.) After repurchasing his old property for not much more than those investors had paid him to begin with, he sold off the clubhouse and a bunch of acres to the park district, which barely had to do any renovating to the cement block building to make it what it still is today: Partonville's largest gathering place.

Louise had been completely taken with the quaint little town, both she and Bob having been born and raised in large metropolitan areas. They'd utterly enjoyed reading the *Partonville Press* while they were there, laughing about "news" like who was visiting who, the corn reports and a police blotter that was made up of one item that week: "During his 8 P.M. rounds Tuesday evening, Sergeant Phillip McKenzie spied a Banty Rooster wandering the sidewalk in front of Richardson's Rexall Drugs. A chase ensued. The rooster was ably apprehended and taken to the station where he was later claimed by Red Cline Jr. who thanked Sgt. McKenzie for saving his 4-H project from a sure demise on square traffic." Bob and Louise were hysterical with laughter by the time Bob finished reading the item to Louise and Rick, the three of them drinking a cup of coffee at Rick's kitchen table.

"Laugh if you want," Rick said, "but Red Jr. has worked hard with that little Banty. Would have been a shame for him to lose it so close to the fair."

"Apologies and point well taken," Bob said, clearing his throat. "What do we city folks know about roosters anyway?" The Del Vechias decided on the spot it would be fun to get a subscription for a year. "Maybe it will help us learn about life in the country."

Every year since their visit, the three of them talked about how they just had to get together again ("Your turn to travel next time," Bob and Louise said), but it just never happened. The one year Rick was on the verge of purchasing his airline tickets ended up to be the year his mother moved in with him and he didn't feel right about leaving her alone so soon, no matter how much she insisted he go. So Rick never traveled and Louise never canceled the subscription. In fact, she and Bob had appeared in the paper twice: once for being the longest-running, never-lived-in-Partonville subscribers, and once in an ad they placed. In a raucously energized three-way phone call, Bob and Louise had asked Harold Crab, the *Press*'s editor, if he could please run their birthday greeting for Rick's sixtieth right next to Rick's ad which had never once in all these years changed. They wanted the ad—complete with a photo they were mailing—to be twice as large as Rick's business ad. Harold laughed so long after he heard what they wanted to say and do that he decided not to take a dime from them; the fun would be worth the space. Not only that, he told them, if it was a slow enough news day, he'd give them the headline—unless there was some actual big news, which there hadn't been.

ATLANTA LAW FIRM CHALLENGES PARTONVILLE AT-TORNEY the headline read, with a small SEE PAGE FIVE following it—which definitely got folks curious and caused Rick to choke on his coffee. The ad, printed in bigger and bolder print than Rick's, read **Del Vechia & Del Vechia, an Atlanta-based law firm, challenges Partonville attorney Rick Lawson to: LIVE ANOTHER SIXTY YEARS! Happy Birthday, you old goat!** The picture was one Rick had never seen before. It was a black and white from their law school days. It was taken from over the couch upon which Rick had fallen asleep, a newspaper spread over his face and upper chest. Even though nobody could see his face, they knew it was Rick by the suspenders and that wild shock of hair sticking straight up from under the paper. The caption to the photo read "Rick Lawson studies for the bar exam."

As his gift to Rick, Harold had the headline and both ads framed in a sort of collage. It still hung in Rick's office.

⚜ ⚜ ⚜

Bob placed his hand on the top of the paper and gently patted it. He retrieved the hanky from his back pocket and wiped tears from his eyes. Not only had he read Rick's obituary, but also the details of the accident that had been reported by Sharon Teller (other than Harold, the *Press*'s only staff reporter) which included a photo of Rick's car upside down in the ditch—a photo Bob wished he'd never seen. He wiped his nose, leaned forward and tucked the hanky back in his pocket. Such a typical day up until he'd read the paper, he thought: he'd played a round of golf; the fragrance of fried chicken was in the air; the radio played softly in the background—the discovery their good friend had been dead for five days before he knew about it.

"Louise, honey," he hollered into the kitchen where Louise was making dinner, "you haven't read the *Partonville Press* yet today, have you?"

"No, dear," came the reply.

"I didn't think so."

Her husband's voice sounded so strange that Louise walked into the living room. That's when he gave her the terrible news and encouraged her not to view any of the photos. After they spent a few minutes consoling each other, Louise said she felt like they should try to go to the funeral, say . . . good-bye. Bob was in agreement. "I'll get online after dinner and see if we can find some last-minute tickets to get us into Hethrow Regional Airport by late Friday afternoon."

🌲🌲🌲

"I don't know how Earl and I can thank you enough, Jacob," May Belle said, swallowing down the urge to shed happy tears. "This has been such a *wonderful* treat." Dinner dishes cleared, crumbs adeptly removed, she smoothed the linen napkin lying across her lap, admiring the fineness of the fabric, then gazed at the delicacy of the chandelier in the center of the room and the crisply pressed seams in their waiter's trousers as he approached the table to refill their crystal goblets. When Dorothy'd called to extend Jacob's dinner invitation and told them to "gussy up" in their Sunday finest, she had no idea they'd be eating at The Driscoll in Hethrow! "The ultimate in fine dining," their radio advertisements touted, and now she knew why.

When they'd arrived at The Driscoll and Jacob helped May Belle shed her coat for the coat-check, Dorothy noticed May Belle's uneasiness. Dorothy whispered, "I see you're wearing your beautiful pin." The gold filigree dove was about the size of a half-dollar. May Belle's parents gave it to her for her high school graduation, her mother saying she believed May Belle was now "officially ready to soar into life with the grace and peace of a dove." The pin, which she wore at her neckline over the top button of her white dress blouse, was not only a touchstone to her parents' love, but it was May Belle's finest piece of jewelry, in fact the only piece of jewelry she ever wore aside from her thin wedding band and a Timex Dorothy'd given her for Christmas several years ago. May Belle gently fingered the pin now, her eyes twinkling with joy and mischief. "You know, we haven't had this much excitement since our Dearest Dorothy took us for our last ride in The Tank, have we, Earl?"

Earl shook his head. Although there were too many strangers, too much activity and too many knives and forks on the table for Earl, he had nonetheless eaten most of his roast beef and Yorkshire pudding before he'd returned to rolling the seam of his napkin between his fingers.

"Well, Mom," Jacob said, leaning back in his chair, "dinner at The Driscoll doesn't hold a torch to a road trip, but it's a nice high-on-the-hog respite from what's turned out to be a busy week. I'm glad Earl's here to help me enjoy the company of two such lovely ladies."

"Go on," Dorothy said. "Don't stop now! We oldsters can use all the compliments we can get, right, dearie?" she said, nodding her head at May Belle.

"Right. But since he's the driver *and* insists on treating us, I say we let him off the hook."

"Would you like to see the dessert menu?" the waiter asked as their chuckling died down. Jacob nodded. The waiter handed them each a leather pad containing the day's selections. May Belle leaned toward Earl and quietly read each one aloud, one sounding more delectable than the next. Then she noticed the prices and gasped. "Goodness!"

"Find your favorite, May Belle?" Jacob asked.

"I think I'll pass on dessert," she said, figuring she could make ten trays of brownies, if not more, for the price of one piece of chocolate cake.

"Nonsense," Jacob said. "I've never known you *or* my mother to pass on dessert." He turned his head toward the waiter. "We'd like the Extravagant Sweets Tray, please, and coffee all around." May Belle caught the price of the Extravagant Sweets Tray just before the waiter whisked her dessert menu away. As much as she wanted to protest, she also wanted to claim dibs on the *Chocolat Éclair* that was part of the mix.

"Jacob," Dorothy said, "the meal was de-lish, the dessert tray is on the way and we thank you, son." She gave her hands a gentle clap, then threw her eyes upward. "And thank *You,* Lord," she all but cheered, "for the gift of family—every single one of them at this table!"

8

⚹ ⚹ ⚹

With papers spread before her, Katie waited for the architect to arrive. She was working on a weathered sign resting on two sawhorses, her green case off to one side. The makeshift table had been the only thing left behind in this old building. It was still sitting exactly how and where she'd found it: precisely in the middle of the first floor. She wondered if the Taningers had simply been too sad to take it with them after Hethrow's mega-furniture stores had finally dried up their business and forced them to sell out. She ran her fingers across the peeling block lettering, FAMILY OWNED AND OPERATED SINCE 1923, and wondered if they'd maybe eaten a tearful last supper on it before departing. Such an odd and sentimental notion for her, she thought, right before another hot flash caused her to fan herself with her legal pad.

In her worst moments Katie Durbin wondered what on earth she'd been thinking buying this building and announcing such an ambitious project; in her best moments she was once again Kathryn Durbin, businesswoman, exhilarated by the challenge, knowing that the more she took on, the more the overload fired her adrenaline. It was so good to feel alive again! For three whole days she'd done nothing but talk on the phone to architects and a few retailers from Chicago she knew well and trusted. She'd surfed the Internet for any information she could find regarding large re-habbed buildings in rural areas, see what kinds of facilities they'd brought in, how they'd thrived, or not—and many had not. But she decided she needed to erase all doubts and sentimentalities and focus her energies on success. "Out with the old and in with the new," she'd heard. Exactly. Under her direction, "the old Taninger building" would be no more. In its place would stand a thriving new beginning.

As Edward Showalter had proven by the previous jobs he'd done for her, he was knowledgeable, thorough, tidy and more than reasonable. He was by far the best electrician and handyman she'd ever worked with, and throughout her years in commercial real estate development in Chicago, she'd been involved with dozens of them. The man could do anything from rewiring a house to building furniture. Although she would love to give the trustworthy Edward Showalter the entire job, or have him serve as contractor, she feared it might be more than he could handle, especially in her frenzied time frame. If he had a year to get it all done, he was no doubt capable of handling everything, pulling in people when he needed them. But in reality, some of the structural projects she'd projected on her legal pad would likely need entire crews. Yes, to transform the old open-floor-plan Taninger Furniture building into a mini mall was going to be quite an undertaking, perhaps too much for any one man—especially a man highly distracted by his new love for Nellie Ruth McGregor. Still, at the very least, Edward Showalter would be involved when it came to projects like special wiring, lighting and painting. Or making shelves and building partial walls, and. . . . She made a note to give him a call to ask him to meet with her, reserve her a huge block of time, talk openly about his limitations. She trusted they could hammer out his role and agree on financial arrangements.

But first, the architect. *Focus, Katie! Focus!* Edward Showalter or *any* contractor would need to see some drawings.

Early on she'd decided the best plan of attack would be to procure an architect from Chicago to draw up a few rough drafts encompassing some of her ideas—like an atrium. Yes, an atrium would tie things together nicely. Whether said atrium should, or structurally could, encompass all three floors (lower level, first and second floors) was going to be one of her first questions, and she'd finally found someone who was willing to travel the distance and commit to staying in the area for a couple days at a time while they worked through the possibilities. Although she'd never met the man, he'd come highly recommended and she told him so. "Likewise," he'd said over the phone. "It will be lovely to finally meet the famous Kathryn Durbin, Development Diva," a statement which he followed with a warm and kind laugh, one she'd liked. She'd booked him a room at the Lamp Post hoping that the motel would help render a sense of what she was after with the mini mall: homespun, vintage, welcoming. He was due to meet her here at the Taninger building within a half hour.

Although the pool of reputable architects in Hethrow was a healthy one (likely cheaper and certainly more convenient), she didn't want any overlapping with the Craig brothers' endeavors. Best to keep all specific plans to herself. She had a competitive history with Colton Craig that was strained by his involvement in a series of incidents that led to her losing her last job, and more recently he'd offered her an obscene amount of money for Crooked Creek *and* the opportunity to consult with him and his brother, an offer that made her reel.

But then, *then* he'd gone and insulted Partonville, a little town and its people she had, in spite of her resistance, become a part of. The land war was on: no, Partonville would *not* be bulldozed and it would *not* become the next suburb of Hethrow. The little town she had once chided as Pardon-Me-Ville would find new life if she had to invest every last cent to her name. The wheels were already set in motion and as far as she was concerned, there was no turning back now. Colton Craig would eat her dust.

Before securing the architect, she had hurled herself into a fury, believing she first needed to decide exactly what type of stores and how many of them she wanted in the mall. This was a whole new ball of experience since although she'd spent much of her professional life in cutthroat commercial real estate development, she'd only bought and sold properties to developers, not *personally* rehabbed and selected the *stores*. Where to begin? She didn't want to openly advertise for lessees and end up with unsuitable occupants, ones that didn't "fit" with her vision. As it turned out, she needn't have worried about finding lessees. Since word had spread concerning her mini-mall endeavor, she'd started receiving calls from seemingly every business wanna-be in and out of the area. Any message she received from a chain store went straight into her circular file; the mini mall was all about grassroots entrepreneurs, the little guy and gal.

Between brainstorming and all the calls she'd been receiving, thus far her "Possible Occupants" file bulged with thirty-three entries ranging from an antique store (a for-sure) to a massage therapist (maybe wouldn't fly here) to a tea room (no doubt, tea room was in), not to mention a bath and body shop, yarn shop (she'd read knitting had made a comeback), candy store, kite store, coin shop, birding supply shop, consignment store for handmade items (a must), art gallery, "adult store" *(Where are* these *people getting my name?),* upscale jewelry store, two tattoo artists. . . . She shuffled the papers until she realized that in order to get moving, she would just have to go ahead and have an architect render a few possibilities for the square footage usage for at least six and up to a possible ten, maybe even twelve?, businesses rather than wait to fill the spaces and then begin building. Before construction actually began she could have potential lessees take a look at their proposed square footage and layout and tweak it a bit as necessary, perhaps even allowing for a few revisions as construction took place.

Flux. Yes, she wanted a plan in place, but she also wanted to allow for a certain creative air to blow throughout the whole endeavor since she wanted each space to have its own unique flavor, shape and feel rather than churn out another building with the atmosphere of a big-box retailer. She was after ambiance, the *right* ambiance to tie each store together, something she hoped she could create with a great lighting scheme and, of course, her atrium. Something else to talk to Edward Showalter about, she thought—although she wondered if he even knew what the word *ambiance* meant. Sigh.

During one of her late-night planning/envisioning sessions she'd started a "reserve shop" folder for establishments outside the mini mall—outside of the town square, in fact. But none of the store fronts or interiors would be allowed to appear contemporary in design; she wanted the entire Partonville area to smack of either historical integrity or down-home cozy. (She scribbled "cozy and comfortable" on her PR page, then "viable and vintage.") She brain-stormed ways she might create marketing synergy among scattered retailers. Perhaps she could incorporate built-in glass showcases throughout the walkways in the mini mall, places to display a few goods and placards from the other shops around town. Something else to talk to the architect about. Scribble, scribble, scribble.

♣ ♣ ♣

Although all the mini-mall stores didn't really *have* to be ready to open at the same time, Katie wanted the grand open-ing to be *so* grand, she'd get press in Hethrow that would cause Colton Craig to sit up and take serious notice. In order to protect her greater plan, she'd also been systematically buy-ing every possible piece of real estate in that fringe area around the square and rural parameters of Partonville. She was *so* determined to protect her financial investments that she'd even tolerated a recent stop at the ever-greasy-spooned Harry's Grill. She'd been circling the square one morning and spied not only Cora Davis, the town crier, in her usual spot at the window, but Gladys was still at the counter, too. Perfect.

Katie seated herself at a table and ordered dry toast and black coffee, about the only thing she could tolerate in this es-tablishment. The more she looked around the place, the more it reminded her of Mayberry, which, she decided, was good. And if she was looking for real vintage characters to lend local flavor, she couldn't *plant* a better one than Lester K. Biggs, or anyone at that counter, for that matter. It made her smile to realize how there was so much to do in Partonville and yet, in some ways, so little.

Upon overhearing Katie's order, Gladys spun on her

stool, noted Katie's inviting smile and said, "We order our toast the same way!" quickly covering the remaining bites of her butter-smeared toast with her napkin. "Something else we have in common," she said in a booming voice. Katie had to work to keep from audibly groaning at Gladys's comment. Surely Dorothy couldn't be right: she and Gladys just could *not* have that much in common. Nonetheless, it was time to fertilize the grapevine, and where was it more rooted than at Harry's?

"Gladys!" Katie said with a painted-on smile, "I'm glad you're here. It looks like you're done eating, but if your mayoral duties can wait a few minutes, why don't you bring your coffee over and join me? I have something I want to talk to you about, and in a way, it is town business." Gladys beamed, grabbed her coffee and stomped (not on purpose, she was just a heavy-footed woman) on over. She set her coffee on the table, tugged at the bottom of her blazer and seated herself. After they exchanged a few words about poor Rick and Sadie and the funeral arrangements, Katie raised her voice a decibel to make sure it reached Cora, whose upper body was already tilting their way. "Here we are, barely past your Centennial Plus Thirty and now we have Rick Lawson's death drawing people together again. Things like this certainly cause us to think about what really matters, don't they?" She paused here a moment as though to let the weight and earnestness of what she'd said sink in.

"You know, Gladys, I've learned since moving here that Partonville is a town that cares." (She made a mental note to write in her PR folder: "Partonville Cares.") "What with Hethrow knocking on our door, it's important we never lose this strong sense of community you've worked so hard to cultivate. I know that in order to *really* help Partonville continue to thrive, you'll be encouraging any residents who want or need to sell their properties to sell to locals, not to outside interests. I wanted to let you know that Herb Morgan and I are both on the lookout for any and all land opportunities." There, she'd dropped Herb's name as though she'd known him forever.

"As you know, Gladys," she said, leaning forward, luring Gladys into what felt like a circle of intimacy, "with your able backing, I'm readying plans for the mini mall. But I'm also," she said, leaning in just the slightest bit further, causing Gladys to do the same, "considering several other possibilities I'd like to talk to you about. Maybe you and I could arrange a meeting with Herb to strategize on how to keep Partonville in the hands of Partonvillers."

Katie was no fool. Although she could have done her own behind-the-scenes canvassing for available property, she did not wish to alienate one of Partonville's own by cutting him out of his livelihood. No, that would assuredly be a fatal tactical move. Plus, she earnestly desired for the locals to succeed since they all needed to be in this together. So she had partnered with Herb Morgan at Morgan's Realty, a nearby independent she'd learned most Partonvillers had done business with the last many years. Although his office was located two small towns west of Partonville, in the opposite direction of Hethrow (which is another reason why she'd chosen him since all land west of Partonville was in her radar), Herb himself lived in Partonville, which made him a known and therefore trusted individual—and one privy to insider town talk.

Of course, from a financial standpoint, she'd obviously rather have people come straight to her, but there were those who still considered *her* an outsider who would be more apt to do business with Herb. She'd contracted with him to act as her buyer's broker, sweetening his incentive by offering to pay him a percentage more than his regular fees. Her hope was that Herb would be motivated enough to tap into buyers before they'd even decided to list. "Nothing wrong with that," Herb had said upon their handshake, especially since she was a guaranteed buyer. From the sellers' standpoints, she'd already gained a reputation as one who must have money to burn. The trick was to get to the farmers before Colton Craig's scouts came knocking on their doors. Near-the-square homeowners would be easier to target since talk flew around town as quickly as mouths could fly open.

Katie checked her watch again. Even though the architect was now five minutes late (she abhorred tardiness), she smiled as she recalled her conversation with Gladys. It was clear from their enthusiastic responses that both Gladys and Herb were in her pocket, two more notches in her property-acquiring gun belt against the Craig & Craig empire. *Enough with the mega everything-is-the-same stuff,* she thought, reviewing her goals. Right under "Partonville Cares," she scribbled a few more notes on her PR page, most of which would probably one day end up in her full-page ad in *BackRoads Illinois,* a startup publication in which she'd invested. "Not your 'same old' but your 'NEW old!'"

9

⨩⨩⨩

Thursday was always a busy day at Your Store since it began the new sale week, but today seemed extra busy for only a week after Thanksgiving. Then again, people were probably either sick of turkey or finally and thankfully out of it. Ground beef and pork chops were on sale and they seemed to be in everyone's carts, including May Belle's hand basket which she picked up inside the store door and set like an infant seat in the top of her folding metal pull cart she always chugged to and from the store, even when Earl came with her to carry the bags, as he had today. Every once in a while Earl would get the notion that he needed to check with Lester about deliveries or stop by the church and realign the pew Bibles for Pastor. Although it didn't happen often, when it did, it was easier to let him go than to keep him with her since all he would do is fret. Yes, May Belle always needed to be prepared to handle the groceries herself, which fueled her concerns about Earl's ability to carry on after her death.

Even though a community member had died, the Christmas season was now officially under way and Wilbur was playing Christmas carols over the loudspeaker. In the wake of Rick's death, it felt good to be reminded that life went on, in Partonville and the rest of the world. May Belle did love the Christmas season, especially because Earl brightened so when the decorations went up. "Earl," she said pointing overhead, "look at the sparkly holiday bells Wilbur has strung up there." Earl looked and sure enough smiled. "Time to get our tree up. Let's do it Sunday after church, okay?" He nodded his enthusiastic agreement. She knew he would start asking tomorrow, Friday, if it was Sunday yet. And once again, May Belle would patiently show him the calendar and count off the days.

Since all turkeys for the community dinner had been roasted sans stuffing, which Lester had graciously provided in his large banquet pans, May Belle still had a bag of stuffing mix in her cabinet. Had she been choosing the chops for her and Earl, she would have picked the thinner pre-packaged ones since they were always a few cents cheaper per pound. But because, as a member of the Care Committee, she was cooking this evening's dish for Sadie and her family, she'd gladly pay the extra for the six best hand-selected butterfly chops in the case. Her stuffing would do nicely in these, she speculated. She decided to pick out a good green apple, dice that up real fine and fold it in just to add a little extra juice and flavor. She would also send along a custard pie, which would be cheap and fun. Besides, people might not recognize her if she showed up without sweets! The chops would all but wipe out her meager food budget for the next several days, but a grieving family needed quality food to help their tired bodies heal. Praying and preparing them a good pork chop dinner were the best ways she knew to express her love.

Earl close on her heels, she pulled her cart to the fruit section of the produce aisle and studied the beautiful, shiny pile of green apples. She selected the one with just the right color, set it in her cart, then picked up a tangerine and gave it a careful squeeze. She held the end of it to her nose and deeply inhaled. She loved tangerines; they always reminded her of her childhood Christmases when her parents would put one tangerine in the toe of her stocking, along with a shiny nickel and a few walnuts. Oh, it smelled so good; but the price was still a little high so she gently set it back down. Nellie Ruth, assistant manager of the store and one who wandered the produce aisle whenever she could, just because she loved the diversity of color and selection, noticed May Belle returning the tangerine to the display.

"Something wrong with the tangerines today, May Belle?" she asked, picking one up herself, hoping her new stock boy had finally caught on to the fact that he should not put out bruised or inferior fruit unless he set it on the "bruised and reduced" shelf.

"Oh! Nellie Ruth! You startled me!" she said, raising her hand to her chest.

"May Belle, I am *so* sorry. You okay?"

May Belle released a great belly laugh. "Of course! Don't worry about a thing. It's good to give the old ticker a jolt now and again, isn't it?"

"Not if it scares you to *death*!" Nellie Ruth said in a knee-jerk response, then gasped and quickly cupped her hand over her mouth. Why was it so many things people said, including herself, sounded . . . *unnerving* in the wake of Rick's sudden death? She and ES—Nellie Ruth was the only person aside from Johnny Mathis (no, not that one) who didn't always address Edward Showalter as Edward Showalter—were going out to dinner tonight and she was going to ask him if he had noticed that very same thing. She released her hand from her mouth and resumed her conversation.

"So, are the tangerines not up to snuff?" She knew May

Belle was not only a discerning shopper, but a very frugal one, always careful with her money. So careful, Nellie Ruth had noticed, that she often bought things from the "bruised and reduced" shelf, especially if they were bananas which Nellie Ruth knew would immediately be transformed into some wonderful goodie like banana cake or banana muffins or banana cream pie.

"The tangerines look *wonderful*," May Belle said. "Absolutely perfect. And they smell so citrus-y, just like I've always imagined the *whole* state of Florida must smell, right, Earl?" Earl briefly glanced from his mother to the tangerine to Nellie Ruth, then down at the floor. He didn't understand how a state could have a smell.

"As long as everything's okay then," Nellie Ruth said, turning her head toward the two checkout lanes, only one of which was open and now had five people in line.

"Nice to see you, May Belle. I've got to go open register two. Pick my lane when you check out, okay?" May Belle nodded her agreement at the same time she heard Maggie Malone's enthusiastic "Yoooohoooo, Maaaaaay Belle!" She turned just in time to see Maggie speed-racing a cart toward her, all but skidding to a halt right in front of her.

"What are you doing in the store on Thursday?" May Belle asked, Thursday being a popular hair day.

"My ten o'clock canceled," Maggie said, patting her hands to her hair, adeptly shifting the entire up-do slightly to the right as though her quick stop had thrown it out of kilter. "I thought I'd run over and pick up a few things for my evening clients. Well," she said, wiping the corners of her mouth with the back of her knuckle, then tapping her dangling Christmas ornament earring causing it to wildly swing to and fro, "the food's mostly for *me*. When I work until seven, I just can*not* make it without a little something more filling than the goodies I usually keep in the shop. Not even my exotic silver doilies can make scones and herbal tea feel like a *meal*! I need something sweeter, saltier *and* crunchier if I'm going to make it through this evening," she said. She glanced in her cart, then tossed her hands in the air, threw her head back and just howled. "I guess," she said, pointing to each item as she rattled through them, "Hostess Cupcakes, a bag of M&Ms—red and green for Christmas you know—potato chips, nachos, *two* kinds of salsa and a roast beef sandwich Wilbur just made me at the meat counter certainly cover the bases!"

What Maggie didn't say was that after her seven o'clock, she'd be packing up her beauty supplies and heading to Casey's Funeral Home to do Rick's hair, then over to Sadie's to take care of her, give her an assuring report about Rick's clothes and care. Sadie was originally scheduled at La Feminique Hair Salon & Day Spa for tomorrow afternoon, which would have worked out well for the wake that evening, but since Maggie and Sadie had already discussed the possibility of Maggie coming over to Sadie's, she wasn't surprised when Roscoe had called on his mother's behalf saying he thought she could use a "good dose of Maggie," and that getting her hair done right in her own home might calm her down, make her feel better. "One less thing to worry about tomorrow before the viewing," he'd said, his voice laced with exhaustion. "*I'll* be glad to see you, too, Maggie. I'm sure you're the same ball of energy you've always been. We could *all* use a little of that around here. And Maggie, this was all so sudden that I didn't have time to get a haircut before I left home either. Think you might be able to give me a trim?"

⚜ ⚜ ⚜

Eugene scurried around Rick's viewing room at the funeral home moving floral arrangements from here to there. Wake here tomorrow night, funeral at the church on Sunday. *The place looks like the Garden of Eden.* He couldn't help but read all the cards; always had, always would. By the time he got to the last bouquet, he simply could not believe it. There'd been no fewer than three FTD arrangements sent to the funeral home that had arrived from two different flower shops in Hethrow. "Honest to gaslights!" he said out loud. "How does a person expect our little Floral Fling to stay in business?" Two of the arrangements were from Roscoe's town in Des Moines: one from the principal of his school on behalf of all the teachers, and he deducted the other must be from his wife's place of employment, since he'd never heard of the corporation before. The third FTD bouquet had originated in California. He had no idea who it was from, in fact needed to call the florist since there had obviously been an error. The flowers, tight round snowball mums, were each died a different color—including a black one!—and arranged in something that looked like a triangular rack of pool balls with one larger white mum (as though it were the cue ball) sticking off to the side, to which the card was attached. "Yours until the eight ball sinks for good. Love, Your Little Red."

⚜ ⚜ ⚜

Where is he anyway? Katie looked at her watch yet again, fanned herself—again, a third wave of hot flashes engulfing her. The architect was now thirty-five minutes late. She *hated* tardiness. She sat at her sawhorse desk on one of two folding chairs she'd brought from the farm and looked around her:

dust everywhere, her papers helter-skelter, windows so dirty she could barely see through them. "Welcome to the office of Kathryn Durbin, mall director," she thought, shaking her head as she fanned a little harder. She recalled her city office which had been huge, filled with solid oak furniture and red leather accessories. She scribbled "Space for mall office?" on her design folder. Another thing to discuss with the architect.

She'd had the building's electricity turned on two days ago now and sniffed every once in awhile, imagining she smelled smoke. She pictured frayed wiring lurking between the walls. She assumed the entire building needed to be rewired, brought up to code. Then, of course, there would be the electrical complications of subdividing the cavernous space and setting up for computers—DSL, wireless maybe—which, to the best of her knowledge, still wasn't available in Partonville but maybe it was time to check again. Dial-up at the farm was making her nuts!

Maybe she should have brought Edward Showalter in here beforehand to run a few checks. Then again, she couldn't even remember if she'd ever checked to see if he was actually a licensed electrician. *I think these hot flashes are cooking my brain!* She scribbled a note to ask him for some documents, furious with herself she'd never thought of this before. Or if she had, she didn't remember it. *Memory loss. Classic menopause symptom.* She flipped to a clean page in her legal pad. "Personal" she wrote at the top. "Make doctor appointment; ask about hormone replacement therapy."

She flipped back a few pages and spotted her "Mall Names" page, which, she thought, she'd also made a folder for. Yes, back to that. "Unique Boutique," she said aloud, seeing how it sounded coming out of her mouth. "Good name but for a store not a mall," she said aloud, shuffling through her green file box to grab a new folder (and yes, she *had* already made a "Mall Names" folder. Gads!), "I should hold a contest to name the mall. Get the people invested before it even opens." Yes, she loved this idea. "Mall de Unique." "Partonville Mini Mall. "Vintage Mall." She shook her head and tapped her pencil on her legal pad, then picked up the pad and fanned some more. Even though the building was plenty cool, she could feel beads of sweat breaking out on her forehead, her cheeks obviously flushed. She imagined Jessica could probably come up with twenty great mall names in a split second.

Katie was good at business deals. Period. It hit her anew how very much she needed to partner with people (architects, contractors, lessees, retailers, advertisers, crafters, employees, creative types . . . advisors?) in order to make this happen successfully, which made her feel very vulnerable. Katie was used to calling all the shots, not asking for help. But this, this wasn't a "do-alone," as Dorothy had gently reminded her time and again. "Given the chance, most folks will rise to the occasion, honey," Dorothy had said with that warm, encouraging look in her eyes. "Trust them."

The only person in town at the moment who didn't seem to have a close emotional tie to Partonville's recent loss was Jacob. She pondered what lousy timing it was that Dorothy could finally spend more than a week with her son, and now there was this terrible tragedy. Dorothy told her Jacob had even suggested they take a mother-son road trip. "Imagine that!" Dorothy said to Katie when she'd called to share the news Jacob would be staying for a spell. "A grown man and attorney son who still wants to take a road trip with his oldster mom! To be honest, I don't know whether that should make me happy or sad—or worried about him." She'd stopped to chuckle there. "But I've decided I'm *ec-sta-tic*! The only problem is I'm not currently available for a road trip, what with all the doings for Rick, which have gotten more involved than I might have guessed. Maybe you could entertain Jacob for me an afternoon or two, think?"

Katie had found herself oddly warmed by the idea of entertaining Jacob. *Or is this just another hot flash?* she'd thought at the time. She'd told Dorothy she'd be glad to help any way she could, that they should just let her know when and how. But she hadn't heard from either one of them since Dorothy's Monday call and it was Thursday already. It had occurred to her that even though she had her own long-time attorney, Jacob was a lawyer, too, and he might have some very good "outsider's" advice about how she might proceed with this type of a grand undertaking, what hidden legal things to watch out for.

Perhaps it was time to check in with the Wetstras, what with the wake being tomorrow evening already. She'd read in the *Press* that the post-funeral dinner (and Katie had learned after her Aunt Tess's passing that in Partonville there was *always* a dinner following the funeral) was, due to the expected size of the crowd, being hosted by Sadie and Roscoe at the park district building. The meal was being provided by a "community effort": United Methodist Church's Care Committee, all side dishes; Harry's Grill, ham; St. Augustine's, beverages and paper goods; and attendees were invited to bring their favorite dessert to share. She wondered what Dorothy and May Belle would be bringing—although she suspected May Belle had volunteered to bring a dessert for both of them, since Dorothy was definitely not a baker.

What could *she* bring, she wondered? The only thing she

knew for sure was that it couldn't be a disaster, not after her failed turkey attempt for the community Thanksgiving dinner. "You remember *that* embarrassment, Katie," she said aloud while shaking her head, fanning her reddened face and neck more swiftly, "the one where, to no avail, you resorted to using a hacksaw!" She sniffed twice, exhaled, then sniffed again. *Smoke?* "Stop imagining things!" she chastised. "Stop thinking about fires, for goodness sake!"

Back to desserts. She'd check with Dorothy's selections first, see how everyone was doing. She'd do that right after her appointment with the architect—who, unbeknownst to her, had entered the building and caught her not only flushed, fanning herself and sniffing, but talking to herself—about a hacksaw and fires! When Katie looked up and saw Carl Jimson's face, she would later describe it to Dorothy as one verging on panic.

🌲🌲🌲

During lunch with an old friend, Carl would later describe *his* first impression of "the grand Diva Durban" as a psycho. It would make Colton Craig laugh out loud.

10

⧫ ⧫ ⧫

Jacob slowly and carefully rolled back in Rick Lawson's desk chair so as not to knock into something and send one of the many piles helter-skelter. He rose, laced his fingers behind his neck, let his head fall back, arched his chest, lifted his arms behind him in an attempt to stretch everything possible. His neck and shoulders ached. He held the extended position for several seconds, then released it. He lifted his shoulder blades toward his ears, held them there, let them fall, repeated the process, then rolled his shoulders both forward and backward several times. It had been over a week now since he'd arrived in Partonville. His body and mind missed his health club routine. "Some vacation," he said quietly, not wishing Helen, Rick's secretary, to hear him. She'd been relentlessly working, too, and was clearly an emotional wreck to boot, what with the loss of her friend *and* her boss—and possibly her job.

It seemed like ten years ago that he'd walked down the hall to hunt for Christmas decorations when the phone had rung and changed everything, tossing both mother and son into a whirlwind of events where, aside from their leisurely dinner at The Driscoll last evening, they'd remained ever since.

The call had been from Pastor. Dorothy immediately shared her exciting news that Jacob was in town for at least a whole week more. Pastor replied how nice—and how timely, since he'd just talked with Roscoe, who was beside himself with grief and in a near panic fretting about how he and his mother would ever even *begin* to handle his brother's office. What would they tell people about their documents? Although Roscoe was an able man, he was a schoolteacher who knew nothing about legalities. Pastor told Dorothy that Jacob might want to give Roscoe a courtesy call, which he did immediately. Although he now wished he'd thought twice about it, he'd been raised to pitch in where help was needed. Next thing Jacob knew, he was shoulder deep in papers at Rick's office.

He carefully maneuvered his way from behind the desk and wove his way toward the window. He needed a breath of air. After banging around on the old warped and wooden window frame, he finally got the second-floor office's window open. This was an interesting view of the square, he thought, one he'd never had before. After a quick survey, he spotted Katie Durbin's SUV parked in front of the Taninger building, strained to see if he could spot her inside. Nope. Although there was evidence a large sign from the side of the building leading onto the square had been removed, a smaller sign above the store entrance remained. "FAMILY OWNED AND OPERATED SINCE 1923," he said out loud. "Good-bye family, hello mini mall." He snorted, then reminded himself Katie'd had nothing to do with the closing of that business; it happened years before she'd arrived in town. He wondered if things were going any better for her this week than they were for him. Maybe he'd stop by on his way out, if her vehicle was still there when he was done for the day.

He turned and leaned against the windowsill to survey

the office. Three straight days of sorting, prioritizing, and where had he gotten? Now rather than Rick's giant piles, Jacob had nearly three times as many smaller ones. Was this progress? It had taken Jacob, a complete neatnik, one whole day just to figure out Rick's filing system, if you could call it that. Tall piles of folders were stacked on nearly every available space, including on chairs and across the tops of open file drawers. It was just the way his mom had described it. There were more files out of the drawers than in them, Jacob decided.

But after endless queries to Helen, who had no idea how Rick sorted things but assured him Mr. Lawson had *never* had trouble finding anything, it finally dawned on him: Rick seemed to have an aversion to alphabetical organization and instead liked to keep things in categories like wills, trusts, dead, alive, real estate, and court cases (which were few) and sorted in stacks of open and closed. The more recent the event, the closer to the top of the pile. Only *really* old cases were *in* the file cabinets, and as far as he could tell, everyone in them had been dead for more than ten years. Finally cracking Rick's "system" had been like finding the magic key, he thought, since at least he had a better handle on how to proceed to sort so that somebody *could* eventually take over. That somebody *could* find an important document, a brief, proof of innocence or ownership. But he didn't envy them. What had the man been thinking, keeping all these legal and binding papers in this chaos, and in this *tinderbox*?

"How did you work with this mess?" he'd asked Helen halfway through the first day. She'd teared up and run back to her office. Jacob followed her, apologized for his careless judgment and lack of sensitivity. She blew her nose while he patted her on the back, feeling like a helpless clod. He'd never been comfortable when women went all . . . emotional. "Really, Mr. Wetstra, it was Mr. Lawson who had to put up with *me*." Blow-sniff. "Do you know I was never once on time and he never once docked my pay or even complained? Not *once*!" Now Jacob really felt terrible. It had taken him less than four hours to bellyache about something.

At least he'd done something right: he'd located Rick Lawson's personal documents including his will, in which, thank goodness, he had named his co-executors, just like Roscoe had said. Jacob went through the document with a fine-tooth comb. Although some things were stated differently in Pennsylvania law (his state of practice) than in Illinois, it was clear all the necessary pages were concise, signed, witnessed and notarized. Roscoe and his mother were in charge of Rick's estate, although neither of them had a clue what to do about it other than *beg* Jacob to *please* step in and help poor Helen, at least until after Roscoe and his family arrived in town. "Of course, we'll pay you for your time," Roscoe said, not having a clue how much Jacob's fees were. Jacob was sure Roscoe would be shocked, so he made up his mind to just charge a nominal fee since Roscoe had *insisted* they pay Jacob for his time. Of course, that was before Jacob had seen Rick's office!

Jacob stretched one more time, closed the window and maneuvered his way back to the desk. He rested his forehead in his palms and thought back over the last few days. Roscoe had been wrong about one thing, he thought: people weren't waiting for the wake to ask questions. The law office phone was ringing off the hook. "Tell everyone not to worry," Jacob told Helen. "Tell them their files are safe and they'll be receiving a letter soon."

And that's exactly what he was going to work on next, a letter for Roscoe and Sadie to send to Rick's clients. The letter would advise clients that they were free to retrieve their files (easier said than done) and obtain other council. Or, should Roscoe and Sadie hire an official attorney to take over the probate for them *before* the letter went out, perhaps even find someone who could take over for Rick, the letter would extend an invitation for clients to make an appointment with the new attorney.

"Helen," Jacob said as he leaned in the doorway between their offices, "is it *possible* Rick or you kept a client roster?" *Please say yes.*

🌲🌲🌲

Pastor Delbert Carol Jr. and his wife had not had a vacation in years. Although during the summers they went to his wife's folks' cottage for a brief stay now and again, and he'd spent a short bout alone at a retreat center, the two of them had not had their own time together for eons. "How long has it *been,* Delbert?!" she'd asked him several times over the last two years. He'd promised her some time alone. "Just let me get through Thanksgiving," he'd said, "and we'll be out of here." His mother- and father-in-law were just awaiting word; if they could bring their cats ("Of *course* you can bring Frick and Frack, Mom!"), they would come stay with the Carols' two children at the drop of a hat.

But now there was a huge funeral and a town of hurting people. A shepherd couldn't leave his flock at a time like *this.* Yet, he knew his wife was right: he'd been under ongoing stress and it was taking its toll. He was not only forgetful and having trouble concentrating, but he was as close to being irritable as he ever came.

"Delbert, do you *know* what your voice just sounded like?" his wife asked him one day. "It sounded like you were reprimanding me."

"I'm sorry, honey, truly I am. I'll try to be more thoughtful. No man should talk to his wife that way, especially not a pastor!" Then he gave her such a quick hug before whirling away to attend another meeting that she'd hardly felt the warmth of his body.

Meanwhile Pastor Carol's wife was nearly just as stressed, building her own case of the blues. She was tired of being such a low priority when it came to his time. Yes, she'd known what she was getting into when she'd married a man of the cloth, but there were limits to these things! She was also tired of always being referred to as "Pastor's wife" instead of Marianne. She wondered if some people in town even *knew* what her name was. "Ask Pastor's wife." "Oh, let me introduce you to Pastor's wife." "Pastor, your wife wants to talk to you." Those who did know her name had not only worn out the old joke "So how have things been on Gilligan's Island lately, Mary Ann?" but they'd spelled it every which way under the sun and almost never correctly. She'd even once been referred to in the newsletter as "Pastor's wife, Mary Beth." It was as if she were invisible, or taken for granted. She couldn't remember the last time he'd looped his arm through hers the way he used to do, or reached for her hand, or. . . . It was time the two of them got away, got reacquainted, renewed their spark.

Although it was only December fourth, Delbert sat at his desk and thumped his pencil eraser on the "December 15" square of his giant desktop calendar. No way around it. Between funeral stuff, the aftermath of emotions, helping Sadie through her grief—not to mention the rest of the town—on top of Christmas preparations like the pageant. . . . No, he couldn't leave now. Marianne was going to be upset, but she would just have to understand: he had no control over Rick's death. *Please, God. Help prepare her heart for this news.*

He removed his glasses and rubbed his eyelids with the heels of his hands, then raked his fingers through his thinning hair. When he went to put his glasses back on, the left earpiece fell off. He rested the glasses on his nose, pinning them at the bridge with his left pointer finger so they'd stay in place while he looked for the screw; he was all but blind without his glasses. After closer inspection, he realized it wasn't just a matter of a missing screw; the hinge was broken. *Is this Your idea of helping me, Lord?* he asked as he shoved back in his chair in annoyance. He ducked down behind his desk to check the floor for the missing part, which he hoped he could tape. "Sorry, Lord" he said out loud, even though he hadn't previously opened his mouth; he knew God heard his every thought and question. *How's this for a better question, Lord?* he asked, running the palm of his hand across the floor, *I promised my wife a short vacation. What am I supposed to tell her? Huh?*

"Your wife just told me she already knows."

Pastor bolted upright. He'd jumped so quickly that he knocked his head on the bottom of his desk and his glasses fell completely off. His heart was about to pound right out of his chest as he retrieved them from the floor. Was God talking to him out loud?

"But she said to give her a call anyway."

Pastor bonked his head a second time before finally settling his glasses on his face, again pinning them to the bridge of his nose with his finger, and looking up. Dorothy was standing right square in front of him. "Goodness! Are you alright?" she asked as he rubbed his noggin. "I didn't mean to startle you!"

"Yes, I'm fine. Did you just say something to me?" he asked, his voice sounding taut.

"I certainly did," she said. "When my jaw flaps, it's usually me talking!" She smiled, although her eyes showed concern as he continued to rub his head. "As much as I enjoy a good ventriloquist, I've yet to work with one!" she said, breaking out into laughter, then quickly shifting to concern. "Are you *sure* your head's okay? Honestly, I am sorry. I didn't mean to startle you."

He just stared at her and nodded. Was it possible Dorothy was working with a ventriloquist of the highest order and *God* was moving her mouth, answering his silent prayers through her? With caution in his voice he asked, "What is it you think my wife already knows?"

"I don't think I know, I know I know. She told me herself—I just passed her in the narthex on my way in. I know for a fact she asked me if I was coming to see you and when I told her yes, she said, 'Oh, Good! You can save me a trip down the stairs. Tell him I already know, but he should give me a call anyway.' I think that's how it went."

"Did she tell you what it is she knows?"

Now it was Dorothy's turn to stare. "Is this a new version of 'Who's on First'?" she asked with a chuckle. "Because if it is, I'm not very good at that sort of game, never have been."

"No, no game. I'm just wondering if she made any reference to what it is she *knows*."

"She didn't say and I didn't ask. I assumed you'd know what she was talking about." Dorothy pulled up a chair and sat down in front of him, staring at him as he continued to jam his finger into the bridge of his nose. "You know, Delbert," she was one of the few people who called him Delbert sans the Pastor part, and she only did so when she wanted to address the man behind the cloth, "I've told you this before, but you need a vacation. And what happened to your glasses?"

Delbert sighed, released his finger and slumped forward, his glasses falling on the desk where he left them. He felt blind inside anyway. Aside from God, his wife and Father O'Sullivan, if there was anyone trustworthy he could talk to, it was Dorothy Jean Wetstra. She'd known him since he was a baby. He'd lost his mother when he was only eight years old and Dorothy always felt as close as he'd come to a surrogate mom. He leaned back in his chair and laced his fingers behind his head, elbows protruding straight out. He closed his eyes, pursed his lips for a moment.

"Marianne and I both need a vacation, Dorothy. And we were just about to take a few days off when Rick died. I've checked the calendar and there is now no way we can go until after Christmas—but I'd *promised* her." He released a great sigh that bordered on a moan. "I haven't told her yet that we can't go, I'm just dreading it." He sighed again. "And my glasses just broke. Too many times of putting them on and taking them off with one hand, I guess. Marianne warned me about doing that. I should have tried the contact lenses when she suggested them."

"Dear Lord," Dorothy said, bowing her head and launching right into what she knew Delbert needed to hear more than anything else from her, "Delbert here loves his wife and we all know it. We all love *him,* and we hope he knows it. *You* know he needs a break—they *both* need a break from feeding this ever-hungry and needy flock. We don't get your timing, God, but we just have to trust it. I ask you to give Marianne an extra dose of understanding and patience, and I ask you to quickly set a new plan in place for them, something they can look forward to in January when this congregation will *make* them take a trip, if I have to preach one Sunday myself! Amen."

Delbert opened his eyes and carefully settled his glasses back on his face, hoping the lenses would hide his pool of tears. He was so weary. He tried not to move his head so the tears wouldn't spill. "Bless you, Dorothy. Bless you. You know, you didn't know *you* knew, but you did," he said, winking. And then he couldn't help but laugh. "The only one who doesn't know is me. And I guess I'll just have to call Marianne to find out what she's talking about. You said you were on your way to see me. What did you need?" He leaned forward, rested his forearms on his desk and laced his fingers together.

"To be honest, I cannot remember. But I think God knew what *you* needed, and that was somebody to pray for you!"

♣ ♣ ♣

At Dorothy's suggestion, Delbert decided not to phone Marianne, which he did far too often. Instead, he made the short walk over to the rectory to give her the bad news in person. No point being a coward. Dorothy's prayer had helped shore him up—although the old King James Version of "O death, where is thy sting?" verse kept running through his mind and he thought, "The sting is going to be in my wife's eyes when I tell her that once again we cannot take our vacation—due to death."

The Carols finally got things sorted out, for better or for worse. Earlier in the day Delbert had left a message for Marianne on the machine saying he'd be late for dinner, then promptly forgot he'd made the call. What with all the last-minute arrangements for Rick's wake, and then the funeral, Marianne had already assumed he'd be tardy anyway. And previous to his message she'd also already guessed their trip would have to be postponed. She wasn't happy about it when he confirmed her suspicions, but one of the things she loved most about the man she had married was his sincere commitment to love God and to do his best for everyone. What more could she ask—aside from an entire week, maybe even *two*, with him in January!

Before he left, Marianne Rebecca Carol, the Pastor's wife, shocked Pastor Delbert Carol Jr. by saying, "And Delbert, I'm going to Hethrow *tomorrow* to start shopping for a new nightgown for our trip. A *black* nightgown." For a guy who was tired, she'd sure put the spring back in his weary step. The first place he walked was to the junk drawer to get some duct tape to temporarily fix his glasses.

"And I, Marianne, am making an appointment for next week to finally get fitted for contact lenses. I don't want to miss seeing a *thing* on our trip!"

11

Joshmeister,

Your e-mail freaked me out, man! You must have just missed being *in* that accident. FREAKED. ME. OUT! No wonder you can't stop thinking about that upside down car. The whole thing—your dead cell-phone battery, that guy in your town getting killed—FREAKED. ME. OUT.

On a related topic, I'm sure Shelby gave you some extra lip-lock after she heard about it. Like they say, everything has a silver lining. ☺ And speaking of lip-lock, I finally got up the courage to try to kiss Jennifer good night—and she let me. It was a kiss worth waiting for and that's all I'm going to say on the subject other than we're going out again Saturday night.

I bet it's too cold for crawdad hunting now but maybe if Jen (sweet, huh?) and I are still together next spring, and you and Shelby are still together next spring, we can all go hunting. I bet Shelby's as good at bagging them as you are (born and bred country girl that she is), but I know Jen (*so* sweet) would hate the slimy things, which would send her straight into my pumped-up arms. Did I tell you I've been working out with weights? I can see some progress. But enough on that topic.

Jen (okay, I admit I can't stop thinking about her) said her family stays home for Christmas. (RIGHT ON!) I think my Uncle Ned and his family are coming in which will be a blast. You remember him, right? He's the funniest and the hairiest relative I have. I like him, but I hope I don't sprout hair on my back like that. You gonna be here visiting your dad at all? Maybe your mom would let you bring Shelby for a day or two—then again, maybe after your last trip, your mom isn't ever letting you drive anywhere ever again.

Back to homework. But oh! How's Dorothy doing? I'm glad her son got to stay longer. I hope they're having a good time. I haven't e-mailed Outtamyway for a long time but tell her I'm thinking about her and that I'm glad her son got to stay.

Adios Amigo (Jen's taking Spanish. Think I'll call her before homework),

Alex, aka Huge Pecks

Dear Alex Huge Pecks (but I sincerely doubt it),

I've read your lovesick letter—my stomach is still rolling. My advice to you is to get a grip. (Just kidding.)

Working out, huh? This MUST be love! Do you remember when we were in sixth grade and we talked my mom into buying me a weight bench? Man, we were pathetic stick men. Hope you're better at it now since you nearly choked yourself to death trying to lift ten pounds, as I recall. Good thing Jen (*so* sweet) hasn't seen a picture of *that* studly muffin—not!

About driving. You aren't going to believe this, but Mom has actually mentioned getting a second car, and there's no way to look at that other than it would be MINE! She said when I was gone for the holiday in the

SUV and she was stranded way out here by herself, she realized how hard it was for me not to be able to get around when she was gone. I tried to stay cool. Got that responsible look on my face. "That might be a good idea," I said, while inside I was screaming YES! She hasn't mentioned it for the last two days, but I might bring it up at dinner tonight—if I see her. She is like obsessed with the mini mall.

Back to my homework. Already called Shelby (awwwww). Since Mom wasn't here we talked for forty-five minutes. It's good to have your homework done when you're lobbying for a CAR!

Joshmeister, who will tell Dorothy hello for you— maybe soon when I drive to see her in MY NEW CAR!

♣ ♣ ♣

Less than two minutes after Josh pushed the send button, his cell phone rang. "ARE YOU KIDDING ME?" Alex yelped. "A car? Get out of town!"

"I am *not* kidding you," Josh said. "I can hardly believe it myself. Shelby and I walked to the corner store today and grabbed a couple candy bars for lunch break since the school's food's taken a serious nose dive, and we also picked up a newspaper so I could start searching the car ads. I figure if I only point out used ones to Mom, that seems more responsible than assuming she'd get me a new one."

"Slightly diabolical, but I like it."

"I've circled maybe a dozen ads. The coolest is a . . . hold on here, let me grab the paper . . . '1998 Mitsubishi Eclipse. Low mileage. Good condition.' Then there's a 1997 Mazda Miata that sounds interesting and an older Pontiac Grand

Am. I didn't bother circling anything that didn't have at least a *minimal* rad factor. But you didn't hear that here."

"You better call me as soon as *this* deal goes down—if it really does."

"Don't worry. I've got Mom in my pocket."

♣♣♣

Nellie Ruth and Edward Showalter sat across from each other in a little Chinese restaurant in a strip mall on the Partonville side of the outskirts of Hethrow. Nellie Ruth looked from one oriental decoration to the other, her big brown eyes as delicate as china saucers, Edward Showalter thought. Her gaze panned from the bright yellow lanterns hanging from the ceiling, to the statues of red dragons with bugged-out eyes, to the octagonal aquarium back in the corner where her eyes landed. "Oh, that aquarium is just so beautiful. I love fish. They always look so relaxed and graceful, like mermaids gliding through the water." Their waitress set a pot of hot tea between them. "Mmmm. Smells good," she said, fanning the steam toward her nose with her hand.

"Allow me to pour," Edward Showalter said. He picked up the pot and served Nellie Ruth first, then himself. "Looks to be pretty dern hot, too," he said, "so be careful." The sounds of their synchronized blowing pleased him. Felt like it might be a sign.

Nellie Ruth turned her head back toward the aquarium. "Ever have any pets?"

"I'd say I've had more than my fair share of them over the years, mostly dogs."

"Oh, what kind?"

He looked thoughtful, executed another quick blow and

took a cautious sip of his tea. "I'd say mostly black-and-white kinds," he said with a chuckle. "I'm partial to mutts, although I did once own a full-blooded beagle. Bubbles was the quirkiest dog I've ever known. Always up to one kind of mischief or another. Did you know beagles can climb telephone poles? Well, at least Bubbles could." Nellie Ruth shook her head in amazement. She'd recently seen an advertisement featuring a lumberjack scaling a tree. She tried to picture a beagle doing the same. "I had this thick fence post—oh, I'd say a good five feet tall—I used to chain her to and I swear to you, I am not making this up: that dog could get up that pole and would sit right on top of it, just as pretty as you please. Looked like a flagpole topper. She'd sit as still as the post and sniff the air. She was one of those dogs that was . . . well, how can I say this? She was a good dog even when she was a bad dog, know what I mean?"

"I can only imagine. I never had a dog—or any pet, for that matter."

"Don't like animals?" he asked, a tone of surprise in his voice. "Allergic to them?"

"Oh, I ADORE animals. And as far as I know, I don't have any allergies. But I've just never had the . . . opportunity to own one."

"Not even when you were a kid?"

Nellie Ruth's childhood had been difficult. There was no point going into it over a question about a pet—or perhaps any time. "No, not even then."

"What keeps you from getting one now?"

"When I moved into my upstairs apartment decades ago, there was a 'no pets' clause in my lease."

"Excuse me if I'm wrong, but isn't there always a cat or two sitting in Bernice's windows?" Bernice Norris was Nellie Ruth's landlord. Nellie Ruth lived on the second floor of Bernice's stately old home.

"Oh, but those are *hers,* and she's the *landlord*!"

"Have you ever asked her if she'd mind if *you* got yourself a cat? Maybe she just bought or borrowed a copy of one of those standard rental agreements that already had that pet clause in it, but maybe she never really cared one way or the other."

"May I take your order?" the waitress asked. They hadn't even noticed her approaching.

"Well," Nellie Ruth said, looking to ES, who usually asked her what she wanted before the waitress or waiter came, and placed the order for her. This had been a hard thing to get used to since she was sixty-something years old and had been ordering on her own her entire life.

"Go ahead," Edward Showalter said. "Tell the lady what you want. You've got a voice of your own, and a mighty pretty one at that," he said, which made her blush. The waitress smiled, nodded her head and stared at Nellie Ruth.

"I think I'll have chicken chow mein," Nellie Ruth said. "That isn't spicy, is it? I see you have some red peppers by some of the dishes, but I don't see one next to the chicken chow mein, so I'm assuming it's not hot."

"No. Not hot. Crunchy noodle come with." Nellie Ruth closed her menu and set it on the edge of the table. "And you, sir?"

"I'll have the number fourteen," he said, his menu already closed.

"Oh, were we supposed to order by the *number*?" Nellie Ruth asked, reaching for her menu again. Both Edward Showalter and the waitress assured Nellie Ruth that any way she ordered was fine.

"Back to the pets. If you did have a pet, Nellie Ruth, would you rather have a cat or a dog . . . or maybe fish, since I see you keep looking at that aquarium?" he asked, nodding his head toward the corner.

"Kitten," she said without hesitating. "I just adore kittens. Bernice has four cats, and my favorites are her two gray ones. I know it's because she let me take care of them right after she got them. She went on a seven-day cruise with her sister and asked me to keep an eye on them for her. Those sweet little fluff balls fit in the palms of my hands when they were young," she said quietly, holding her cupped hands out in front of her as if the kittens were still nestled there. "I was so sad when Bernice got home. Well, I mean I was glad to see Bernice, of course, but I missed not spending that special time with those munchkins. While she was gone, I'd go down to their laundry-room inn," she said, giggling, her eyes bright with memory, "and visit them several times a day. Even though I still sometimes get to baby-sit with them, I'll just never forget how much I adored them at that kitten stage. So vulnerable," she said, her voice fading, as though the thought had touched something deep within her.

"And fish? Would you like an aquarium, too?"

"You can't have an aquarium with cats, can you? Weren't the cats always dipping their paws into the fishbowls in those old cartoons? Remember those cartoons they used to show before the movies, back when we were kids? I miss those."

"I surely *do* remember the cartoons. Mr. Magoo was my favorite. Laugh? I thought I'd bust a gut at that portly little guy. But back to pets. You know, they got so many fancy fan-dangled aquariums now that I think most of them even have lids on them. Lids and lights. I think a cat would have to be a safecracker to get into 'em these days! So," he said after a short pause, "a kitty or two *and* a fish or five. If you had your way, is that how it would be then?"

"No sense getting myself excited about something I can't have," she said, studying her cup of tea. "I have a full life the way it is, though. Nothing to complain about, really. For the most part I've learned to be content with what I have. And what about you?"

"I've been keeping my eyes open here lately for a 'free puppies' sign along the roadside. I had to put Wiley, my last dog, down about a year and a half ago. Cried like a baby, I did. I've cried every time I've lost a dog and Wiley was among my best. Poor guy got cancer. The vet at Hethrow gave him some pills that looked like they might be helping for a spell, but . . ." His voice trailed off. "I thought I could do without a dog, but turns out I can't."

The waitress carefully settled a cup of egg drop soup in front of each of them. "Egg rolls be right out."

"Oh! I'm sorry but I didn't order soup," Nellie Ruth said, apologizing for someone else's oversight.

"Soup and egg rolls come with meal."

Chow mein, soup, egg rolls *and* ES with dinner. Did it get any better than this? Nellie Ruth wondered.

As if he had read her mind, Edward Showalter said, "Not only that, but when we're done with our meals they'll bring us each an almond cookie *and* a fortune cookie."

"Oh!" Nellie Ruth exclaimed and clapped her hands. "A fortune cookie! I can't remember when I last had one of those! I wonder what's in store for us?" She could have fainted with embarrassment. She'd meant to say, I wonder what's in store for *each* of us, but the way it came out. . . .

Edward Showalter raised his eyebrows, then his entire face smiled. He was beginning to suspect he might just know the answer to that question.

⚞ ⚞ ⚞

"I don't know, Jessica. I'm thinking I'm going to make a fresh fruit salad, see what I can find at Your Store—although I have a feeling I might need to run to Hethrow for the star fruit."

"Star fruit? Is that a type of *fruit*? It sounds like something out of the ocean. Oh, wait! That's a star*fish*. But you know, I'm not even sure a starfish is actually a fish. Oh, well. What does a star *fruit* taste like?"

Katie switched the cell phone to her other ear and scooted down in the metal folding chair—her back was killing her. Bodies weren't made for metal folding chairs without padding. Plus she needed to work out. She felt stiff, tight. She'd just finished her first marathon meeting with the architect and hadn't realized how tense she'd been.

"You've never seen a star fruit? They're about as big as a kiwi and taste a little tarter, but when they're sliced, the slices look like stars. They make a pretty topper on a fruit salad. You'd love them." Jessica twirled the hair at the nape of her neck with her fingers; it had slipped out of the scrunchy that held her ponytail. She didn't have the nerve to admit she'd never had a kiwi either. "I'll put a little bowl of yogurt on the side, bring a spoon so people can drizzle some on top, if they like. Maybe get some chopped walnuts. . . . I figure there'll be enough calories at the dessert table to keep everyone up like kids on Christmas Eve. I, for one, am always glad to see some fresh fruit mixed in with all the rich stuff. Then again, if May Belle brings her double chocolate brownies, they are hard to resist!"

"Oh, I wish brownies sounded good, or anything for that matter," Jessica lamented, her morning sickness still haunting her. "About the only thing that sounds good to me right this minute is one of those hard, round peppermint candies. My grandmother taught me they can settle your tummy as well as most of those expensive products. I keep forgetting to have Paul pick me up a bag."

"How about I spare you any cooking, then, make a double batch of fruit: one for each of us to take?"

Jessica didn't answer right away. "You know, if you don't mind, I'm going to take you up on that kind offer. Paul says I just have to get better about accepting help when it comes my way, now that we're going to have two munchkins running around. But I'll pay you for my share, so keep track."

"Done deal. Two batches of fruit it is—and you are not paying me a cent. But speaking of money, how much do I owe you for the gift basket?" Katie had asked Jessica, who was talented at such things, to put together a special welcome basket on her behalf for the architect's room. At the time Katie also thought maybe the mini mall could use a gift basket store and she'd jotted a few notes. May Belle's double chocolate brownies would undoubtedly be a top choice for including in the gift package. She could already picture the individualized baskets brimming with unique items and goodies, May Belle's brownies right on top.

"Let's call the fruit salad and the gift basket a wash," Jessica said, "unless you think you're getting the raw end of the deal. Last time I was in Now and Again Resale they had a three-for-one basket sale to clear out some of their overload and I just couldn't resist: I came home with *nine baskets*! I've got baskets tucked just everywhere in our teensy place! One of them was the perfect masculine size—it didn't

have any round, more feminine corners; it was more boxlike—
and it didn't cost me a penny. And my friend just left me
some new Avon samples of men's products I tucked in the
basket—the first time she's thought to add men's samples to
her mix and I told her how timely *that* was—and most of the
other items I picked up at Wal-Mart, like a small bag of mixed
nuts and a sleeve of Oreo cookies, couple bottles of water, a
bag of chips, an apple, a banana, yesterday's *Partonville
Press.* . . . Oh, and I put in our Centennial Plus Thirty booklet!
I thought he might like to read about our town, get more of
an idea of our history to help him understand what you're up
to with the mall renovations. I printed 'Office Copy' on it so
he'd know to leave it, but it got me to thinking that I should
ask Harold if there are any copies left. Maybe he could sell
them to me at a discount so I could leave one in each room."
She stopped talking a minute, didn't hear anything, realized
she'd been prattling on. "I'm sorry, Katie. I know you have
lots to do and I'm just rambling."

"Jessica, you're *brilliant.* Hold on, I'm writing this down.
The Centennial Plus Thirty booklet is just the type of thing
I've been trying to come up with for the mini mall: how do
we help promote each other? Everybody did such a good job
on that booklet, too. There are some *wonderful* stories in
there! Funny, warm, sad, triumphant." She quickly recalled
being named an heir of the late Pastor Delbert Carol Sr., her
paternity claimed and affirmed in print. No details, just her
name. It had been perfect. "Let's talk to Harold together
about an extra print run if he doesn't have an ample supply,
maybe a special edition just for tourists, one with space for
more advertisements in it—which could pay for itself! I'll put
that in my 'Plan ahead' file. You know what else struck me
while you were talking about the basket? Wouldn't it be

great to have a mug? A 'Welcome to Partonville' mug. We can sell the booklets and the mugs and any other Partonville items we can think of in the mall—all around town, really."

"No!"

"Excuse me?"

"I didn't mean no to your idea. But you know what would have more buying appeal—well, I know *I'd* buy one, if the price was right: a 'Welcome to Pardon-Me-Ville' mug! That would be *funny* on a mug!"

"Jessica! It's *brilliant*! You are a marketing genius! Look, I know you have your hands full now, but let your mind start percolating a name for the new mini mall, okay? I'm going to run a townwide contest to name the mall, but I already have a feeling you're going to win."

"Mall names. Hm."

"Table that for now. Let me tell you my most exciting news. Carl Jimson, the architect, thinks my atrium idea will work. He said he couldn't be sure until he checked a couple structural points, but he sounded very optimistic." Katie shared a few more ins and outs of their labors and speculations, said he was going to draft a few rough sketches this evening for her review tomorrow. Jimson had told Katie it would be good if she could call in the contractor for their meeting tomorrow, too, to have him take a look at their ideas, get some of his input. She told Jessica that before she'd thought it completely through, Edward Showalter's name had rolled off her tongue as though she already had him under contract. "I sure hope he's available and can handle it or I'm going to look pretty stupid. I'm going to phone him as soon as we hang up."

"Oh! This is all so *exciting*, Katie! I'm sending good thoughts your way about Edward Showalter. Oh, and I see a big black car pulling in right now. Must be your Mr. Architect! Gotta go! And don't worry about a thing here; I'll take extra special good care of him for you."

⁂

When the waitress delivered the dessert plate containing two almond cookies and two fortune cookies, Edward Showalter let Nellie Ruth select first. She set an almond cookie on a napkin in front of her, but she was most excited about the fortune cookies. "Eenie, Meenie, Minie, Mo." She allowed the game to select the cookie on the left. Edward Showalter thought he would just melt watching her sweet, childlike enthusiasm. She ripped open the wrapper, cracked apart the cookie, read the paper fortune and simply could not believe her eyes. *Your love life is on track.* She folded it in half and said, "Interesting." She was too embarrassed to read it aloud, but Edward Showalter insisted.

"Smart cookie, if you ask me!" Without thinking he reached out and the palm of his hand briefly alighted on the top of Nellie Ruth's, which was resting on the table. It was their first intentional, intimate contact; he had not even dared to hold her hand as of yet. Such a warm and powerful jolt ran up his arm that he immediately pulled his hand away and busied himself opening his fortune cookie. He hoped Nellie Ruth hadn't thought him too forward. He ripped the cellophane, broke the cookie in half, popped the halves in his mouth, gave it a few crunches and swallowed. " 'Your financial situation is about to improve,' " he read aloud.

Little did he know just how much.

12

As soon as May Belle arrived home from wheeling the pork chop dinner to Sadie's, she'd phoned to invite Dorothy and Jacob over for a piece of custard pie. She'd baked two of them: one for the Lawsons and one to share with the Wetstras. It seemed the least she could do to repay Jacob for treating them to such a lavish dinner the other night, although a simple pie seemed a meager offering compared to the Extravagant Sweets Tray. Dorothy said Jacob wasn't home from Rick's office yet. He and Helen had ordered carry-out sandwiches from Harry's so they could work straight through and hopefully call it a night around seven or so, but now he wasn't so sure they'd be done by then either. "He didn't want to leave until some kind of a letter was under control. He sounded bushed, but that son of mine has always been diligent when he sets his mind to something. Guess that's what makes him such a good trial lawyer. But if you've got custard pie on the table, I'll be right over! My sweet tooth has been talking to me all day. I'll leave Jacob a note, tell him to come on by your place when he gets home, if it's not too late."

≣≣≣

Dorothy and May Belle sat at May Belle's kitchen table sipping a cup of decaf coffee. Sheba was curled up on the throw rug in front of May Belle's sink, the place she often settled in hopes May Belle would head toward the counter and toss her a crumb or two, which is usually how it went. "I think we have everything under control," Dorothy said. "Well, under as much control as we can ever have, since I imagine Rick thought he had control of things up until the moment he hit that black ice."

"Yes," May Belle said quietly, goosebumps racing up her arms.

"Eugene has everything set up at the funeral home for the viewing tomorrow evening, the altar for the funeral at the church is taken care of and it sounds like the food is covered for the dinner. Oh, and Theresa said St. Auggie's would also put out a few centerpieces on the tables, too. I'll tell you, I love this community partnership we've formed with St. Auggie's, and that Theresa Brewton continues to marvel me! She's always one step ahead of things, cheerful, enthusiastic and kind. A true leader."

"I quite agree with you about Theresa. And speaking of one-woman marvels, it sounds like Maggie's got everything under control with the Lawson family, considering their circumstances," May Belle said, shaking her head sadly. "Sadie told me Maggie would be coming to their house after dinner tonight. First she's going to Casey's to attend to Rick's hair and to make sure his clothes are in order, then she's coming by Sadie's to do her hair and give Roscoe a trim. You know I saw Maggie in Your Store today and she didn't say a word about volunteering to do all of that, and after a busy Thursday at the shop! Just like Maggie to keep on goin' and goin', doin' and doin'."

"And just like you," Dorothy said.

"And just like *you*," May Belle chimed, reaching into her

apron pocket to see what was bulging there. She almost always wore an apron around the house, kept it tied tightly against her soft roundness. She often picked up one thing or another that needed to go here or there and tucked it in her pocket. This time it was a three-prong adapter she'd used for her heating pad.

"Well, if I'm so wonderful, then where's my pie?" Dorothy teased. "I expected to see it on the table by the time Sheba and I got here. I do believe she's the only one who's received her treat so far."

"The way you talk to me," May Belle said, pretending to be shocked, "you'd think you've known me for eight decades or something!"—which, of course, she had. "I just thought if we waited a few minutes, Jacob might be along, but I guess not." When May Belle stood to cut the pie, Dorothy noticed she'd done so gingerly. May Belle's back was obviously better, but Dorothy could tell it was still bothering her some. May Belle placed two cloth, plaid, fall color placemats at their usual spots, as Dorothy had always had "her" chair at May Belle's, then quickly retrieved another one for Earl who must have heard the word "pie" clear from the living room since in he came. May Belle's kitchen was small and she kept her table pushed up against the wall. She and Dorothy always sat across from each other; Earl didn't like sitting against the wall so even when Dorothy wasn't there he sat in the chair toward the center of the room facing the window.

"I told Earl that we're going to get our Christmas decorations up pretty quick now," May Belle said while she retrieved the napkins. "I've got some of the happiest snowman placemats—I'm sure you remember them, Dorothy. After so many years they're starting to look a little ragtag from all the washing and ironing, but I just love them. Every year after the holidays I think I'm going to toss them out, but I just can't bring myself to do it."

Try as she might, Dorothy couldn't picture them. "Do you remember placemats with snowmen on them, Earl? I don't."

"Yes, Dearest Dorothy," he said, seating himself between the two women. Although Earl addressed everyone as Mr. or Miss plus their first name, he'd never called Dorothy anything but Dearest Dorothy. It was an endearing remnant from his earliest childhood days. Although Earl didn't usually warm to people, he'd melted right into Dorothy's lap. May Belle had been so touched and joyful to see her son take to someone, she'd said, "Oh, my. He sure loves his Dearest Dorothy." After that, Earl never called her anything else. "The snowmen are right here," he said, pointing his index finger to the lower right-hand corner of his placemat.

"That is exactly right, Earl!" Dorothy said. "I couldn't picture them myself, but when you said that, I knew you were right, by golly. I can picture them now. Three of them, right? And the placemats are green, right?" Earl nodded and beamed.

"Earl does love the Christmas decorations," May Belle said as she stood at the counter using her pie cutter to slip the slices onto the plates, Sheba standing by just in case.

"Now *that* I remember! You know, Earl, I don't have my decorations up yet either. Four days ago Jacob was on his way to help me find the boxes, but then the phone rang and. . . ." She didn't want to bring up Rick's death again. "But by golly, we're getting them up this weekend, no matter what!"

"Can I see them?" Earl wanted to know.

"Of course you can. We'll give you and your mom a call as soon as we light up the tree, Earl. Or better yet, maybe you'd like to come help us decorate it!" When she lived out on the farm, she'd always had a huge fresh tree. Every year people at her Christmas open house would rave about it. "Where'd you get such a big tree?" they'd want to know. "Got it at By George's," she'd always answer.

♣ ♣ ♣

George Gustafson owns By George in Partonville and since the first year he opened the filling station, as most in Partonville still refer to it, he's set up a tree stand in his side lot right after Thanksgiving. He drives his big old flatbed pickup to his cousin's tree farm in Wisconsin and cuts them himself. When Hethrow began its expansion, many of their chain garden stores started selling cheaper trees and his business dwindled so much he thought he might have to give it up. But after a few years, most of his regulars—who had trouble looking him in the eye during the holidays, they felt like such traitors with their store-bought trees—decided that By George's trees smelled better and sure enough lasted longer. "I reckon if a feller ain't had enough sense to grow his own Christmas tree, he should at least, by George, buy it from By George!" Of course, Arthur was always in George's corner since George had sent a lot of auto repair business Arthur's way when he was still running his shop. But still, time and again Arthur would say to Dorothy when he saw her tree, "*I never saw one that big on George's lot when *we* went looking.*" Dorothy didn't tell them that George always spotted, cut and set aside the biggest one just for her—for her party, really—since he couldn't imagine the holidays without her lavish hospitality and figured it was the least he could do to contribute his share. He cut her a discount, too, but he swore her to secrecy lest word got around.

Where would she put even a *tiny* tree in her living room now? She'd have to talk to Jacob about it. This was just one more in a long string of changes for her and it made her sigh. *Surely* she wasn't old enough for one of those little trees that sits on top of a table! She used to tease about folks who had those, saying they must not have a very big Christmas spirit to have such a tiny tree. She remembered asking her own grandmother why one year she suddenly had a small tree and her grandmother had said something like, "At this age, it's all just too much bother. A small tree can bring as much pleasure as a big one." *Lord, let it be so!*

May Belle sat down at the table, having served the largest pie slice to Dorothy, the second largest to Earl and the one that hadn't cut exactly right to herself. "May Belle, how big was your tree last year?" Dorothy wanted to know. She couldn't envision it and was beginning to wonder if she needed to check into that memory vitamin she heard about and kept forgetting the name of.

"How big *was* our tree last year, Earl?" The Justices' moderate trees were so different each year: some years fat, some years skinny, some years taller than others (although never too tall), some more lopsided than others. . . . Same as he did for Dorothy, George always set one aside for May Belle, one slightly larger and therefore more expensive than he knew she could afford, but he only charged her for a smaller one.

Earl set his fork down and held his hand about three feet above the top of the table.

"Well, now, I'm afraid that's about the size I'm going to have to get this year, not including the table!" Dorothy said.

"Jacob can help you rearrange a few things," May Belle

said, casting her memory around Dorothy's living room. "I'm sure you can work something out. Maybe you could fit a tall, skinny one in the front window where we moved that card table for your Hookers' night."

"Do you foresee a Charlie Brown tree in my future?" Dorothy asked, sounding almost forlorn.

"Now, Dorothy, there's worse things than that. Think how we all love Charlie Brown."

"Thank you, dear. That's just what I needed to be reminded. And you know, I bet if I put my mind to it, I could have a *dandy* Charlie Brown tree. Might even be fun trying to create one!" Yes, the quirky notion was already percolating in her imagination. *Thank you, Big Guy.*

"Say, speaking of Christmas, did you ever talk to Katie about maybe hosting your Christmas party out at the farm?"

"The right moment hasn't presented itself yet," Dorothy said between swallows, then she stopped to smack her lips. "How *do* you make simple custard taste so good?"

May Belle ignored Dorothy's question about the pie; she still had concerns about the present lack of a December gathering. She'd heard Dorothy offer one excuse or another as to why she hadn't approached Katie about it yet, and she wondered what was *really* going on there. It wasn't like Dorothy to procrastinate. "I've had a couple folks at church ask me whether I know anything about the annual party. I told them to ask you. I'd say that party has been one of the highlights of *everyone's* season all these years. Hard to imagine Christmas without it. When and where else would the Hookers present their 'Best of Happy Hookers Moments' to the townsfolk if not at the party?" It was a long-standing tradition in which riotous moments throughout the year were instantly collected with a "Well, THAT one just made the 'Best Of' moments!" The last entry this year was when Maggie had arrived direct from the hair convention in Chicago with a REAL TATTOO!

May Belle took a bite of pie and rolled it around in her mouth for a moment to decide whether or not she'd added enough vanilla and cinnamon. Just right, she thought with a satisfactory smile, which made her happy for the Lawsons. "If we weren't all so distraught and distracted by Rick's death, I imagine we'd be hearing much more about the lack of a party plan. If Katie's *not* hosting the open house, do you think she'll at least host the Hookers for a December night of bunco, or maybe a potluck dinner or . . . ?" Dorothy's annual Christmas party always took the place of the usual Hookers' meeting. "If we don't have anything at her house, I can't remember who's in line to host the Hookers next. Can you?" Dorothy shook her head and took another bite of pie. "Hard to think we don't even have a Hookers' meeting in place yet and here it is well into the first week of *December* already! And folks get so busy, what with shopping and school plays and out-of-town company, I wonder if we'll even be able to coordinate anything this late in the game," she said. "Wonder if we might have to just skip it."

"Can't speak for Katie one way or the other, May Belle, but to be honest, I've had more than a few inquiries about the party myself. Between the two of us, probably all the Hookers have asked, as well as half the town."

"I wonder if any of them have actually asked Katie?"

"Good question. I'd bet we'll get a question or two about it during the doings for Rick this weekend. It *would* be a swell time to make an announcement about a party though, give folks something to mark on their calendars and look forward to after such a sad turn of events. And this I know: no matter how last-minute the invite, if you offer food and fellowship, people will come. I guess I'm just going to have to give Katie a call either this evening or in the morning and approach the topic head on."

⚏⚏⚏

Jacob followed Helen down the steep second-floor stairs from the law office; it was 7:45 P.M. "I don't know about you," he said as they walked, "but I *feel* like we've put in a very long day. I think we got a lot accomplished, though, which makes me feel good. How about you? How are you doing?"

Helen came to a sudden halt in the landing at the bottom of the stairs and Jacob nearly crashed into her. She was staring at the metal mailbox mounted on the interior wall just inside the door. "Rick Lawson" was handwritten on the yellowed and curling piece of paper that was taped to the front of the dented box. Although it was usually locked, the lid was open and envelopes of all sizes were sprouting out the top. This was the first time in the four days since Mr. Lawson's death that she'd either noticed or thought about the mail. Her boss had always brought it up before she'd arrived for work. "I must have been living in a daze," she said more to herself than to Jacob. She was still frozen in place.

"Under the circumstances, I'd say you've been doing extremely well," Jacob said, a gentle assuring tone in his voice. She sighed and started to reach for the bundle, realizing she'd have to retrieve it one piece at a time to keep it from toppling out, the mass was so tightly wedged in. "I have an idea," Jacob said. "Let's pretend we didn't see this tonight either. We're both tired, you've got a big weekend in front of you with the funeral and all and we need to be *done* for the day. That pile of mail isn't going anywhere."

"Do you think it'll be okay? How will they even leave tomorrow's delivery? Not a single thing more will fit in there," she said, continuing to stare at it like it was a ghost, or maybe a mummy or a tombstone.

"How about you give me the office keys and I'll come in before the mailman arrives tomorrow. What time will that be?" She stared at him for a moment and her eyes began to well; it wasn't clear why. "Don't worry about it, I'm an early riser. I'm sure I'll beat him here."

"Her."

"Her. I'm sure I'll beat her here." Helen looked concerned. "Or how about this?" he said enthusiastically. "How about you go on ahead, I'll get a plastic bag from upstairs—I saw a couple stuffed somewhere—and I'll take this to Mom's tonight."

"If you're working, I'm working," she said, her voice leaving no doubt about it.

"Okay. I promise you I won't work either. I'll just put all the mail straight in a bag and I won't look in the bag tonight. I'll just bring the bag back with me tomorrow morning." She studied him, thinking it over. "But here's the caveat: neither one of us will look in the bag tomorrow either. Since tomorrow is the wake and you've been such a trooper to work under so much duress, we will only work on the letter until noon so you have time to catch your breath before the wake. When we're satisfied with it, I'll find out if Sadie and Roscoe have found an attorney to handle the probate for them yet. If so, we'll add that information, make the copies—your copy machine is up to snuff, right?" She nodded her head. "Good. Then we can spend the morning try-ing to ready the mailing so all the Lawsons have to do is sign the letters and send them off." She gave a small nod. "Right now I'm scheduled to fly out on Monday and I feel pretty sure I'll need to be on that plane, so I'm hoping we can get things at least that far." Panic began to fill Helen at the re-minder he'd soon be leaving. Then what? He could see the concern in her eyes. "At least we'll have the framework in place. Then whoever steps in can handle everything, includ-ing what's in the mystery bag of mail," he said.

Helen chuckled and dropped her shoulders. "Mystery bag of mail. Mr. Lawson would have liked the idea of *that*," she said, a faraway look enveloping her. And then she be-gan to cry—again.

For the third time that day, Jacob pulled out his mono-grammed hanky. "Do you have the keys to the mailbox?" he asked her.

Helen blew her nose so loudly that it echoed in the stair-well, then she pulled herself together. "I'm taking this hanky home and washing it for you," she said, her voice still crack-ing a bit.

"You'll get no argument from me," he said, which turned up the corners of her lips. She reached in her handbag to re-trieve the keys from where she'd plunked them after locking the upstairs door to the office. Three keys on a metal loop: one key for the office, one for the mailbox and one for Mr. Lawson's top desk drawer—which he never locked anyway, she thought as she gingerly fingered them. There was a two-inch round wooden key fob on the ring with only the mer-est evidence of print left on it, so little print you couldn't tell what it had originally said. Since he always carried the keys by the fob, often rubbing it like a touchstone when he sat idle, he'd worn a smooth and shiny groove in it. She ran her thumb down the groove now, wondering at the fob's origin. She'd once asked him about it, but all he said was that it was a special gift from a special friend. It wasn't right for her or Jacob or anybody but Mr. Lawson to have this set of keys which suddenly felt like such a personal item. Mr. *Lawson* always opened and locked up. That was *his* job. These were *his* keys, *his* special fob. Her eyes welled again, but she reluctantly handed the keys over to Jacob since Mr. Lawson would not be coming back. She hated how that truth kept hitting her anew.

"I'll give them back to you tomorrow," he said. "Don't worry. I'll make sure not to lose them." Helen left without another word. If she spoke, she would surely sob again, and she was simply too wrung out.

Jacob, on the other hand, felt a spike of renewed energy when he noticed Katie's SUV still parked in front of the Taninger building.

13

⚑⚑⚑

"Yes, I remember mentioning a second car, Joshua," Katie said into the cell phone wedged between her ear and shoulder. "Yes, I know you are currently stranded out in the country like I was when you were in Chicago—although you are being a little dramatic since I'm only a couple miles away. And I also know you're supposed to be doing homework."

"Done."

"Have you cleaned your room?"

"Done."

"Have you checked the mousetraps, emptied any . . . corpses, put fresh peanut butter in traps?"

"Done. Corpse report: one. Escape report: one tripped trap."

"Have you had something to eat?"

"Done. Had a PBJ, a cheese sandwich and a *salad*," he said, hoping to score a few points with his few leaves of iceberg lettuce and three tablespoons of Thousand Island dressing. "Have you had any dinner, Mom?"

"No. I'm just finishing up here."

"Want me to make you a salad while you're on your way home? I can use one of those bags of weed-looking stuff you keep in the fridge and cube some of your gross-smelling health cheese. Sprinkle a couple drops of your low-fat raspberry dressing on it."

"I'm surprised you've noticed."

"You think I don't pay attention? I pay close attention, so close it might scare you." He chuckled. "While you eat the dinner I will have prepared, we can go over a few ads for used cars I've circled. Okay?" He was sure the "used" part sounded particularly wise.

Katie was just about to consent when she heard the door opening, looked up and saw Jacob. He was wearing a white dress shirt with the top two buttons undone, a pair of black slacks, shiny cordovan loafers, a cordovan belt, a lightweight beige jacket and a smile. Why is it he was always taller—and broader-shouldered—than she remembered? "Let me get back to you on that," she said, her Mother Voice having vanished, suddenly replaced by a business tone. "Someone just came in."

Josh sighed. It seemed like more and more every day, his old Chicago Mom was reemerging. Not coming home for dinner was beginning to be a habit—and a sure sign of things to come. "But you won't be long, right? And we'll look at the ads when you get home, right?"

"Joshua Matthew Kinney, do not start pushing me. We will talk about all of this later," she said, her lips pressed as closely to the cell phone as she could get them in an effort to keep her words private. She said a quick good-bye and flipped her phone closed.

"Whoa. That sounded like the same tone I heard my brother use on my nephews a few times over the holiday, but only when they were crossing a line—or threatening to."

Katie stared at him. She didn't like the idea he'd heard her, and she liked it less that he'd made a point of letting her know. *Not very tactful.* "Just one of those parenting things," she said casually. "We'll work it out."

"I have no doubt about it, especially since you used his full name. Mom always stopped me dead in my tracks when she pulled *that* one out of her bag of tricks."

Great. I remind him of his mother. "What are you doing on the square at this hour?" she asked, sneaking a peek at her watch. "I thought maybe you'd left town by now. Are you just getting back from a road trip with your mom? I understand you invited her."

"Actually," he said, "Mom's been pretty busy with funeral stuff and I've been working in Rick Lawson's office all week, trying to help poor Helen and his family by making some sense out of his mounds."

"You've been working right over there? Up there in Rick's office?" she asked, nodding her head in that direction. She wondered if he'd been spying on her from the front window.

"Yes," he said, seating himself in the metal folding chair across from her without first asking if she minded. "That would be the place. Ever been up there?"

"Unfortunately, yes. But I have to admit, it *was* surprising how well Rick handled my aunt's estate and how he seemed to know what was in every stack. He might have been a slob, but it's clear everyone in town is really going to miss him."

"Slob? That's kind of harsh."

Oh, so now you're Mister Nice Guy? "It was a bad choice of words. Disheveled might be a better word, or maybe just eccentric. You know what I mean."

"If you say so," he said flatly, again baffling her as to whether he was being rude or if this was just his wry sense of humor. Then he gave her a wide smile, letting her know he was just teasing her. "Amazingly, Helen has assured me that her boss never had any trouble finding a thing in that mess.

And Mom does nothing but brag on the man. She's told me lots of stories about the great things he's done for people. Kind of a quiet, behind-the-scenes guy, I guess. Didn't like to draw attention to himself. I don't remember too much about him, although I've met him several times over the years. Mom says there was nothing boastful or showy about him, just a guy who always got the job done and did it from the heart." A silent moment passed. "You know," he said, his voice lowered and laced with sincerity, "when all is said and done, that's a pretty good testimony to a man's life, isn't it." He noticed the look on her face and added, "Or a *woman's* life."

Katie studied his face a moment, then nodded. "How long you in town for again?"

"As far as I know, I'll be on a plane Monday—although there is an outside chance I can extend my stay a little longer. I talked to my law partner today and she said there's been another postponement on the biggest trial I've got on the docket. I do have to get back pretty soon, though, wrap a few things up. I'm hoping to come back here for at least a couple days over Christmas. But you know, I feel bad for Helen. She's pretty stressed out and she's sure got her hands full. Going to have them full for some time, I'm guessing."

"I don't think I knew you had a law partner."

"Brenda Stewart. We went into practice together about twelve years ago now. She's as tough as they come and incredibly smart."

Maybe she's *why he never married.* "Do the Lawsons have anyone stepping in for Rick yet?"

"Don't know. It would sure make it easier if they did, though. It's quite a burden and worry for them, especially with Roscoe being from out of town. I'm sure they've got extended family coming in this weekend and their phone's probably been ringing off the hook, so I doubt hiring someone to handle the probate has been at the top of their list. After all, they're burying a son and a brother. I can't even imagine . . ." He shook his head and looked down at the floor.

"How'd you get involved up there?" she asked, pointing her cell phone toward the window. "Did you just volunteer?"

He laughed. "Volunteer? *Volunteer* to work until after seven P.M. every night on my *vacation*? Do you think I'm *that* swell of a guy?"

"To be honest, I don't know you well enough to know what type of a guy you are—really. I do know that if you're anything like your mother, you volunteered."

"Let's say Mom sort of volunteered me. Plus Roscoe sounded desperate on the phone and I had a little time. . . ."

"How's the labor going?"

"Once I cracked the code, things got a lot easier."

"The code?"

"Rick's filing system."

"You're not telling me that all those piles actually represented a *system*, are you?"

"Indeed. Quite a fascinating system, too. Say," he said, looking at his watch again, "have you had dinner yet?" Never mind he'd already eaten; he could go for a light sandwich or bowl of soup. "We could grab a bite and I'll tell you all about it."

Shocker! "No, I haven't. Josh volunteered to make me a salad, but he's just trying to bribe me."

"Bribe you? That's due cause for legal action and I happen to know a good attorney who's in town for a few days."

She laughed in spite of herself. "Yes, bribe me with a bag

of salad and some cubed cheese. It's my own fault, though. A few days ago I made the mistake of mentioning we should get a second car."

"*Now* I see. A little anxious, is he?"

"A lot bugging me is more the truth."

"Can't blame him. I remember when I got my first car. Interesting story. So would you like to go grab a bite with me and hear that saga, too? Josh could join us if he likes."

"He's already eaten."

"Mom's already eaten, too. She's over at the Justice household, no doubt pounding down custard pie as we speak. I'm supposed to drop by for a piece, too, but to be honest, I need some protein."

"Where would you suggest? Harry's is already closed, thank goodness."

He chuckled. Personally, Jacob found Harry's Grill a comfortable place laced with fond memories, which always made him feel nostalgic for good old Pardon-Me-Ville. During his youth, he and his buddies used to go to Harry's on their way home from school—when Partonville *had* its own schools—for French fries and cherry cokes. Now, kids didn't get off the buses from Hethrow until late in the afternoon. He'd hardly seen any youth on the square since he'd arrived. Sad. "To be honest," he said after his mini reverie, "aside from dinner at The Driscoll the other night, Mom's kitchen—and, of course, May Belle's—I'm pretty out of touch with food offerings around here. Can you recommend a place?"

Katie yawned, looked at her watch again. "You know, I'm not sure if it's open for dinner but there's a new little restaurant in Yorkville that's supposed to . . . OH! I've got a phone call to make!" Since Edward Showalter had helped Johnny Mathis transform the old feed shed into a restaurant, thoughts of The Piece sent a hot *zing* through her. She had to call Edward Showalter right now! "Would you mind waiting while I make my call? It's pretty urgent."

"No, go ahead. Or . . . I've noticed you've been yawning," he said, standing, "and I'm pretty bushed myself. Maybe we should just skip it."

"Hold on a minute," she said, lifting her index finger. It occurred to her he might think she was just blowing him off. "Let me make this call, then we'll evaluate the time, our energy and our choices." She was already pushing the buttons on her phone to bring up her contacts.

Turns out Edward Showalter had just walked in the door to his ringing phone. Yes, he was available in the morning, and yes, he was "indeed honored and mightily blessed" she'd invited him to sit in on the meeting. She should not worry about a thing; he'd see her at nine sharp.

"Whew!" Katie said when she hung up, feeling suddenly wide awake from the close encounter with humiliation over almost forgetting to phone him. She looked at her watch again. "Okay, how about this. How about we head to Hethrow to the Olive Garden? I love their soup and salad, and at this late hour, that's about all I want to eat before I get in bed. Since it's the direction of the farm, I can drop off my car, ride with you and you can drop me off on your way back to your mom's."

"Sounds like an excellent plan."

⁂⁂⁂

Dorothy and Sheba walked home from May Belle's, two slices of custard pie in tow. They were on real plates (May Belle didn't stock paper plates; too expensive), each wrapped in plastic wrap placed side-by-side in a big brown grocery bag from Your Store. One piece was for her and the other for Jacob who she hoped wasn't wearing himself out working until midnight since he'd never shown up at May Belle's and it was now past nine-thirty.

Strolling along, she couldn't seem to help but obsess about the Christmas party again, now that May Belle was pressing the issue. Dorothy prayerfully examined herself about her lack of follow-through when it came to the matter of the Christmas party. Had it just been about asking someone a favor, that would be one thing. If she could simply move the party to her new house, that would be another. If she asked to host the party herself at Katie's. . . . She'd envisioned that possibility many times, and did so again now, but her vision always ended the same way: at the end of the gala it would simply feel too sad not to be able to venture up the familiar old creaking stairs to her cozy bedroom, sit in her prayer chair by the window and have her evening moment with the Big Guy while she looked out over the barnyard and toward the creek line of trees (rather than into the neighborhood street), whisper good night to Weeping Willy, Woodsy and Willoway, the trees down by the creek she'd named as a child, then fall quickly asleep to the aromas of the land and the sounds of a chirping cricket wafting through her good old country window.

Oh, for goodness sakes! Crickets don't even chirp in the winter! Lord, snap me out of my mire of self-pity. I'm allowing my own emotions to interfere with a whole town's tradition!

"Dorothy Jean Wetstra," she said aloud, causing Sheba to stop her trotting for a moment and look at her, "it's time you buck up and stop imagining a mountain of mayhem, woman! This town deserves its annual Christmas party. Get over yourself and see what you can do!"

14

⁂

The Del Vechias pulled into the Lamp Post drive with only forty minutes to spare before the wake was to begin. Just enough time to freshen up, catch their breath and head to the funeral home. Even though their burden was heavy, they couldn't have been more delighted with their room. Some time ago they'd read in the *Press* about the Joys buying the old place and all the improvements they'd made. Things looked just the way they'd imagined them after reading the descriptions so aptly reported by Sharon Teller. Jessica Joy, although looking somewhat peaked and tired, was much more beautiful than they'd remembered her appearing in the newspaper picture. Sarah Sue, who was in a little bouncy seat in the lobby when they checked in and whom they'd read about in the birth announcements, looked like a beautiful miniature version of her mom. Paul Joy escorted them to their room after Jessica handed them the key; it was clear they were a couple working hard not only for the money, but to make everyone feel *at* home while *away* from home. If everyone in Partonville was as dear as this sweet family, no wonder Rick wouldn't leave.

Whether she knew the occupants or not, Jessica had handwritten notes of condolences for everyone in for Mr. Lawson's funeral (six rooms out of twelve) and left them on the beds along with Wednesday's *Partonville Press* since it contained everything she thought visitors would need to know about all of the arrangements, including directions to the locations, which Sharon had thought to provide in a sidebar. ("You had a raise lately?" editor Harold Crab had asked her when he read her submission. "No, sir." "Well, you deserve one." "I accept," she'd jokingly replied. The very next week she'd received twenty more bucks in her envelope.) Sharon had also included the hours to Harry's Grill with an asterisk that explained "*Opens 6 A.M.; Closes 6 P.M. sharp, which means SHARP!"

When Katie read the sidebar, she laughed out loud remembering the way Lester had stuck by his guns the night she and Josh first arrived in town to deal with her aunt's estate. They were travel-weary, starving and he was the only dining establishment in town, other than the snack bar at Wal-Mart which Jessica had so warmly told her about and which Katie refused to even consider. It hadn't mattered how loudly she'd knocked on the locked door to Harry's Grill; all Lester finally did was come to the door and point to the sign. All anyone in the restaurant did was to stare. 6:01. CLOSED, Lester's sign said. And that was that. It had been a terrible beginning to what turned out to be a life-altering change. She'd had no idea at the time that she would end up not only living in Partonville, but fighting for its very survival.

Some days that incident seemed like a million years ago to Katie and on other days it only felt about ten minutes ago. The truth was, it had been about seven months, although she hadn't officially moved to Partonville until close to when school began, she and Josh first having rented two rooms at the Lamp Post for quite some time, which is how

she and Jessica had come to be friends. They were an un-
likely pairing: a rich, divorced, well-educated, hard-hitting
businesswoman in her forties with a teen son and a somewhat shy, married, high school graduate in her twenties
struggling with a new business and a new baby. What they'd
learned from each other, however, was that you cannot
judge by circumstances, social standing or appearances.
Everyone has vulnerabilities, needs and gifts; all moms are
often utterly lost when it comes to knowing what to do in a
given situation—no matter what the age of their child. The
friendship had become a tight, rich, fun, honest godsend
for both of them. It was an odd-couple friendship the Del
Vechias would take note of during their stay, citing it as an
example of how people who might not otherwise ever make
a connection have a *chance* to get to know one another in
small-town living.

≠≠≠

Usually at wakes, people come and go. This time, people gathered early and most stayed until the end. There was an un-
spoken need to draw close, affirm each other's grief—affirm
each other's lives.

Sadie stood at the foot of her son's casket and refused to
sit down, her facial bruises now more green and yellow than
a few days ago, her battered body aching, her mother's
heart pierced clear through. Roscoe held on to her elbow,
his family lined up beside her, as the reception line kept
moving along. Sadie kept looking over her shoulder at her
son. *So still. My baby looks so still.* "He looks real good." "I
just can't get over it." "What will we do without our Rick?"
"How long can you stay, Roscoe?" "Rick looks real nice."

"How you feeling, Sadie?" Such trite things people say and ask, Sadie thought when she realized that they were talking to her. But then, what else could they say, she wondered.

Oh, my baby boy is gone! How can I go on living without you?

Dorothy motioned for Roscoe to move down for a moment so she could squeeze in. She sidled up beside Sadie and took her hand. She stood there for a long while saying nothing, just gently holding Sadie's hand, rubbing her arm, occasionally nodding as if to respond to people on Sadie's behalf. When Sadie finally dared to look at Dorothy—and she feared doing so might cause her to crumble—she heard in her heart everything Dorothy had not uttered aloud. She knew Dorothy's spirit was groaning along with hers. This was a mother who had lost a child. This was a mother who knew.

🌲🌲🌲

The next day at the funeral dinner in the Park District building, the Del Vechias stepped up to the microphone and shared some of their wildest stories about Rick. It warmed Sadie's heart to know her responsible son had, at least at *some* point in his life, simply let loose and partied. In fact, learning *those* stories reminded her of several raucous stories she knew about her deceased husband, stories they'd never dared tell their sons. It was time, she decided. She could barely eat for all her table talk, sharing every last anecdote she could think of. Her only regret was that Rick wasn't there to hear these things about his father, too.

"Dorothy's right," she said wistfully. "If it wasn't for our stories, what would we *really* know about each other? What would we leave behind?" Encouraged by the Del Vechias' sharing, no less than a dozen more folks eventually stepped up to the microphone to share something about Rick, and in doing so shared pieces of themselves. They talked about how he'd made them laugh, saved them from this, helped them do that, fought for them against one thing and another—even though they couldn't always pay him his regular fee. May Belle could hardly be heard when she tried to talk about Rick's generosity to her son, Earl, all of these years. "How many dollars . . ." she wondered aloud, her voice cracking and fading off.

‡‡‡

Near the end of the dinner, Dorothy approached the microphone and asked if she could have everyone's attention. "Folks, we are mourning the loss of one of our own. But thanks to the Del Vechias' kick-off," she said, motioning for them to stand up and be acknowledged, "we have also celebrated Rick's life in grand style, if I do say so myself." Acknowledgments and a few chuckles rippled through the crowd. "Thank you, Bob and Louise, for making the long journey back to Rick's beloved Partonville.

"Folks, there is nothing like the death of someone we love to remind us that life is fragile—that we are *alive*—and that ready or not, the sun will continue to rise tomorrow, life will go on. So in keeping with the idea of a celebration of life, it seems a fitting time to make a joyful announcement! Katie Durbin here," she motioned for Katie, who was seated beside her, to stand, "has asked me to do the honors. So here ye! Here ye! The annual Happy Hookers' Christmas party will once again be held out at Crooked Creek Farm!" She stopped talking to allow for the applause. Silence. Seemed people needed a moment to digest the news that either the City Slicker was hosting their annual tradition or allowing Dorothy to; it hadn't been made clear.

This lack of information, some of them thought, would be a topic for conversation at the U on Monday. But in any case, they decided to go ahead and clap since obviously that's what Dorothy was waiting for them to do. And after all, it was good to know that the party was on no matter who was hosting.

"Here are the particulars, which will undoubtedly be printed in the *Press,* but we want you to mark your calendars now. As usual, the party will commence at two P.M., Saturday, December twentieth—which is exactly two weeks from today—and end when the last of you leaves." *And don't we all know who* that *will be?* she wanted to say aloud but stifled herself. It was always Cora Davis who didn't want to miss a single thing! She and her husband, who wasn't much for gatherings, always came in separate cars since he came late and left early and she was first to arrive, last to leave. "Come when you want, leave when you want. But make sure you're there by five, since you don't want to miss the Best of Happy Hookers Moments. If we can talk our Maggie into it, we might even have a moment of show and tell for the most shocking entry!"

Maggie leapt up from her seat. "Excuse me, but I simply *must* interrupt here, Dorothy. I hereby *promise* you a show-and-tell moment. The line will start forming around four, gentlemen. Ben says you can look but not touch!" This drew a huge laugh and a few hoots and catcalls. Although the tattoo was only on her ankle, it was public and much talked about knowledge that since she was twelve years old, Maggie had the best gams in Partonville and had never been afraid to show them off. Plus, you had to be living in a cave not to have heard about her tattoo.

"Thank you, Maggie! Along with Maggie's *Ta-dah!* moment, as usual, food and beverages—and a short supply of an especially cheerful eggnog, if I know Doc," another short but fervent round of applause went up, "will be supplied. Board games, decks of cards, no doubt a little Christmas caroling and general merry-making will be had by all, I'm sure. And now, I'd like to lead us in a special cheer for our new hostess with the mostest."

"Ah-hah! So Ms. Durbin *is* hosting!" Cora whispered to her husband.

"If you'll all stand, please," Dorothy instructed. The sounds of murmuring and metal chair legs scraping against cement filled the room. Since Dorothy was the official cheerleader for the Wild Musketeers, Partonville's mostly senior citizens softball team, as well as the town's unofficial and much-respected matriarch, whether they cared for Katie Durbin or not, they'd sure stand up for Dorothy. Katie had reseated herself after her first acknowledgment and it didn't feel right to stand for a cheer about herself, and at a *funeral* dinner no less, but Dorothy grabbed her arm and up she came. Katie was visibly aghast at this whole idea, which she could see was highly entertaining to Jacob, who was seated next to her.

"You know, folks, now that we're all standing, let's all lift our hearts and any glasses you see in front of you." Everyone did as they were told. Pretty soon iced tea, empty glasses and cups of coffee were held high in anticipation of a toast to Katie.

"Dear Lord," Dorothy said, surprising everyone. She kept her eyes opened and looked up, water glass lifted over her head. A few people bowed their heads when they figured out she was praying; it just wasn't respectful not to bow your head when praying. A few others stared at her unsure of what to do, prayer not being part of their everyday routine—especially not what they perceived to be a toasting prayer! "We give You thanks and praise for the life of Your child Richard Lawson who is the reason we are gathered here together. We will miss him dearly." Her voice cracked and she had to swallow and pause a moment before she could continue. "His mother, Sadie, will miss him. His brother, Roscoe, will miss him." Roscoe released a short audible sob, the first he'd allowed himself in public. There was just always something about Dorothy's prayers. "This town will miss him, Lord. We can't even imagine what we'll do without his presence. The band won't be the same. *We* won't be the same." A few quiet releases of *Amen!* swirled among them. "But we take this moment to lift high our glasses and celebrate his entry into heaven!" She stopped talking and took two toasting gulps of her water. Others followed suit, even those who'd closed their eyes. "*Thank You,* Lord! Thank You for giving us Rick, even for so short a time." People started to set their glasses down, their arms a little weary.

"And *now,*" Dorothy said, surprising everyone yet again, "we lift our glasses to give You thanks for sending this bright new resident, Katie Durbin, to Partonville. We thank You for the heart of a woman who will help us keep our traditions alive, even in the midst of our grief. We ask You to bless *all* of her efforts on behalf of our little town. Thank You, Jesus! *Amen!*" She took another gulp, as did everyone else—including all who'd had to air sip for both toasts.

When people started to sit, she said, "*Please* remain standing. We're not through yet. I promised you a cheer and you're gonna get one!" She walked to the buffet table, grabbed two paper napkins and shook them out, placed one in each hand and moved toward the front of the room.

"Watch out, now," Doc hollered, teasing her. "I hope you got yourself a nitroglycerin handy!" He was only *half* joking.

Dorothy waved one of her makeshift pom-poms at him. "Not to worry. I hear there's a good doctor in the house!" She paused a moment and cast her eyes around the room. "Doctor Nielson! Could you please make your where-abouts known to us, just in case?" Well, she brought the house down with that one. The young Doctor Nielson was as embarrassed as Katie, but what the heck. If he was ever going to become a true part of these people's lives, be em-braced by them, he'd better join in, and so he lifted his arm and waved.

"Ready?" Dorothy asked. The crowd acknowledged its enthusiasm—including Sadie, who, even though numb, re-leased herself for the briefest of moments to a short burst of joy. Had it been anyone *but* Dorothy inviting this moment into her son's funeral dinner, it would have been unbearable. Instead, hope itself stood before Sadie in the form of a five-foot ten-inch, merry-making, eighty-eight-year-old waving napkin pom-poms. More than once she'd heard Dorothy say you never get over the loss of a child, but you eventually learn to live with it. Yes, Dorothy was a beacon of hope that she herself could survive.

Dorothy threw her arms in the air and wildly waved her napkins. *"Give me a Katie!"*

"KATIE!" the crowd chanted.

"Give me a Durbin!"

"DURBIN!

"What does it spell?"

"KATIE DURBIN!"

"No, it doesn't!"

People stared at Dorothy with confusion.

"IT SPELLS THE CHRISTMAS PARTY'S ON!"

⚜ ⚜ ⚜

For all Dorothy's fretting, this remarkable turn of events about the Christmas party had unfolded without any of her doing. In fact, it was highly possible several good things had been set in motion, she'd told the Big Guy during her evening prayers Thursday night. "I do believe You're working overtime again, Lord. But then again, when don't You?"

Jacob hadn't arrived home Thursday evening until a little after ten. "Sorry I didn't make it to May Belle's, Mom. I hope she sent my pie home with you—and that you didn't eat it already." He drew his eyebrows together, gave her an admonishing look and opened the refrigerator door.

"Pish-posh on your pie. I've got my own piece. I don't need yours!"

"You're not telling me you brought your piece *home* when I didn't show up, are you?" he said, backing out of the fridge with a wrapped plate. "Because if you are, I don't believe it for a second."

"No wonder you're a lawyer, you always sniff out the truth. In fact, I *did* eat a piece at May Belle's—although neither of us could believe we were desserting again after indulging ourselves in that Extravagant Tray!—but she sent another piece home for me anyway."

"Is that what I'm eating here?" he asked as he began to move around the kitchen retrieving a fork and napkin.

"Nope. I hid mine in the back of the fridge in case I was sleeping when you got home. Didn't want you to eat both of them." Dorothy stared at her son while he unwrapped the plastic, silently giving thanks for his presence in her kitchen. Although he did have the same tired eyes he used to get when he was a boy, at the same time he seemed uncommonly . . . what? Energized? Maybe he was so tired he was punchy. "You must be exhausted," she said. "What time did you go up to Rick's this morning anyway? Nine? That makes a thirteen-hour day, son, which is too many for a guy who's just helping out. I'm starting to feel sorry I got you into this."

"Don't feel bad, Mom. I admit it's not my idea of the dream vacation, but to be honest, it makes me feel good to do something for someone else for a change."

"What on earth are you talking about? That's all you do all the day long! The reason you became an attorney was so you could help folks! And from the sounds of it, your law practice keeps you *more* than busy helping your clients with this cause and that."

"*More* than busy," he said, taking a seat at the table across from her and plunking down with a sigh, "helping fat cats get fatter." The tone in his voice sounded . . . she wasn't sure what.

"Jacob, honey, what is it?"

He finally took a bite of his pie which was yet untouched. He swallowed, took another bite, swallowed. "Mm. This pie is delicious. I thought you said it was custard pie. Can't be, this tastes too good. What does she put in here?"

"I asked her the same thing but she didn't say. Just May Belle Magic, I guess. But don't change the subject, Jacob. What's bothering you?"

He looked up at her, pushed his tongue into his cheek until he'd settled something in his mind and tucked away his vulnerabilities. "Oh, nothing really. I'm just tired. Things feel exaggerated when I'm tired. Mostly, though, I don't want you fretting you did something wrong getting me involved with this because it's been good for me. Besides, I'm getting to spend time with you every evening. And after the funeral dinner on Saturday we'll have the rest of the day and all day Sunday before I'll probably fly out. I've decided to go with you to all the *doings* this weekend." He gave himself an internal smile, "doings" being a Partonville word he wouldn't be caught dead using on the East Coast. "Originally I wasn't going to, but after working at Rick's office all week, I feel kind of invested, as though I've gotten to know him better through his secretary and so many phone calls from people talking about him, sharing what all he did for them, how kind he was. The man handled everything from injuries to adoptions to real estate!"

"It'll be good for you to go to the wake and funeral, Jacob. I'm sure your presence will be comforting to Roscoe and Sadie." Dorothy was now hungry for her second piece of pie, which she retrieved after removing the gallon of milk and sliding over a pickle jar and a can of soda, all which she'd used to hide it. "Glass of milk?" she asked.

"Thanks."

She poured two glasses, served them and settled back down.

"Also, it'll be a good chance to see other folks I know from high school and haven't caught up with for decades. Pastor Delbert—it feels strange to call him that since I knew him in high school when he was just a rebellious preacher's kid!—asked me during the Thanksgiving dinner if I'd seen Hank Bentley yet, which got me to thinking about some of the old gang. It'll give me a chance to wax nostalgic, see if anybody else remembers stopping at Harry's for French fries and cokes after school. I started thinking about those days earlier this evening when Katie mentioned her distaste for Harry's."

Whoops! He hadn't really meant to mention her tonight. It's not that he was planning on hiding his dinner with Katie, but he knew his mom's antennae were up about him and Katie and he didn't like that. Dorothy raised her eyebrows, smiled and shoveled in another bite of pie. "Quit smiling," he all but growled. "We just went to dinner because we'd both worked so late and were both on the square and she hadn't eaten and . . ."

"There's no need for you to explain your whereabouts or *who*abouts with me, son. It's a small town, easy to run into somebody on the square. I'm glad you had some good company. Where'd you eat?"

"Hey, thought I didn't need to explain anything," he said flatly.

"You don't. But you know better than to think I don't want to know!" They both chuckled.

"We went to the Olive Garden in Hethrow. Soup and a salad sounded good to both of us at that late hour." He smiled, stabbed his last bite of pie. "And because I'm sure inquiring minds still want to know," he said, pausing to eat the last lingering bite hanging in front of his mouth, "she dropped her car off at the farm and I drove. I went in and visited with Josh for a minute when I dropped her back off. That's why I'm so late."

"How's her mini-mall project coming?" Dorothy asked. *Absolutely no personal questions.* "I feel badly I haven't talked to her all week."

"She mentioned that. She seemed curious as to whether or not we'd gone on a road trip. Wonder how and where she might have gotten *that* idea?" Although he was trying to sound annoyed with the obvious inside informant, Dorothy could tell he didn't really care.

"A little birdie."

"A big bird, I think. A big tough old bird," he said, bonking her on the head like she was ten.

"Hey! Watch yourself now!" She hadn't seen him this animated since his brother and nephews were here a few days ago. Seemed as though spending time with Katie had perked him up. "So, how *is* the mini-mall project coming along?"

"She'd just finished her meeting with the architect when I dropped by and I gather they're getting together with Edward Showalter tomorrow."

Dorothy would have to remember to tell Maggie the new hairdo she gave Katie seemed to be doing wonders for her—although she'd never tell her exactly what she meant by that lest the whole town fill up with gossip.

"She's hoping he can serve as a general contractor. Funny, a woman with her experience trusts this goofy guy who drives a camouflage van," Jacob said.

"Let me remind you that goofy guy did all my renovations here, helped move me, does excellent work and is currently dating our very own Nellie Ruth McGregor."

"Nellie Ruth. She's the redhead. A Hooker on your altar guild, right?"

"Very good! Stick around here another week and you'll know everybody's business, too!"

"I met Edward Showalter at your auction. I have to say I did like the guy, even though he is quirky. You've bragged on him enough for me to know Edward Showalter is a man of his word. But, Mom, why *does* everyone always call him by his full name?"

"Don't have a clue. Here's something unusual, though: Nellie Ruth has taken to calling him ES. I'm *sure* that means they've got something special. But enough speculation. What else did Katie have to say about her project?"

"She said the architect thought her atrium idea would work. She seemed very enthusiastic about that."

"Good. *Good!*"

"She also said she's going to hold a mall-naming competition to get people invested in the idea. And she asked me for my opinion about the legalities of having lessees."

"I'm sure you were helpful, son. Between Rick and Katie, turns out you arrived in town just in time to become Superman, helping the downtrodden and distressed whenever the need arises!"

"I'd hardly call Katie Durbin downtrodden and distressed. By the way, she said she'd be happy to host the Christmas party. Or co-host it. However you want to work it. She doesn't care. She said to just let her know."

Dorothy's jaw dropped open. "How'd *that* come up?"

"I brought it up. You'd mentioned it the other day, remember?"

"You asked her about that? *Please* tell me you didn't say 'Mom wants to know.'"

"Let's just say there was a natural segue when she and Josh and I were chatting. And by the way, did you know there's talk of him getting a car? He's really bugging his mom."

"Oh, he's told me all about that. It's a 'shoe-in' the way he presented it in his e-mails. He's even sent me a few lines from ads he's cut out. I told him he should go shopping with Arthur. Arthur can give any car a good listen-to and know if it is a gooder or not, to use one of his words."

"I don't know Katie very well, but I told Josh on the q.t.

that he should back off a tad. Katie definitely doesn't seem the type you'd want to bug if you were trying to get something from her. I offered to help once they work something out, but I'm not exactly a genius at spotting a good used car. Arthur would be perfect. Now if Vinnie were here, he'd be a good help, too. He was always better at tinkering than me."

"So Josh is really bugging Katie, huh? I figured he'd be smarter than that."

"He's eager, that's for sure. When I mentioned we didn't have your Christmas decorations up yet, Josh jumped in and volunteered to go get their tree while Katie was busy with the mini mall—if he only had a car." Jacob chuckled and shook his head at the memory. "Katie reminded him they had a perfectly shaped fake tree, I believe were her exact words, in the attic. Josh responded with something like 'you don't have a fake tree on a *farm*, Mom!' Then he tried to rope me into backing him up with both the tree and the car."

"Did you?"

"Not exactly," he said with a devilish grin. "I did tell them about the giant fresh trees *we* always had out there. To be honest, it made me kind of lonesome for the old place. I told them how George always set the biggest one aside for us because he so enjoyed our party—hear my windup coming for the segue, Mom?" Dorothy grinned, gave her head a small nod. "Then she asked what was happening with the party this year, so I said you'd been wondering the same thing."

"Jacob Henry Wetstra! You didn't!"

"I did. And wait till Josh hears *this*."

"What?"

"That both our moms pulled our full names out of their bag of parenting tricks today!"

⨶ ⨶ ⨶

Katie called Dorothy at 8:30 the next morning, asking Dorothy why she hadn't brought up the annual Christmas party before. Hosting the party would give her a reason to stop obsessing about the mini mall for a change and serve as an incentive to finally decorate her new home. "After so many years in the same place, it becomes easier once you have a handle on just what goes well where," she'd said, "and try saying that three times quickly!" Dorothy laughed and agreed on all counts.

⨶ ⨶ ⨶

Just like that, the party was on and now the whole town knew about it. *Why do I worry, Lord, when You're always one step—make that fifty million—ahead of me!*

15

⁂

Sunday morning's church service was more crowded than usual. Pastor Delbert wasn't surprised: Christmas was coming and attendance always went up a week or two beforehand. Folks who believed in God Almighty and His Son but didn't believe in getting themselves to church every Sunday nonetheless managed to do so around Christmas and Easter. Over the years Pastor had also noticed that death brought questions of faith to the forefront. More than once he'd heard skeptics say, "There was something about that funeral service that got me to thinking."

When Josh and Katie entered the sanctuary, Josh quickly spotted where Jacob and Dorothy were seated. Dorothy moved around every Sunday; she liked to make people feel welcome, and she'd never taken to the idea that some families thought they *owned* a pew. "It's good to shake things up a little," she always said. This Sunday she was sitting with Wanita ("That's the way my mother spelled it on the birth certificate!") and her three-year-old twins. Her husband didn't attend church since what kind of God, he wondered, would allow them to encounter such hard times financially. Josh thought Dorothy's seat selection was very brave since from what he'd seen of Danny and Dougie (what *anyone* had seen) they were likely to start socking each other and accidentally land one on Dorothy. Josh walked around to the other end of their pew, Katie behind him, slid in and plopped himself down next to Jacob who looked up and smiled at them.

"Got a car yet?" Jacob asked in a low voice as he leaned toward Josh.

"Nothing."

"Hang in there, sport."

Even though Katie was reading the announcements in the bulletin, she leaned forward enough to make eye contact with Jacob. "I heard that. Sunday morning doesn't seem like a good time to be playing devil's advocate now, does it?" Her voice sounded neither chastising nor playful. He just smiled at her and shrugged his shoulders, lifted his eyebrows, as though he didn't have a clue what she was talking about.

"You leaving tomorrow?" Josh asked.

"I won't know for sure until noon tomorrow."

"Keep us posted. But if I don't see you before you go," he said, thrusting his hand forward, "I hope you come back soon. You still got my e-mail addy, right?"

"Yup. And my plans are to be back for Christmas."

"If you e-mail me, I'll keep you posted about the car."

Katie sighed loud enough to cause Danny and Dougie to lean around Jacob to see what was going on. That kind of sigh was usually reserved for them.

⁂

Nellie Ruth, who sat in her same pew and position every Sunday, was a jumble of nerves, which wasn't like her. No, it was not like her at all. Her heart had not stopped racing since the funeral dinner when Dorothy made the announcement about the Christmas party and ES leaned right over and whispered, "Can we make it a date?" Without thinking, she had agreed. But in hindsight, she could hardly believe he'd asked her to attend something with him a whole two weeks in advance, which, after about five weeks of dating, certainly must speak as a sign to his growing affection for her. Plus, he'd told her after the funeral dinner that he couldn't think of anyone he was happier to tell about his long-term job on the mini mall than her. "I'm going to be the contractor, Nellie Ruth, on the whole mini-mall project! I have a retainer!" he'd said. "A steady income for months to come! Ms. Durbin even talked to me about maybe serving as the official maintenance man in the building after it opens! I'll be darned if that fortune cookie wasn't right! That cookie was like a direct Word from the Lord!"

Yes, all his news had been wonderful, especially when he shared that he'd told Ms. Durbin of his one prior commitment, and "that is to paint Nellie Ruth's place. Ms. Durbin said after Monday's meeting we'd have to wait a spell for final drawings anyway, so I should just go ahead and get that Splendid Pink on your walls."

Nellie Ruth still had mixed feelings, however, as this long-range date plan for the Hookers' Christmas party felt like a commitment of sorts, which unnerved her. Yes, she enjoyed his company. Yes, he was a man of faith, which was important to her. Yes, he was a hard worker, and obviously a trustworthy one if Katie had entrusted him with such a huge undertaking. And he certainly was good to her. But since her father had been so horribly abusive to her when she was growing up, a portion of her couldn't help shying away from the trust of commitment. In all her sixty-some years, she hadn't really dated anyone more than once or twice (and to call those encounters "dates" was a real stretch of the word), so after five weeks of seeing Edward Showalter on a pretty regular basis, she found herself swimming in new, unsettling waters.

It's not that she'd even had much of an opportunity to steadily date before, pickings for single men in Partonville—out of which she hardly ever ventured—running slightly slim. She had not, in fact, ever even been properly kissed, which seemed pretty embarrassing for a woman in her sixties. But seeing ES on a regular basis, and now this two-week-ahead date, was making her jittery. Why was she suddenly starting to feel like fleeing from him when they had such a good time together, when it seemed the exciting tingle that had run up her arm the other night when he'd laid his hand atop hers would never leave? She'd thought for a second that he was going to try to kiss her when he'd last walked her to the bottom of the outdoor stairway leading up to her apartment. He said good night to her and told her what a great time he'd had. He looked at his shoes, he looked at the sky, he stared into her eyes—then he paused, leaned toward her just a hair. The moment was so startling she thought her heart was going to explode, which unconsciously caused her to stiffen. Suddenly, he backed up that same hair he'd just leaned in, said good night and then he was gone. Between replaying the wonderful tingles, the panic at the thought he might soon try to kiss her *again* and the long-range date, her heart-hammering simply would not cease.

Although Edward Showalter attended church every Sunday and often went to Wednesday evening prayer meetings, he didn't attend UMC. He worshipped with Johnny Mathis and his family (wife and two grown daughters, one now married and a mother herself, the other still living at home) at a Baptist church in Yorkville. Even in her confusion, Nellie Ruth realized she wished he was sitting there beside her. But she was content to know they were both worshipping the same God at the same hour, which made her feel close to him even in his absence. With each hymn she wondered if he might be singing the very same song, maybe at this very same moment—which caused her a slight pang of guilt since she'd been thinking about ES instead of the words. She'd have a chance to ask him about the hymn selections when he came for a visit at three this afternoon, a thought that jolted her heart back into overdrive.

When they'd first begun seeing each other—if she dared to think of it in those terms—she didn't think it would be right for him to come up to her place until he officially came to paint it her choice of Splendid Rose, what with them both being single and her landlord always seemingly spying on their comings and goings. Last night ES said on the phone, "Nellie Ruth, we are both over sixty years old. If I can't come for a mid-afternoon visit—if we can't be trusted alone together *now*—when can we?" It was the first time he'd pressed an issue. She'd told him she'd pray about it and let him know what God said—and everyone who knew Nellie Ruth McGregor knew she was a prayer warrior. Turns out God seemed to have said YES, or at the very least He hadn't said NO! So she called ES back and told him 3 P.M. would be fine. She'd make them a cup of tea, perhaps even a mid-afternoon snack.

Although her upstairs apartment was as neat as a pin, after she hung up she spent the rest of the evening cleaning, polishing, double checking, putting out a few tasteful Christmas decorations here and there. No tree yet, but her handmade papier-mâché angel (she'd followed the directions explicitly and it looked exactly like the picture) was on the bookcase and her Christmas globe with ice skaters in it was in the center of her kitchen table. But what if he didn't like her taste? What if he'd pictured something more . . . *whatever*? What would her apartment tell him about *her*? She walked from room to room trying to become a stranger in her own home, to see everything through fresh eyes. *Hmm. She must like pastels. Hmm. Is this a music room? Hmm. She must not be very fun.* Gads! Her place was b-o-r-i-n-g through the eyes of a stranger, at least as "stranger" as her own eyes in her own place could get. She was now more glad than ever she'd risked picking out such a bold paint color and wished he'd already painted it before this first visit, which made her laugh at herself.

She'd once heard someone's home referred to as always being *so* neat that it looked as though no one lived there. Recalling this, she sat down in front of her tidy, short stack of crafters magazines and decided to splay them, then realized she'd busied herself arranging a perfect fan. *No!* She tried to make them look like she'd just tossed them down on her coffee table. *Better.* But she couldn't stand it and soon evened up the corners again. *I am who I am. He will either like my home the way it* really *is, or he won't.* She recalled the state of Edward Showalter's van on their first date, empty pop cans and snack wrappers everywhere. Since then, he'd cleaned it up, but she wondered if he'd done so because of the look on her face. She hoped not. She hoped *he* could just be who he really was in her presence.

She sat in the church pew scolding herself for her own ridiculous actions and her continually racing heart. *Lord, don't let me be afraid to receive the kind but* appropriate *affection of a man who loves You as much as I do and who is so very good to me, and whom I've grown to care a great deal about. Help me to be nothing more or less than the Nellie Ruth McGregor You created me to be, and give me eyes to see the real Edward Showalter. He is not my father, he is Edward Showalter.*

⁂

Edward Showalter sat at the Mathises' kitchen table. They'd invited him back to their house for a bite of lunch or brunch—or whatever he wanted to call it, Mary said (Johnny said he'd call it sandwiches)—after the service. The pastor's sermon hadn't been one of his best, they'd decided, but nonetheless, he'd certainly given them food for thought and conversation.

Edward Showalter always loved the comfort of their kitchen table. They were, in his mind, the perfect example of a family, something he sorely missed. Mary and Johnny always made him feel embraced by their circle of love, and made him feel like a part of *their* family. In fact, were he ever to bring Nellie Ruth "home to meet the family," this was as close as he could get. Not that Johnny and Mary were perfect. They had rocky times in their marriage, *terrible* times, in fact. Edward Showalter had also been a part of those in a way, since he and Johnny used to be drinking buddies. "Drunks is the only way to put it," they'd admit to anyone who asked. Mary had once left Johnny, told him this time she wouldn't come back until he'd stopped drinking for good. With the help of AA and each other, both men finally left the booze behind, and months later Johnny and his wife were back together, had been ever since. Johnny and Edward Showalter still attended AA meetings together. They approached staying sober one day at a time, as they always would.

"How are things going with Nellie Ruth?" Mary asked.

She'd always been the direct type and both men liked that about her.

"I'd say they're going mighty fine. Mighty fine, indeed." He beamed.

"I haven't seen you look this happy for a long while," she said. "If you keep this grinning up, I'm going to have to meet this lady pretty soon. Johnny says from what he's seen of the two of you at The Piece, he thinks this could be *The One.*"

Edward Showalter shot her a broad smile. "Whoa! I don't want to get ahead of myself here. But, so far, so good!" Even though he was a Godly man of faith, he still honored the old "don't jinx it by talking about it" superstition. Johnny knew this about his friend and quickly veered Mary off her prying by changing the subject.

"Hey, remember when you mentioned the other day you were thinking about getting another dog?" Johnny asked. "Were you serious?"

"I was."

"Right after that I saw a sign out on County Y that said FREE DOG TO GOOD HOME. I almost called you."

"Didn't say what kind?" Johnny shook his head. "Didn't say free *puppy,* huh?"

"Free dog. D-O-G dog. Funny thing was, I didn't notice the sign on the way to East St. Louis, but I did on the way back. I wonder if the dog did something bad in between and the owner said, 'That's it!'" He laughed his great belly laugh.

"How long ago was that?"

"Monday . . . no Tuesday evening's when I went. I'd say the farm with the sign was about halfway down County Y."

"What were you doing in East St. Louis? Pretty long drive for a quick turn-around."

"Needed a few restaurant supplies and one of the bigger places was having a one-day tent sale until nine."

"Get anything?"

"He did!" Mary said. "He got a wonderful pasta cooker for the restaurant. Have you tasted his spaghetti sauce lately? My, it's good! He's jazzed it up a bit, added a few secret ingredients." Johnny loved the light that shone in her eyes when she was proud of her man. He hoped to see that same look for ES in Nellie Ruth's eyes one day.

"I haven't tasted his new sauce. Maybe Nellie Ruth and I can swing by next Saturday. Will you have it on the menu?"

"You betcha!"

"Say, did you get a New York City dish figured out yet?" When Johnny first opened his restaurant, his sign outside read A LITTLE PIECE OF NYC, which, much to his disappointment, everyone assumed meant New York City, even though the front of his menus clearly said "A Little Piece of New Yorkville Cuisine." He finally tired of correcting everyone and decided to go ahead and feature a New York City dish on his menu, conversation about the possibilities becoming its own good advertisement. As of yet, however, it hadn't been announced.

"I *do* have one concocted."

"And?"

"And, why don't you find out on Saturday? Spread the word about the great unveiling, okay? Mary, maybe you can swing by, too, just happen to be there when ES comes by, and check this Nellie Ruth out."

16

After a week's delay, Sunday afternoon Jacob finally made it back to his mother's spare bedroom closet to hunt for the Christmas decorations. Dorothy wasn't sure what, in her frenzy, she had kept before the auction, but she thought maybe a couple boxes were hidden amidst the many unlabeled ones stuffed in there. At least none of the boxes were very big, Jacob thought, but he hated to think she'd have had to wrestle them around by herself if he hadn't been home. Then again, maybe she'd have had Earl come and help her. He was good at things like that. At least Jacob *hoped* his mom would be smart enough to ask for help, what with her heart condition. But she could be stubborn about things like that.

At last he'd checked each of the boxes, ultimately scooting three old Del Monte green beans shipping cartons out into the middle of the room, all appearing to have Christmas decorations on top of whatever else was in them. He was brushing the dust off his hands when Dorothy entered the room.

"Oh!" she said, applauding. "You found them! Now that I see those Del Monte boxes, I should have remembered," she said, giving herself a gentle whap on the forehead. "Out of all the boxes I was packing I picked those matching boxes for the decorations because I figured that the D in Del Monte would remind me of *decorations.*"

"No comment," he said.

"You can take me to the Supreme Court, Attorney Wetstra, but I shall say no more since clearly I was out of my mind." He shook his head, his crooked grin warming her heart.

"Where do you want them?"

"Just set them up there on the bed so we can save our poor backs while we're looking through them."

"You got an old throw or something to cover your bedspread? The boxes are kind of dirty."

Dorothy scurried off and returned with a sheet. "Not old, but easily washed." She shook out the floral flat sheet and let it float down on the bed, then smoothed it with her hands. Jacob hefted the boxes up. "Let's have at it," she said with glee. "I have no earthly idea what's in them. To be honest, making decisions before the auction and the move got harder and harder, and at some point I just had to make up my mind to either toss or gloss. 'Dorothy,' I said to myself, 'either toss it or gloss over it and put it in a box to take with you. You do not have the time or the stamina to process all of these memories!'" She sat down on the edge of the bed. "I hope I don't start missing things, realize I made some terrible decisions."

"Like?"

"Like what if I can't find Esmeralda!" She looked horrified at the thought.

Jacob sat down beside her, put his arms around her and drew her close as he kissed the top of her head. "I remember how hard it was for me to come *help* with the auction, Mom. So *many* memories. . . . I can't imagine how hard it was for you, having been born in that house and living there all your life. You held up like a champion, though. And I have a sneaking suspicion that even though it was tough, you made all the right decisions. When haven't you?" They turned to face each other. "Let's see what we've got here," he said, ramping up his enthusiasm. "Which box should we start with? Today, you have time for however many emotional journeys you feel like taking. It'll be a good chance for me to hear some more of the stories."

She stood and stared at the boxes for a moment, then tapped the one on the right. "Let the fun begin!" she said, tossing back the flaps. It felt a little like opening gifts on Christmas morning. As if God desired to calm her heart, the very first thing she withdrew was her beloved hand-carved wooden doll her grandfather, Granpy, had made for her fifth birthday. Esmeralda was wrapped in one of Dorothy's mother's old dish towels and carefully tucked inside the stable for the nativity set. "Esmeralda!" she exclaimed as she clutched the little doll to her chest, the dish towel falling by the wayside.

"*I* would have missed Esmeralda if you'd left *her* behind," Jacob said fondly. "The nativity set wouldn't be complete without her. See, I told you. You made good choices."

"Do you remember exactly *where* in the nativity she goes?"

"With the Wise Men, of course. How could I ever forget? Don't you remember when my Sunday school teacher asked me where I'd ever gotten the odd notion that one of the Wise Men was named Esmeralda?" Dorothy smiled, nodded her head, kissed Esmeralda's cheek. Jacob continued, "I can't believe that after all these years I'm only now thinking to ask how Esmeralda came to be one of the Wise Men . . . Wise *Woman*. A Wise *Person*," he said, chuckling, landing on what he decided must be politically correct—at least for a wooden doll.

"When Granpy—who had already named her Esmeralda, and now I sure wish I'd thought to ask him why—gave her to me, I could not put her down. I was only five, remember. I took her to bed with me, I stood her next to my plate when I ate, I took her to church, I talked to her all the time. In fact, it started to fret my mother a little just *how* attached I was to her. It was hard to know at the time if I loved her so much because she was cute," Dorothy held the doll at arm's length and studied the curlicues Granpy had meticulously carved into the wood for her hair, "or because Granpy had given her to me. He was, and will always remain, one of my favorite people in the world. My dad was just like him . . . so gentle and caring." She drew the doll to her chest again. "Anyway, since I'd gotten her for my birthday, I'd been carrying her around for a month before Christmas came around. That year Santa brought me Baby Bunting. She came sealed in a box and was certainly a more lifelike doll than Esmeralda—who immediately got set aside." Dorothy's tone of voice dropped, as did her spirits as she recalled the details.

"Then one Sunday in late January Granpy came to visit and of course I was dragging Baby Bunting around. Granpy asked me if she and Esmeralda had become friends yet. The question caught me up short because I hadn't even thought about Esmeralda for weeks. For the life of me, I couldn't even think where she was. We *all* looked high and low, but no Esmeralda. I thought I'd sob myself to death, not only for losing her, but from five-year-old guilt. Even though Granpy assured me she'd show up when she was good and ready, his eyes looked so. . . ."

"Anyway, the next Christmas when Dad got the nativity set out of the attic, low and behold, Esmeralda, who was the same size as the Wise Men, was in the box with them! I was so happy! My mom cried and said, 'Oh, we must have accidentally tucked her in with the Christmas decorations when we put them away. Wait until Granpy finds out we found Esmeralda! We'll have to invite him for dinner and surprise him!' And so we did. We set her up with the Wise Men, then asked him to come see the nativity set and see if he noticed anything new. Of course, he did."

"What did he say?"

"He said, 'By golly, that doll must be smarter than all of us put together after hanging around with the Wise Men all year. I bet she'll miss them after Christmas when they have to go back in the box—although maybe that's a good safe place for her, you think?' Oh, how that man knew how to cover a little girl's carelessness with grace! And that was that. Every year, back in the box with the Wise Men she went. She just keeps getting smarter and smarter, don't you, Esmeralda?" She gave the little doll a pat on the head. "I don't know why I fretted I might have lost you in the auction. You're too smart to let me have done such a dumb thing, aren't you?"

She gently stood Esmeralda on the dresser in front of the mirror facing toward the center of the room. Dorothy could see in the mirror that a little piece of her heel had chipped off and she rustled through the dish towel looking for it. Nothing. She'd have to look in the bottom of the box after it was emptied. She'd glue it back on if she could find it. Then again, it could have been missing for years and perhaps she just hadn't noticed.

"How do you like it here?" she asked the doll after folding the dish towel and leaning down to look at her face. "Yes, I know, the whole place *is* much smaller. But having you here surely does make it seem more like home. Maybe Christmas *can* come to Vine Street as well as the farm! We'll get you set up with your buddies after we finish unpacking and figure out where to put you. Promise."

"What else you got in that box, Mom?" Jacob looked at his wristwatch. "How about we finish scoping things out, then get ourselves over to George's for a tree?"

"Sounds like a plan. You be good," she said to Esmeralda. "We've got work to do."

‡ ‡ ‡

"Wonderful! We'll have to come over and have a look-see," Dorothy said to May Belle, who had called to tell her that she and Earl had finally finished decorating their tree and that it was just beautiful.

"George has outdone himself with this year's selections, Dorothy. This is one of the best trees we've ever had! It's so fragrant that our whole house smelled like Christmas when we woke up this morning, didn't it, Earl?" Dorothy knew Earl was sitting right there on the couch staring at the tree. He loved the lights so May Belle left them on all day. "George inquired about you. He told me he missed seeing you and The Tank come roaring into the station. I don't wonder why. I bet you burned more gasoline tearing around than anyone else in town!"

"I wouldn't argue *that* point."

"Anyway, if I were you, I'd get right over there if you want to have a selection. You wouldn't believe the crowds."

"We were just saying it was about time to do that. Jacob probably has to leave tomorrow and he wants to get Christmas in order for me before he goes. We've spent the last hour or so going through the Christmas decorations—well, at least what we *thought* were all Christmas decorations. Honest to goodness, everything in those boxes has a story! What a surprise we had when I discovered my sequined Easter eggs—remember when we made those with the kids?—and my St. Patty's Day figurine, *and* my stick-um window Valentine hearts, all in the same box! Some packing job. I pulled them out one at a time, holiday after holiday appearing before our very eyes. At one point Jacob said, 'Well, Merry EVERYTHING, Mom!' I tell you, we laughed until our sides hurt.

"You know that ancient little two-inch fuzzy yellow chicken I put out every year for Easter, the one with the orange wire legs and the funny little misplaced beak, a silly cockscomb down too low on his forehead and black beady eyes?" May Belle acknowledged that she did. "I'm sure you had one when you were a girl—in fact I think everybody had one back then—but this one looks especially goofy. Well, when I pulled out my little wicker Christmas sleigh, that little Easter chicken was sitting in it as big as you please, looking like he thought he was Santa Claus! Imagine a goofy chicken driving the sleigh! Merry Everything, indeed!"

"What a picture!"

"I'll tell you, we've got stuff strewn and sorted all over the back bedroom. It's hard to believe it all came out of three boxes. What fun we've had. But we *better* get crackin' with the tree and get the decorations up tonight or Jacob won't be able to crawl in bed, it's so covered with all that Merry Everything!"

"Wait! First you have to tell me. Is Esmeralda even smarter this year?" It was May Belle's annual question.

"Sure is! Would you believe she was in the first box we opened? I don't know where I've got room to put my nativity set, though. We talked about maybe setting up one of the bunco tables in the corner next to the tree. We decided we should get the tree first though, see how much room I end up with in there. And speaking of getting the tree, I'm going to sign off now. If we get done early enough, we'll come and see yours. I'd invite you over to help, but I imagine we'd have a hard time dragging Earl away from the lights, especially since you just got the tree up today."

"You know him well, Dorothy."

"That I do. Well, good-bye, dearie."

"Good-bye."

Before the receiver had barely hit the cradle, Jacob was already reaching for his car keys. "Ready to go, then?"

"Hold on a minute. Do you mind if we invite Josh and Katie to go tree hunting with us? When I checked my e-mail earlier, Josh said he'd talked his mom into leaving the fake tree in the box this year. I'm thinking I should personally introduce Katie to George, see what he might be able to do for her—as a favor to me."

"I guess that would be fine," he said. "Just have them meet us there in say, twenty minutes? We can grab a quick sandwich before we go. While you were talking to May Belle, I noticed we still had some meat loaf left. You get the bread and I'll get the mayo."

⧫ ⧫ ⧫

"Katie Durbin, meet my good friend George Gustafson. George, this is my good friend Katie, the woman who bought Crooked Creek from me and who is kind enough to host the annual Hookers' Christmas party out there on the twentieth. I'm sure you heard the announcement at the funeral dinner."

"If I hadn't heard the announcement I sure couldn't have missed your cheer!" George said. Although he'd stood and toasted for Rick, he had only begrudgingly followed along for Katie's since he wasn't sure this woman was deserving of a cheer. On many occasions he'd noticed that big gas-guzzling Lexus SUV driving right by his station, never once pulling in for gas. He figured she must travel all the way to Hethrow or maybe Yorkville for gas. She probably had one of those chain station's credit cards. "That's how they do, those city people." When Katie held out her hand, however, George took it and gave it a shake. It wouldn't have been right not to treat one of Dorothy's friends with respect.

"And this is her son, Josh." The two of them shook hands and exchanged a greeting. "And you remember Jacob!" she said, throwing her arm around her son's waist and beaming.

"Jacob Wetstra!" George said, giving Jacob a hearty whap on the back. "I heard you've been helping Sadie and Roscoe out." This reminded Jacob that in a small town, nothing much happened people didn't know about. "That's awfully swell of ya," George said, meaning it.

"Here for a tree, Dorothy?" George asked. She nodded her head and George went on to tell her about how he'd been out chopping and seen the most beautiful, giant tree and thought of *her* and then remembered she didn't live out at the farm any more so he let it be.

"Katie's here for a tree, too, George," Jacob said, speaking before Katie had a chance to open her mouth, which ruffled Katie's feathers just a teensy bit. She'd been finding her own way with the people in town, thank you very much. She didn't need help from him.

"Yes, George. I'd like to keep as many of the lovely Hookers' party traditions alive as possible," she said. George shot her a skeptical look. *Such fancy talk.*

"In other words, George," Dorothy said while she touched his arm, "we'd like for Katie to have a wonderful tree for the party, as wonderful as you've always selected for me all these years."

"Like I said, the biggest and best tree I saw is still growing in the forest. If," and he'd said the word just short of exaggerating it, "Ms. Durbin here is still around and hosting the party again next year, I'll keep that tree in mind for her."

When Sam Vitner had stopped by the lot earlier today to buy his tree, he was fired up about Ms. Durbin since the funeral doings and just *had* to mention it to *some*body. He gave George an earful about a potential "snake in the grass," and by golly, some of it had rung true with George—even though he'd never even officially met the woman. Well, now he had met her, and he realized he might just agree with Sam Vitner's theory one hundred percent. Why, just like Sam had said, she'd even cozied up to Dorothy's son to take advantage of Dorothy's influence! She'd make her money on her mini mall and all the properties he'd heard tell she was buying up, then leave town. Yessiree, Sam was exactly right.

Josh suddenly captured their attention by, tree in hand, trotting up and stomping its trunk on the ground. "What do you think about this one, Dorothy? Mom? Jacob? Does this live up to the party?"

"Not by a long shot," Dorothy said, "or at least not by a foot." He jaunted off to return it, the branches pumping up and down with his every step. "Help us out here, George," Dorothy said. "You know every single tree on this lot. Or have you maybe got any around back you're saving for something as special as the party?" Dorothy winked at George, trying to lighten him up a little. He didn't seem quite his usual jovial self today. Must be tired, she thought. Tree work was hard.

"How about *this* one?" Josh asked from behind a taller and bushier tree than the last, not a speck of him visible.

"Close!" Dorothy said.

"I believe that's as close as you'll come this year," George said. "If I was you, I'd buy it before somebody else does."

"SOLD!" Jacob said, reaching for his wallet. "Now let's find one for Mom."

"Hey!" Katie yelped. She lowered her voice. "As the hostess of this party, and, may I remind you, a certified Happy Hooker, *I'm* buying this tree for *our* party. But leave your wallet out. You can buy your mom's, right, Dorothy?" She shot Dorothy a clever smile.

"Right!" Dorothy said.

George took note of Katie's ability to boss everyone around. His eyes flipped back and forth between Jacob and Katie. *Yup*, he thought. *I can almost hear the slither. Leave your wallet out, indeed!*

17

⁂

After such an emotionally charged weekend, the last thing anyone expected over breakfast at Harry's Grill Monday morning was an angry exchange. Sam almost never came to Harry's for breakfast since he opened his business early, but this morning he'd stuck a hand-scrawled note in his shop's door window that said "BACK AT 10" and all but blew into Harry's with an axe to grind and a mission to accomplish: start a *revolt* against the mini mall.

Who could have guessed how activated Sam Vitner could become? To the best of anyone's recollection, Sam was a mild-mannered, if somewhat eccentric, salvage-selling story-teller. But the longer Sam thought about it, the angrier and more threatened he'd become, especially after he vented to George Gustafson yesterday. It had been like uncorking a bottle of shaken champagne. After a sleepless night, he was now prepared to do battle with the mini mall, especially since he'd heard tell at the funeral dinner that an antique store was most assuredly going into the mall. In his mind Katie Durbin was entering into direct competition with him, trying to steal his *clientele*.

"Why don'tcha jist say *customers*?" Arthur wanted to know.

"What does that fancy woman—that invader to our town—know about antiques anyway?" he asked Arthur while, with a tad too much frenzy, sawing his sausage into miniscule bits, as though he was trying to make sure it was dead.

"What does that fancy woman know 'bout antiques? Why don'tcha ask her direct, Sammie?"

Sam hated being called Sammie, but he'd long ago learned that expressing that to Arthur only egged him on. Arthur only did it when *he* was wound up enough to want to get Sam's goat, and this morning he'd already had three cups of coffee so his buzz was on and the pickings were too easy to pass up. "But if I was ta guess," he said, staring into his empty coffee cup, "I'd say she knows enough ta know they're popular, and you must, too, otherwise *you* wouldn't still be trying ta sell them to us now, would ya!"

"*Here* now, Arthur Landers! I do not sell things to people that they don't want! And as I remember correctly, you've been one of my biggest customers over the years." Arthur gave a single nod, acknowledging the truth of it—although he generally spent his time in the junk piles looking for one specific thing or another to make repairs, not perusing for collectibles. "She'll probably charge too much for everything. Try to get those big city prices. Folks around here can't afford such nonsense."

"Welp, then what's ta worry 'bout? You'll sell 'em cheaper and that'll be that. Everybody wants ta save a little money, especially when they's buyin' stuff they don't rightly need to begin with. Also, Sammie my boy, I don't expect she'll be sellin' old toilets in *her* fancy place. You've got the corner on that market!" Arthur laughed, as did Harold. Gladys snickered. Sam did not even crack a grin, even though it was true. Swappin' Sam's outdoor lot was sprinkled with toilets—one parked *exactly* on the corner of the lot—most of them having been in exactly the same spot for years, tall grass and weeds grown up around them.

"Sam Vitner, as Acting Mayor and someone who is one hundred percent behind the mini mall, I'd like to think an antique store will be a good *complement* to your business," Gladys said, using her most knowledgeable and mayorly voice. "Everybody knows that a single store might attract *some* shoppers, but two of the same type of store will *definitely* draw them." Sam and Arthur just looked at her, clearly neither of them able to split that odd hair. She picked up her napkin and daintily (for Gladys) dabbed at her mouth. "Gentlemen," she said knowingly, "business draws business. Why do you think people go to the malls?"

"Cuz they don't know how ta rightly entertain themselves playing the harmonica," Arthur said, swiveling to wink at Sam and patting the Hohner he always kept in the front center pocket of his coveralls.

"People go to the mall, Arthur," Gladys said with a sigh, choosing to ignore his remark since she knew he was trying to antagonize her, too, "because they want several stores to choose from. Say I wanted to buy a pair of shoes to go with a certain outfit that was say a certain shade of ... yellow," she said, after looking down at her yellow blouse.

"Yeah, Sam, say you and me needed us a new pair of shoes ta go with our new yeller outfits," he said, placing his hands on his hips and cocking his shoulders, as though striking his new yeller outfit pose.

Again, Gladys chose to ignore the old goat. "Rather than going where there's just *one* shoe store, my odds of finding the *right* shade of yellow would be considerably higher at the mall since the mall has *several* shoe stores. It'll be the same with antiques, Sam. People will come to Partonville to shop in our new mini mall and they'll have to drive right by your store to get there! I bet the mini mall improves your business since more people will learn about it who otherwise might not have. More shoppers at the mall, more shoppers at Swappin' Sam's. More shoppers at Swappin' Sam's, more shoppers for the mall. See?"

"What I see, Gladys," Sam said, his volume rising, "is an acting mayor who as much as said she'd rather go to the mall in Hethrow than give her business to our very own Hornsby's Shoe Emporium right here on our very own square!" Gladys's eyes bugged. She had unwittingly made a *huge* faux pas. "What I see sitting right here in front of me, Gladys, is a traitor to her own office!" Gladys gasped. Sam threw down his napkin. "Lester! How much do I owe you?"

"If the bill were a snake, Sam," Lester said over his shoulder since he was pouring pancakes, "you'd have fang marks on your left wrist." Although Lester was always happy to see new business, he was perturbed Sam had chosen his establishment to stir up dissention, especially on the heels of Rick's death, and was anxious for him to blow back out the door.

Sam mumbled something under his breath, snatched up his bill and stormed to the cash register. "I need some change," he barked.

"Just hold your horses until these pancakes are done, Sam," Lester said. "My griddle's acting up this morning and I gotta stay right with things."

"Besides, Sammie boy, don't let our fine mayor here run ya off!" Arthur said, seizing the opportunity to get in one last jab. Gladys had yet to find her voice. Although she'd sputtered a few times, she'd simply been talked over (no small accomplishment) when she did try to speak.

"The only thing I'd *really* like to see running," Sam said

as he shifted his weight from one leg to the other, "is some-body, *anybody*, running against our Mayor come the election next spring. Otherwise we're all liable to find ourselves out of business—including *you*, Lester K. Biggs! You do know there's plans for a *tea* room in that mini mall, don't you? Last I looked, you had tea and sandwiches on *your* menu. Or does Gladys here think people will also drive to Partonville just to run around from one place to the next drinking gallons of tea?"

"Sam Vitner, I did not mean to suggest that . . ."

"Save it, Gladys," Sam said cutting her off. "I have wit-nesses."

Gladys cast her eyes around the patrons gathered at the U. Surely they knew she was just using an *example*. Surely they knew she wasn't trying to take business away from their very own Hornsby's! Try as she might to collect the words to explain herself, they simply would not string themselves to-gether in her head. She took in such a large gasp that the buttons of her blazer pulled so taut across her ample bosom, it looked like it might be ready to blow. Her flummoxed ap-pearance struck Harold as funny and he tickled himself imagining the next day's headlines he would never print: "Sam Vitner Tongue-Ties Acting Mayor McKern Who Blows Her Blazer." He started to laugh, which really made Gladys angry. Her face began to turn eggplant, her bosom heaved even higher and the buttons gaped all the more, drawing a perpendicular line of ovals between the buttons exposing her "yeller blouse."

Lester lifted the edge of one pancake with his spatula to check its doneness, then scooped up all eight of them and flipped them onto two of the plates he had warming on the corner of the grill. He started to reach for his butter knife but decided to dig in his utensil drawer to retrieve an implement he hadn't tried since the day he'd impulsively bought it.

"You think I can't compete with a lousy tea room?" he asked, incensed Sam would think he could feel threatened by such a silly thing. His voice was full volume in order to be heard over Harold's guffawing, the rigors of which had now caused Doc to start laughing as well as Arthur. The more people laughed, the more Gladys puffed up, the more dangerous her bosom appeared. Harold had to hold in the urge to shout "STAND BACK!" "Just look at this," Lester said, brandishing the metal contraption in his hand as if it were a sword. "I've got me a *melon baller!*" he said, dipping it into his rectangular stainless steel container filled with butter and dropping a perfectly round dollop on top of each stack.

With that, Harold laughed so hard he had to hang on to the counter to keep from falling off his stool.

⁂

The Del Vechias had made their Lamp Post reservations through Sunday night in order to give themselves a chance to physically and emotionally recuperate for a day between the funeral and heading back to Atlanta. After the funeral dinner they went back to their room to nap, the weight of the travel and events catching up with them. Then they spent late Saturday afternoon on into the evening driving in and around Partonville, amazed by the changes that had taken place. On their last trip decades ago Hethrow was a long drive from Partonville with all fields and open spaces in between. This time they couldn't believe how one housing development and shopping center after another now linked their way right to the outskirts of Rick's little town.

Through different conversations that weekend they'd learned Crooked Creek Farm had almost been gobbled up, which would have been the beginning of the end of life in Partonville as everyone knew it. But thanks to Dorothy and Katie Durbin, "the hungry machine was stopped," as Cora Davis had told them.

Whenever given the chance, Cora stuck like flypaper to the Del Vechias, who were a captive audience for all her *information,* as Cora would put it. Of course, the Del Vechias were already familiar with Dorothy Wetstra, having met her their first visit. And they'd often read one thing or another about her in the *Press.* Thankfully the Del Vechias had had a chance at the funeral dinner to spend some time chatting with Dorothy again, the exchange making Bob lonesome for his mother, who had Dorothy's same spunk but who had sadly passed away several years previously.

Katie was only vaguely familiar to Bob and Louise, having once been written up in a "Meet Your Neighbor" column by Sharon Teller. The weekly feature was short, stating only a few facts and the interviewee's opinion about a question Sharon dreamed up. The feature ran with a photo to help people recognize one another—although the Del Vechias found that funny since everyone seemed to already know everyone *and* their business. They'd been introduced to Katie by a few people over the weekend in many different ways. She was once referred to as the City Slicker, a couple times as the mini-mall lady, and jokingly identified as "my fancy neighbor" by Arthur Landers, who remarkably had taken a liking to her—in spite of the fact she drove "one of them foreign ve-hicles." Of course, Jessica had referred to her as "my best friend."

When the Del Vechias checked out and turned in their

room key (when was the last time they'd traveled and received an actual *key*, they wondered), they thanked Jessica for a lovely stay and assured her if they ever came back, there was no doubt as to where they'd make their reservations. They picked up a handful of business cards, saying they'd pass them around to their retired friends who liked to travel.

"Don't thank us," Jessica said. "It's we who need to thank you again for coming all this way to pay your respects to Mr. Lawson and for sharing your stories about him. I know everyone in town is as grateful to you as Paul and I are."

"Thank you," Bob said. "We wouldn't have missed it. We're just sorry we didn't make it here more often over the years, before Rick. . . . Well, anyway, you take care of yourself, you hear?"

"At the dinner Katie told us you were pregnant, and here you've already got your arms full," Louise said, genuine affection lacing her voice. Jessica turned crimson. Sarah Sue, who was perched on her hip, grinned at Louise, long strings of drool spilling over her bottom lip. "Pregnancy is nothing to be embarrassed about," Louise said, taking note of Jessica's red face. "Why I myself had *five* children, nearly one right after another!" Jessica looked like she might faint at the very idea of it. "All you need is a little help and you'll find your way," Louise said with assurance. "We all do."

Great! Jessica thought. *Everyone keeps telling me I need to get help, but how can I afford it?*

⚝⚝⚝

"Good afternoon, ladies and gentlemen, this is your captain speaking . . ." Bob tuned him out. This was the second time the pilot had blared over the intercom to inform the passengers as to what river was down to the right, what state border was off to the left. He pulled his newspaper back far enough to speak out of the side of his mouth to Louise, who was sitting to his left in the window seat. "What's the point? We're above the cloud cover," he griped. Without opening her eyes she shrugged and uttered a quiet "Hm." Bob looked at her, thought for a moment he might have awakened her with his question, although perhaps the captain had beat him to it. "Sorry. Didn't mean to bother you," he said, burying his head in his paper again.

Louise had not been sleeping. She was simply resting her head on her fluffy neck cozy, eyes closed, thinking about how intriguing one particular flower arrangement at the funeral had been. She had fantasized no less than a dozen possibilities since reading it. *Yours until the eight ball sinks for good. Your Little Red.* Her breath had caught in her throat when she'd fingered the card to read it, her curiosity getting the best of her. She'd discretely elbowed Bob for a look-see and his eyebrows had snapped straight up. They knew who it had to be from, especially after they'd learned nobody in Partonville had ever known Rick to play pool.

"Come on!" Louise said to Bob the minute they got in the car after the wake. "Little Red? It just *has* to be! Imagine. After all these years."

"Just the same," Bob responded, taking her hand, "I'm glad you didn't say anything when people asked if we knew who it might be from." He chuckled. "Those Pardon-Me-Villers will probably be trying to solve *that* mystery for decades!"

"At least we finally got *our* answer: he obviously *did* call that little redhead. Do you think they dated secretly? But why didn't he tell us? Such a mystery, but *so* romantic."

Ninety minutes into the plane ride home, however,

Louise had to fight off a sudden sorrow that threatened to engulf her. Had Rick spent all of these years *unable* to be with the Little Red who had captured his heart? Pining for her? Was she married? Did he feel he couldn't leave his mother? She wished she'd thought to pay attention to the florist who had delivered them. Would there have been a way to try to track down the sender?

In the end she decided that if Rick had wanted them to know who she was, and what they'd been up to (or not) he would have told them. A person had a right to their own secrets. Whatever Rick and Little Red had shared, it was obviously special and long-lasting. And *whatever* the circumstances, she was glad that they'd been able to stay in touch.

She rolled her head to the left and looked out the window. There was a sudden break in the clouds through which she viewed the first slice of planet earth since their initial ascent. If there was a pool hall in heaven, she concluded, writing her own ending to their story, Little Red and Rick would watch that eight ball for eternity.

🌲🌲🌲

In the next week's *Press,* the last edition the Del Vechias would receive, Harold wrote in his editorial, "The Del Vechias' willingness to travel this long distance to say good-bye to their good friend is a powerful testimony to the power and pull of Rick's spirit." He tucked a personal longhand note in with the paper before he mailed it. "Thank you for being a subscriber all of these years and for helping us to celebrate Rick's life. Stay well. Harold."

18

⧫⧫⧫

Edward Showalter kept his eyes peeled as he drove down County Y. It was dusk, barely enough light to spot a FREE DOG TO GOOD HOME sign, especially when he didn't know exactly where to look. He wished he could have made this trek in better light, but his meeting with Katie and Carl Jimson had run later than expected.

They'd worked hard all day reviewing and modifying the new sketches Jimson had put together over the weekend. They talked about support beams, licensing (and yes, much to Katie's obvious relief, Edward Showalter had assured her that he *was* a licensed electrician), permits, whether or not to open the atrium from the basement, which smelled plenty musty, or just keep it to the main and second floors, plus several other aspects of the overall rehab. Edward Showalter was plumb tuckered out when they finally called it quits, but the leisurely drive in the country served as a relaxing transition.

"If somebody's already taken the dog, I could be driving back and forth till the cows roost looking for something that isn't here," he said to no one. (Edward Showalter was known for his discombobulated expressions.) When he got to the state highway he figured the dog already had a home so he turned around and headed back. But just before County Y intersected with County EE, his headlights flashed on a white sign leaning against a big boulder. FREE DOG TO GOOD HOME!

"Bingo!" he said aloud as he hit his brakes and flicked on his blinker. No wonder neither he nor Johnny had noticed it when heading south—the sign only faced the south, the back of it hidden by the giant boulder. He slowly rolled up the long drive, stopping just outside the rundown farmhouse's back door and parked his van between an old Chevy pickup and an older Chevy sedan. As soon as he finished swinging his legs around he found himself nose to nose with a tall, long dog who seemed to appear out of nowhere. The dog's entire body was wagging back and forth so hard it reminded Edward Showalter of the agitation cycle in his mother's old ringer washing machine. The red dog—he could vaguely make out the dog's color now that his eyes had adjusted to the dark—set one foot up in his lap as though to pin him in his seat. He used both hands to scratch behind the dog's long silky ears, perhaps the softest ears he'd ever felt, and the dog moaned with pleasure. "Good boy," Edward Showalter said, wondering if this could possibly be The Dog. If it was, this hound dog was going straight to his or her new home. It was love at first sight.

🌲🌲🌲

Joshmeister (at least that's what Mom said to call you when she gave me your e-mail address),

I'm sorry I didn't get to say good-bye but you were already in school by the time I got the conference call from my partner and secretary this morning. For a minute it looked like I might get to stay, but after circling a particular case from several angles we realized it would be best if I came back and presented in court myself this Friday. I have my work cut out for me, but work always feels good to me so that's okay.

But now to the important topic: get a car yet? I pictured you coming straight home from school and putting on the full-court press, maybe wearing your mom down enough that you'd go check out some of those ads. It would have been fun to car shop with you and your mom, but I know you're in good hands with Arthur. If my mom trusted him with The Tank, that says it all.

I hope to see you for the Christmas party. A short trip back will be better than no trip.

Best,

Jacob, aka legal10245

PS I phoned my mom when I got home, just like she instructed me. No, you never get done having to obey your parents. ☺

Jacob (Sorry, legal10245 doesn't do it for me. Too stiff.),

Thanks for the e-mail. Nice surprise at the end of another day when I DID NOT GET A CAR.

What else is there to say besides thanks for being in my corner, even after Mom gave you her evil eye. She said if Arthur is available one evening this week, we'll go "browse." What's the point in that? I'd rather hear we'll go "buy," but I'll take what I can get.

Hope to see you Christmas. Will keep you posted on the wheels.

Joshmeister, aka Josh, aka He Who Needs a CAR!

PS Mom's e-mail addy is Katie.Durbin (Soooo original) with the same @ as your mom and me.

⁂

Dorothy sat in her prayer chair, Bible closed in her lap, fingers laced on top of it, and stared out the window at the muted streetlight, trying to pretend it was the moon. She was wearing the new pink pajamas she'd picked up at Wal-Mart when she and Jacob had stopped there this morning. She'd already washed them with a small load of laundry after he left to give her something to do besides feel sad.

After Jacob learned he *did* have to be on the plane today, he'd asked her if there was anywhere she'd like to go before he took off with the transportation. She'd told him Wal-Mart, since she needed a new pair of PJs, then Long John Silver's for lunch, if he had time. "I already had May Belle replace the elastic waistband in my old PJs once. Now the fabric is worn so thin my bony old knees are popping through. And I haven't been able to get out to Long John Silver's for way too long a time. I'm just *craving* those crunchies." Jacob had waited in the car for her at Wal-Mart in order to make a few phone calls. And although he ran out of time for them to go in Long John Silver's and eat, they'd ordered carry-out for Dorothy. He assured her he'd get a bite at the airport. He looked at his wristwatch nearly the whole time they waited for their order to come up. Although it only took a minute or two, she knew he was cutting it closer than usual, especially since he had to return his rental car. And now here she sat staring at a streetlight feeling bluer than blue.

Lord, the house feels so empty now. And yet I have so much to be thankful for. Why, my whole family was here for Thanksgiving and Jacob got to stay a whole extra week. My Christmas decorations are up and I even like my little tree. And yet . . . I feel all alone and whiny this evening, like another good dose of Poor Me is brewing. But then You already know that.

Sheba jumped up into her lap and startled her. Her Bible

thunked to the floor. "Right on cue," Dorothy said to Sheba when Sheba laid down, stretching her body along Dorothy's leg and resting her head on Dorothy's knee. "Jacob Henry told you to take care of me when he left, didn't he? And here you are."

Thank You, Jesus, for putting up with me and for prodding Sheba to remind me that I am never alone. You are here, making Yourself known in thousands of quiet ways. Dorothy continued to stroke Sheba's head with her left hand while she bent over to retrieve her Bible with her right. She opened to Second Corinthians and rested the Bible on Sheba's back, who was used to this drill and didn't budge. Dorothy flipped the pages looking for her blue highlighter marks. Was it chapter eleven? No, it was twelve. There it was. *"My grace is sufficient for you, for power is perfected in weakness."* Well, I feel as weak as an overcooked noodle, so power me up, Big Guy! Amen.

"It's time for bed, Sheba. My prayers are done. God is in the heavens and in this room. My partial plate is in the soaker, and I'm tired. What else is there to say or do?"

Sheba jumped off Dorothy's lap and hopped up on the end of the bed. Dorothy crawled under the covers. She shut her eyes, and try as she might to feel drowsy now that she was all tucked in, her mind skittered from here to there. She whapped her pillow a couple times and curled up on her side, determined to think about all the things she had to be grateful for this Christmas season. There was the nativity set with all four Wise People. The delight on Earl's face when he watched *anyone's* tree lights. The old glass ornament Jacob seemed as happy to find in the box as she'd been to set her eyes on Esmeralda. It was hand blown and appeared to be some kind of a hummingbird. The bird had a one-inch, very red, very pointy beak which was the brightest thing about it.

The rest of the paint was worn off its silver body, aside from glimmers of a much softer red across its back and a hint of green on its stomach. Whatever had been stuck into the open back end for a tail had been missing for as long as Dorothy could remember. So long, in fact, she couldn't recall what it had even looked like. And the poor bird only had one wing, which was a soft bristly fan of sorts. Come to think about it, she couldn't remember the treasure ever having two wings. It was pathetic looking, really, but she just could not bring herself to throw it away. It always gave her an odd satisfaction to see the ornament nestled in the tree.

"Of course I remember *this*," Jacob said when they'd taken it out of the box. "I'm glad you kept it."

"We've had the poor bedraggled thing since before you were born."

"Did you ever hear the story Caroline Ann invented about this bird?" he asked, finding a place of prestige near the top of the fragrant little tree.

"Never."

He carefully placed the hook over a branch, then gently tugged on it to make sure it was securely in place. "She said the bird would *always* be on our tree, that it couldn't fly away if it wanted to."

"Is that right?" Dorothy's eyes instantly burned, picturing sweet little Caroline inventing a story to tell her big brothers about this tiny bird. She was so tenderhearted and how she loved playing pretend. And oh! how they'd all— Mom, Dad and her two big brothers—adored Caroline Ann, their surprise child.

"Caroline said she'd seen the bird try to fly off the tree late one night when we were all asleep." Jacob stared off into space as though picturing her over there near the chair where his eyes landed. "But he had to come back, because he could only fly in circles. And she said it with that pouty look on her face, you know the one." Dorothy nodded her head. "Then she broke out in a smile and said, 'But that's okay because he *likes* flying in circles. It's *fun*! And he *likes* our tree. And he specially likes *me*.'"

Dorothy sniffled, tears beginning to spill onto her cheeks, especially after Jacob's voice hitched. "What a fine memory, son. I am so grateful you shared it with me," she said as they both stared at the treasured bird. Dorothy lay in bed recalling that special moment she'd spent with Jacob and teared up again.

She looked at the glowing red numbers on her bedside clock. *Come on, sleep!* Then for the first time since Jacob had dragged her boxes out of the closet, her mind flickered to something they *hadn't* found.

When Katie and Josh were going through Tess's home after her death, the home that had since become Dorothy's, they'd discovered an old dented bedpan with dirty plastic poinsettias sticking out of it. The flowers were so faded and filled with dust that they were more brown than red. It was a mystery as to whether Tess had the "arrangement" as a joke or an actual Christmas decoration, or if perhaps one day she'd just stuck the flowers in the first place she'd looked, or, well, it was such a fun curiosity that Dorothy thought she'd set it aside for herself at UMC's annual Fall Rummage Sale. However, the next time she saw it was at the auction, and before she knew it, she was in a bidding war with some stranger, a guy who wanted it for a joke. Since it was her auction she hadn't bothered to get a number, but Arthur agreed to bid for her. Once Arthur got a look at who they were bidding against—a guy who had ticked him off earlier in the day—Arthur decided that bonehead was not taking that bedpan home with him, whether his friend Dorothy wanted it or not. The next thing they knew, they'd run the bidding up to $35 before the other guy finally backed out. Arthur split the cost with Dorothy and jokingly said they could have joint custody. She was sure Arthur had told her she got first visitation and he'd take it the next year. But where was it?

She tossed and turned thinking. She *knew* she'd seen it since the move, but *where*? She flicked on her bed lamp, threw the covers back, slipped her feet into her pink terry house slippers and went on the prowl through her bedroom closet. Sheba lifted her head and looked at her, then put her head back down with a look that said, "I thought we went to bed." Pretty soon every light in the house was on, but no bedpan. Now she was not only wide awake but determined, so she turned on the tree lights and sat on the couch, thinking, thinking. "Esmeralda, you're so smart," she said, turning her head toward the nativity set which Jacob had set up on the card table in the corner, just like May Belle recommended. "Do you know where the bedpan is?" Silence. She drummed her fingers on the arm of the couch, thinking, thinking. Then it struck her: it was on the bottom shelf of her little bathroom closet! B is for bedpan is for bathroom, she'd said to herself when storing it, using the same logic as D is for Del Monte and decorations. She'd taken to trying that system after she heard some guy on a news program talking about helping your memory through association. But too bad her association tactics never seemed to kick in until *after* she'd already remembered—or found—whatever it was she was trying to remember. Obviously, the guy didn't know what he was talking about.

≜ ≜ ≜

Dear Joshmeister,

It's 1:30 a.m. and you won't believe what I've been doing. I've just finished hanging that bedpan with the poinsettias in it (remember the one you found in your Aunt Tess's house, now MY house?) on my bathroom wall and just had to tell somebody about it since Sheba wasn't interested. HA!

First I remembered I had it. Then I couldn't find it. Then I remembered where it was. Then I took it all apart and washed every inch of it, including the underside of the plastic flowers—although I probably should have replaced them, they were so dark. Then I reassembled it and got some ribbon out of my wrapping paper box and made a bow for it. Then I hammered a nail into my wall between the vanity mirror and the toilet. Then I had to wrestle around to figure out how to hang a bedpan on a nail since it had to face forward because of the flowers. (Bad planning.) So . . . I rummaged through my junk drawer and found a three-penny nail, I got out my hammer (Hey! You think I don't have my own toolbox?!) and would you believe I pounded a hole in the back of that bedpan? I kept waiting for Mac to pull up to my house in his squad car, I was making such a racket so late into the night. Anyway, I got it hung and it looks so FUN in there, and now I can't sleep.

I gave Jacob your e-mail address, I hope you don't mind. He's awful busy so not sure if he'll e-mail or not. He was sorry he didn't get to say good-bye to you, which means he liked you. Nice to know you two get along.

Keep me posted about the car. Jessie called me this evening to thank me for telling her you could use Arthur's help. (Anything to get him out of the house, she said!) She also said your mom had called him and I guess you're all going out Wednesday night. I know you thought maybe your Uncle Delbert could help with a car, but trust me on this one. Although he can preach a whale of a sermon, his mechanical abilities and sensibilities aren't as big as a minnow. HA!

Good Night, Sweet Prince. I'm going to try going to bed again now that the pee pot (well, not really since genuine pee pots don't look like this; they look more like a giant teacup) is on the wall.

Outtamyway! Especially when I have a hammer in my hand!

Thank you, Jesus! Dorothy prayed after she settled back into bed, finally feeling relaxed and content. *I've got friends all around me and through the wonders of electronics, I can talk to some of them day or night. My* best *friend makes the best desserts in the whole county, including the likes of Extravagant Trays!* She had put her partial plate back in and downed a glass of milk with two cookies May Belle had brought over when she and Earl came to see the tree this morning. *I can still hammer a nail, clean my own house and stay up until two A.M. if I feel like it. And Lord, THANK YOU, but I don't want to stay up until 3 since I'm tired now so I'm going to sleep. Amen.*

19

⁂

Arthur sat in the passenger seat of Katie's SUV feeling like a captured barracuda. He wasn't used to being a passenger and he felt like a traitor sitting in a foreign-made vehicle, even if it wasn't his. He fiddled with the seatbelt that pressed his Hohner into his chest. Arthur didn't take to wearing seatbelts. He didn't care if it was the law, he never strapped himself into his Buick or his good old Ford truck he'd bought used twenty years ago. However, Katie said she would not move the SUV until he buckled up. "I don't see any human way possible ta make this seatbelt and my harmonica work together," he said, letting go of the seatbelt and allowing it to quickly retract.

"She means it, Arthur," Josh said from the back seat, "so you might as well just do it if we plan on looking at cars today—or within my lifetime." Josh was embarrassed. Who did his mom think she was bossing an old man around? He shot her a dirty look into her rearview mirror when he caught her eye.

"I have two words for both of you gentlemen," she said, keeping her tone of voice light, "Richard Lawson."

"The *Press* said he done *had* his seatbelt on, Ms. Bossy Durbin, so I got two words fer *you:* didn't work." Josh snickered under his breath, but he wondered how his mom would react. He hoped they didn't get in an argument and blow his chance to go car hunting. Nonetheless, Arthur finally wrestled around with the contraption again until Katie heard the click, at which point she turned over the engine.

As much as Arthur's rebuttal irritated Katie, it was also the truth. She shot him a half smile as if to let him know he was impossible, which she could tell from the way he looked back at her he already knew. She appreciated Arthur Landers. He was a man of strong opinions and convictions and he wasn't afraid to express them, and he was about as ornery, to use one of Dorothy's words, as they came. And yet, she'd always felt he was in her corner. Plus, he was such a good friend to Dorothy, who she knew missed spending time with Arthur almost as much as they both missed The Tank, which had always given them the chance to visit. Katie occasionally noticed Arthur's truck parked out in front of Dorothy's, or Dorothy would mention Arthur had stopped by to see if she needed anything or a ride anywhere. Underneath all his grumbling, he was a kind man with a tender heart who was always looking out for Dorothy. His gruff facade didn't fool Katie for a moment. She'd actually been looking forward to spending this time with him, maybe even see what he thought about the mini mall, if there was a way to bring it up. One thing she could be sure of: he would have an opinion.

"Mom, I was just thinking. Maybe we should have asked Dorothy to come car hunting with us."

"Now that there is a much more sensible idere than seatbelts!" Arthur said, turning his head to face Katie, who was holding the newspaper in one hand and driving with the other. They'd made a few calls and charted a route, numbering the order of their stops. It occurred to Arthur to chide Katie about the safety of driving with one hand, but he decided to play nice—at least for now. "Hows 'bouts ya let me have a look-see at that list. Might save us some time."

"You want me to call Dorothy on my cell?" Josh asked, already reaching for his belt clip.

"If you want. But don't think for a moment you're gathering a team to bully me into coming home with a car today if we haven't found the right one." It was her turn to shoot him a look in the rearview mirror, but he was already dialing Dorothy's number. How is it moms were also mind readers? he wondered.

⚜ ⚜ ⚜

"I like the color," Dorothy said to Josh as they stood in front of the Mitsubishi, "and that's about as worthwhile of an opinion as you'll get from me."

"All opinions matter," he said. "I like the color, too." He also liked the leather seats, the sporty dashboard and the reputation it had for cornering.

"Trouble," Arthur said, his ear toward the running engine.

"What kind of trouble?" asked Katie, who was standing beside him thinking how nice and clean the engine looked.

"Sounds like a tappet." He slammed the lid down and brushed his hands together as though ridding them of debris, even though he hadn't touched a thing under the hood. His ear told him all he needed to know.

"Are you sure?" Josh sounded like he was on the verge of arguing with Arthur, his patience (which he really didn't have to begin with) running thin. This was the fourth and final car they had seen today and Arthur had vetoed all of them. Not only that, he'd crossed three more off the list before they'd even gotten to Dorothy's house, saying he'd read one thing or another about them in this car magazine or that, or that he "knowed somebody who had nothin' but trouble with 'em." Josh thought the one before this stood a chance since it was the only one Arthur took out for a ride, inviting Josh to come along if he wanted. *Man! Who does this old geezer think is going to be driving* my *car? Whose idea was it to bring him anyway?* Although Josh didn't say anything, he climbed in and slammed the door a little too hard, making it clear to all of them that he thought Arthur was being unfair. Arthur just looked at him and said in a high-pitched voice, "I ain't ah movin' this ve-hicle one inch, sonny boy, till ya buckle up." Josh couldn't help but grin at Arthur's high-pitched imitation of his mom, but still. . . . He wanted a car and he wanted it today. Who knew when they'd get out again? And now Arthur had nixed this one, too. As far as his mom was concerned, that was that. Dorothy was no help at all, simply repeating that Arthur knew his business and assuring Josh his patience would be worth it.

"Since we're way out here by Yorkville," Dorothy said after they were all back in the SUV, "how about as my thank-you for letting me tag along I treat us all to a root beer float at Harley's? At least we'd get some consolation out of the day."

"Harley's?" Katie asked.

"You ain't heard ah Harley's?" Arthur asked. "And here I thought ya was startin' ta know the neighborhood."

"No, Arthur, I have not heard of Harley's, but I'm sure you're going to let me know all about it. So, somebody better tell me which way to go."

"Make a right at the stop sign. It's about two miles down," Josh said in a pouty, disgusted voice.

"And you know this because . . . ?" Katie asked.

"Because Kevin, who *has* a car, took us there one day on the way home from school."

"Us?" Arthur asked.

"Shelby and Deb. Deborah Arnold. That was when Kevin and Deb were still dating, which, as of yesterday, they aren't any more."

"Really?" Katie caught Josh's eye in the rearview mirror for a moment.

"Really."

After another dramatic wrestle with the seatbelt, Arthur whipped his Hohner out of his pocket and began to play a soulful verse of an old Brenda Lee song. "I'm sorry, so sorry," the words went, which Dorothy began to sing. She'd always loved that song. "Love is fickle, ain't it?" Arthur asked when he came to the end of the tune.

"Never mind love," Josh said. "I'm sorry I still don't have any wheels."

"Speaking of love, Arthur," Dorothy said, stopping Josh from igniting a feud with his mother, "how's Jessie? I haven't seen her since our last Hookers' meeting." Jessie was Arthur's wife of nearly sixty years. "She needs to get herself over for a visit, or maybe you can take me out to your place some time."

"How's Jessie? ya ask," Arthur said, drawing his thumb and forefinger down on his very short (hadn't shaved for two days) but very gray chin whiskers. "Well now . . ."

"Mom! Slow down, Harley's is right up here," Josh said.

"Saved from *that* saga by a root beer float!" Arthur said.

"Is this the closest place to Partonville to get a float or a good cone?" Katie asked anyone who wanted to answer.

"I believe it is," Dorothy said. "Well, of course you can make your own with the fixings from Your Store. But not even Lester serves root beer. I've tried to talk him into it a time or two, but he said he's not interested in becoming a soda jerk."

"He opened hisself up for some teasin' there, I tell ya,"

Arthur said. "Like what kinda jerk does he wanna be?" A group chuckle rustled through the car. Even Josh had to set aside his pouting for a moment.

"Wonder if I should consider an ice cream parlor in the mini mall," Katie said, pulling into a parking place in front of Harley's, which looked to be more old and rundown than quaint.

"Speaking of your min-i-scule mall," Arthur said, finding himself very funny, "ya sure got old Sammie stirred up!"

"Sammie?" Katie asked as they all climbed out of the car, Josh running around the SUV to open Dorothy's door for her.

"Sam Vitner. Swappin' Sam's."

"What do you mean he's stirred up?" Dorothy wanted to know.

"He showed up fer breakfast at Harry's the other day yammerin' on 'bout this and that. He thinks Miss Bossy Durbin here," he said, winking at Katie as he stood back to allow her to enter Harley's first, "is tryin' ta run him outta business. Not only that, he's lookin' for somebody ta run against Gladys come the next election."

"Run him out of business?" Dorothy asked. "I don't understand."

"He says yer gonna have an antiques store in yer mall," Arthur said, studying Katie's face as he spoke, testing the waters.

"Yes. That's my plan for one of the stores," Katie said as they moved toward the counter to read the board of the ice cream flavors for the day.

"Well, ol' Sammie sees that as di-rect competition. Oh! And by golly if he didn't try ta git Lester worked up about yer min-i-scule mall, too!"

"Lester?" Katie asked, her face showing surprise.

"Yup. Sammie told Lester yer fancy schmancy tea room idere could like ta cause *him* ta go belly up."

"I'm going to have the Gallon Guzzler," Josh said, a note of bitterness in his voice. They were supposed to be finding him a car, not talking about his mom's mini-mall project. He was beginning to hate that place and it wasn't even built yet.

"What did Lester say?" Katie wanted to know, feeling a twinge of nervousness.

"He said—and I do believe this is a di-rect quote—'I got me a melon baller.'"

🌲🌲🌲

"What on earth is Sam Vitner thinking trying to stir up trouble, May Belle?"

After Katie had dropped Dorothy off at her house, Dorothy let Sheba out to do her business, then they both walked straight to May Belle's, even though it was only thirty minutes until both of their bedtimes and Dorothy was still catching up on her sleep from the night before last. "Nobody can compete with Swappin' Sam's. I bet there's not another thing like his place in the tri-county area. For goodness sakes!" Earl left the living room where they'd all gathered. Even though the tree was still on, it made him nervous to see his Dearest Dorothy upset. "Sam's got salvage and parts and junk and interesting whatchajiggies and toilets and even that building with nicer stuff in it. To see a little antique store as competition is ridiculous! And carrying on about it at Harry's, trying to get *Lester* excited. *Shame* on him! If he wasn't so far on the edge of town I'd walk right over there first thing in the morning and give him a piece of my mind."

"Now, Dorothy, I haven't seen you take a nitroglycerin tablet for a while. You're going to set your heart to misbehaving if you don't calm down. You're taking those other pills every day, aren't you?" Dorothy nodded. Try as she might to fight her dependence on drugs, much to the satisfaction of the good Doc, she'd finally broken down and started listening to him. "Would you like a nice cup of chamomile tea?"

"No tea this late, thank you. I just downed every last slurp of a giant root beer float from Harley's and if I had another drop to drink I'd be up and down to the bathroom all night. Besides, I've already tested the edge of my bladder's elasticity enough for one day." May Belle chuckled. "I tell you, I just can*not* imagine what Sam's thinking! Why, Katie is working so hard to do good for this town. She doesn't need that kind of friction."

"Were you this riled up in the car? *Good*ness me! What did Arthur say? Or Josh?"

"I bit my tongue and veered the conversation back to car hunting, which is probably why I'm so wound up now since I held it in for so long. I could see Josh was not taking it well when we were all carrying on about the mini mall. It was hard enough on him that he didn't even get to drive one car this evening, but then to have the night end with all of this. His mom's always pretty stoic, but once she started asking Arthur questions about who else he thought might be against the mini mall you could tell she was getting upset. And you know Arthur, he just loves to torment. I hope she knew he was kidding when he said just about *everybody* could find a reason to not like the idea if they set their minds to it. Oh! And then he went and mentioned he'd also heard some talk about her buying up other properties around town. He said somebody wondered if Partonville might soon become Durbinville! Now you *know* he made that up. As much as I love that man, honestly. . . ."

"I'm sure it'll all work out, dear. You're fretting about too many things."

"I wanted to talk to Arthur privately but Katie dropped me off first. Who knows what all he filled her head with. I'll give him a call tomorrow, see what else he said and how much of it was true. See if he might want to take me over to Sam's so I can have a word with him. Pure and simple, Arthur Landers was gossiping. Since when did he become a gossip?"

May Belle stared at her friend. She couldn't remember the last time she'd seen her this angry. "Dorothy Wetstra, this isn't like you to be so upset over something like this. What's going on?"

May Belle's tone of voice caught Dorothy up short. Dorothy stared at her friend, then at her hands, then at May Belle's beautiful Christmas tree, taking note of the pipe cleaner angel, an ornament she'd given May Belle when they were kids. "I think I'm just tired. You know how crabby I can be when I'm tired. And I'm not only physically tired, I think I'm emotionally worn down from the excitement of my boys being here for Thanksgiving, and Jacob getting to stay, and then Rick's passing. Now I'm missing my boys and was up half the night the other night. I guess hearing Arthur carry on about Sam was just my last straw. I'm sorry. I didn't mean to sound so out of sorts. You know I adore Sam Vitner and to be honest, I can't even imagine him being an instigator. You're right. It's not fair to make judgments and work up a head of steam when I haven't even talked to him myself."

"Goodness, Dorothy, nobody would ever accuse you of being judgmental."

"Well, I guess my own conscience just talked to me then, because I surely was."

May Belle slowly stood up and smiled at her friend. "I don't mean to chase you out, but I think we *both* need to go to bed." She looked down the hallway and saw that Earl's bedroom light was out. "Earl's spent so many hours staring at the tree his eyes are probably crossed." She shook her head and smiled warmly, her heart so filled with love for that child of hers.

"Thank you, May Belle. Thanks for listening and understanding and setting me straight. When Earl wakes up, tell him I didn't mean to upset him."

"You know Earl, Dorothy. He won't remember anyway. And I doubt you could ever *really* upset that son of mine; he adores you. Your tone probably just took him by surprise. He was tired, too."

"I'll talk to you soon," Dorothy said, leaning toward May Belle to give her a hug.

The women embraced and then stood in silence staring at the tree and May Belle's small plastic nativity she always set up under it. "God bless us every one," May Belle said. And those were the last perfect, poignant, quieting words that were spoken before Dorothy and Sheba headed down the street toward home, bed and a good night's sleep with the full moon of a lamppost light glowing into her bedroom.

20

♣♣♣

"You can believe it or not, Maggie Malone, but I'm telling you that Sam Vitner, Fred Hornsby," (Cora had trotted straight from Harry's to Hornsby's Shoe Emporium right after Sam and Gladys had at it day before yesterday) "George Gustafson, the folks at the doughnut shop and who knows how many others are hopping mad about this mini mall threatening to destroy our town," Cora said while Maggie washed her hair. Maggie had heard other murmurings in her shop the last couple days, but none on so large a scale. "To tell you the truth of the matter, Maggie" (Maggie had to stifle a giant HA! Since when did Cora ever tell the whole truth?!), "I can't blame them. That Katie Durbin is just a little too slick for her own britches, if you ask me. I mean, co-hosting the Hookers' party—at least that's what they're calling it, *co*-hosting—just to get in good graces with the whole town? How dumb does she think we are?" Maggie bit her lip. "And now she and *Gladys*—a *turncoat* in our own *community*—are all buddy-buddy. It was nearly *shameless* the way that Durbin woman lured Gladys to her table, buttering her up one side and down the other. I tell you, that woman is not to be trusted. Neither of them are. Partonville's *acting* Mayor McKern is *acting* more like a starstruck groupie than a leader. When she as much as *tells* people they should buy their shoes at the mall in *Hethrow* rather than from our very own hardworking *Fred Hornsby* and his *poor* wife, Frieda, it's a sad, sad day for Partonville."

"Now, Cora," Maggie said, hoping the warm rinse running down the sides of Cora's head would calm her, "I think you might be making a tad more of this than is actually true. For instance . . ."

Cora sat straight up in the chair, mindless of the streams of water that began to run down her face and into her mouth. She squeegeed the water out of her face with the heels of her hands, mascara now streaking clear to her ears. "Maggie Malone! I am a paying customer and I deserve to be treated with more respect than to be accused of *lying* right here in your chair!"

Maggie handed Cora a towel to wipe her face and grabbed another to dab at her wagging head. "Now, Cora, settle down. I accused you of no such things. I have no reason to think you are *lying.* I just think there might be another side to the . . ."

"Think what you want, Maggie," Cora yelped, cutting right into her sentence. "Just know your thinking is very clouded if you do not believe there's going to be a fight—maybe even picketing!—over this mini mall." She dropped the towel she'd used to wipe her face into her lap and batted Maggie away from her head. She began patting a spot over her right ear. "Honestly, Maggie! You didn't rinse this side of my head! Can you hear those bubbles popping? I can hear them in my *ear.* Is this how you treat people who don't agree with you?"

"You're the one who sat up while I was rinsing, Cora."

Cora would hear none of it. "How about you just stick to business and finish the job right." Cora leaned back and settled her neck in the sink's neck cradle.

Maggie put her hands on her hips and sighed. She'd been taught that when you were a business owner, the customer was always right. When your business depended upon repeat customers—and Cora had a standing weekly appointment—you needed to go the extra mile to be nice, she reminded herself. She drew a deep breath and held it a moment. In spite of all she knew to be true, she was fighting the urge to pick up the sprayer and give Cora a wet what's-for. *How dare she talk to me like that! The old gossip deserves a . . .*

"And you are waiting for *what?*" Cora asked, never once opening her eyes.

Maggie picked up the sprayer, making sure she held it down in the sink while adjusting the water lest it shoot up out of the sink and dowse both of them. She turned the faucet to as cold as it would go while she argued with herself. *Now, Maggie, you are above doing what you're thinking.* BAD ANGEL: *Wanna bet?* GOOD ANGEL: *Angels do not engage in betting, Maggie. You know that. We spend our time nurturing, guiding, making life beautiful—same as you. You make people beautiful, remember? You do not spray cold water up their noses. You beautify.* BAD ANGEL: *Cora has it coming.* GOOD ANGEL: *Perhaps, but you also want her to keep coming to your shop. Now turn that faucet to warm, Maggie, and take care of your client.* BAD ANGEL: *Soak it to her, Mags!*

With each argument, Maggie steered her faucet as though it was the rudder of a speed boat running an obstacle course. From right to left and back again it went until she finally got a hold of herself. "How's the temperature, Cora?" she asked as she set the spray to Cora's head.

"Fine."

"Good," Maggie replied through gritted teeth. "Now

let's get you good and rinsed, dried, curled and ready to carry on with your day." *You old gossip!*

The BAD ANGEL just had to have the last word, didn't she? Maggie thought while she kept her lip zipped and set her heart back to beautifying.

♣♣♣

Edward Showalter simply could not believe his good fortune. He looked into Kornflake's rust-colored eyes and felt a swell of gratitude so powerful it almost made him cry. He'd had his new dog for less than twenty-four hours and already he felt like he'd known him his entire life. There was just something about this gangly pooch that extracted a very high "awwwww" factor, even from the likes of Edward Showalter. Kornflake could sit, stay (better than any other dog he'd owned), fetch, drop (well, most of the time) and shake (either paw you pointed to) with the best of the Good Dogs. He was housebroken and at least thus far he hadn't chewed on a single thing that wasn't one of the dog toys Edward Showalter had bought at Wal-Mart on his way home. He'd also picked up dog food, treats, two toys and a collar—camouflage to match his camy-van, of course. And Kornflake wasn't even a yapper. When he did bark—which he'd only done once when somebody rang the doorbell—he only let out two low, hound-sounding *Woof!*s, then he'd looked at Edward Showalter as if to say, "Do we care about the guy at the door or can I go off duty?" Edward had looked out his window, saw Rooney standing there and said, "It's okay, boy," and that was that.

"Awwwww, ya gotcha a new dog, Edward Showalter," Rooney said as he scratched Kornflake behind the ears. "It's about time."

Edward Showalter gave Rooney the whole story, from Johnny's sign sighting to the way Kornflake ("Never thought to ask him why they'd named him such a goofy thing, but it just kinda suits him.") had jumped right into his van right up into the passenger seat where he sat "as big as you please," to the way he'd curled up and laid down in the back when Edward Showalter went into Wal-Mart ("Waited so patiently, didn't ya, boy?") and then curled up on the throw rug next to his bed when it was time for light's out. "Slept like a baby. Didn't get up till I did. Ate a good breakfast and hasn't once tormented the kitties."

"Kitties?"

"Look at this," Edward Showalter said, motioning Rooney to follow him to the bathroom. Curled up together in a box were one pure white kitten, a boy, and one jet black furball, a girl. They were so wound around each other they looked like a skein of angora yarn.

"Where'd ya get them?" Rooney, a giant of a man, asked as he adjusted his red bandana a little higher on his forehead, his bleach-blond curly locks spilling over the top.

"Same place as Kornflake. After Kornflake jumped into the passenger seat the guy said, 'Hey! Want a couple kittens for the road?' I said *sure*. The guy took off running toward his front screen porch yelling, 'HONEY! HE'S GONNA TAKE THE KITTENS, TOO!' Before he could pass through the porch to get into his house his wife opened the front door and handed him a paper grocery bag folded down at the top. The bag was rockin' and rollin', I tell you. I set it down behind Kornflake's seat and started my engine. Before I had it in reverse, out the door the wife came runnin' to the van. She had another big brown grocery bag in her hand. I was half afraid to ask what was in *this* one."

"Don't tell me ya got ya another pet someplace!"

"Matter of fact," Edward Showalter said, and that's all he said.

"No!"

"No. I was just pullin' your leg," he said, slapping his knee. "Three's enough for now. She'd packed up one dented can of cat food along with a catnip toy that was so dirty it looked like a *real* dead mouse. To be honest, looking at the dog's ribcage, I don't know that any of them have had much to eat for a couple days. Hard story, really. They've been renting that property the last couple years, until he got laid off from the mines and couldn't find another job. They're fixin' to move to Kentucky to live with his brother's family."

"Dog doesn't look to be that old. What were they thinking gettin' a dog when they were in financial straits?" Rooney picked up one of the kittens and snuggled it under his chin next to the dagger tattoo on his neck. Kornflake was leaning into Edward Showalter's leg while he held a kitty to his chest with one hand and scratched Kornflake with the other.

"The guy said one morning he got up and there was Kornflake rolled up in a tight little ball at the base of a big tree in their backyard. Due to his red color and the fact he was half coated with mud, at first the guy thought he was a fawn. But then Kornflake stood up and wagged his long tail. Guy said he looked half starved so he gave him a few scraps. His wife was fit to be tied since they didn't have scraps to spare. Had four kids, ya know." Rooney shook his head as he gently set the kitty back in the box. "She told her husband he should shoot the dog but he said he just couldn't bring himself to do it since Kornflake had such pleading eyes. Thank goodness, 'cause you were meant for me, weren'tcha guy?" Edward Showalter said to Kornflake whose whole body started its wonderful agitating. "Then this pregnant cat showed up and delivered on their front porch. Got in through a hole in the screen, he said. Momma disappeared one night and left her kittens. His wife said that was the last straw. She's the one who made the sign."

"Must have torn the guy up to see such a good dog go."

"Actually, he was relieved and very grateful. It made him happy to know Kornflake was going to a good home. Said these animals weren't long for this world. Couldn't even look me in the eye when he said it."

"Edward Showalter, animal rescue man!" Rooney teased. "But enough of the animal stories. What'd ya want to talk to me about?"

"I'm putting a construction crew together—already got Smackman, J.R. and Sherlock—and I only want the best guys I know, guys who aren't afraid to work overtime." Rooney smiled and nodded his head. "Guys who want the job done right. Guys who can work for a woman." Rooney raised his eyebrows. "You're one of the best blueprint readers and carpenters in the area and I'm hoping you're available for kind of an undetermined amount of time. The one thing I *can* guarantee you is good money."

"Starting when to do what for who?"

"Let's get out of the bathroom and take us a seat at the kitchen table."

21

⁂

Katie headed for the Taninger building as soon as Josh got on the bus.

"If I had a car. . . ." He'd moaned one too many times.

"One sure way to make sure you *never* get a car is to keep bugging me about it!" she'd snapped to his back as he huffed out the door. They'd spent so much time squabbling about the topic this morning that they'd both lost track of the time. When Katie looked at the clock and realized the bus would be there in less than three minutes, she'd said, "And if you miss the bus this morning, you're going to learn what it feels like to walk miles to school, never mind driving!"

"Whatever." The door slammed behind him.

Katie opened the door and yelled, "And if you ever do get a car, you'd better be thinking about how you're going to pay for gas and insurance!" Although this topic hadn't thus far come up in all their car conversations, she decided his attitude needed a little adjusting. That boy expected everything to come easy. She'd spoiled him.

But never mind all that. For now Katie had to concentrate on the space around her, which wasn't easy since not only did she have Josh to contend with, but she'd kept getting distracted all week putting up decorations and making plans for the Hookers' Christmas party. She knew the townspeople would be inspecting her every corner and she realized she'd opened herself to even more personal scrutinization. *What was I thinking?!*

She sat at the makeshift desk working on a production schedule, such that she could given the limited facts at hand. It would be a while before Jimson got back to her with final renderings, but in the meantime she wanted to figure out what Edward Showalter and his crew—he'd phoned and told her not to worry, that he had all the hands they'd need—might be able to start chipping away at, if anything. If interior demolition was to get under way any time soon, she had to get the restrooms working (a porta-potty on the square simply would not do) and get a thorough checkup on the heating system, although Jimson had already mentioned she needed to consider getting rid of the old boiler and upgrading the building to forced hot air. *I'm in over my head,* she thought again, but quickly pushed the thought from her mind.

Although Partonville definitely wasn't as cold as Chicago this time of year, she'd nearly frozen herself to the core yesterday and she'd only been in the building a few hours. She walked to the front window to warm herself in the little bit of sunshine coming through the dirty glass. She felt confined in her overcoat, like a child whose mother had bundled her in a giant snowsuit. She blew on her hands and glanced across the square at Rick Lawson's window. She wished Jacob was still in town so he might be up there, catch a glimpse of her and wave. She could use a friendly face about now. But plow on she must.

By three o'clock, even though the water looked like pure rust, she had flushing toilets in the building, but the heating man said he needed to "scout up a part" and come back tomorrow. She'd hated the tone in his voice when he'd talked to her, as though he doubted she had a clue what she was doing since why fix the boiler if she was going to replace it. She should have had Edward Showalter deal with these guys. She made a mental note to never get herself in this position again: *all* construction matters should go through Edward Showalter. *How scary is that?!*

The ring of her cell phone startled her. She checked the caller I.D. before flipping open her phone. Morgan Realty. "Katie Durbin."

"Ms. Durbin, Herb Morgan here."

"Hello, Herb. Please call me Katie. What can I do for you? Found me another property?" She couldn't believe what she heard herself saying. Wasn't this one enough for the moment?

"No. No. That's not why I'm calling. Ms. Durbin . . . Katie. We need to talk."

"About what, Herb?"

"Maybe you haven't heard then. . . ."

"Heard what?" Arthur's "warnings" sprang into her head. Surely Sam hadn't rallied *Herb* against her!

"It seems you . . . we . . . the idea of a mini mall . . . your land acquisitions . . ."

"Just spit it out, Herb."

"Word around town is that lots of folks are not happy about your projects. I've received four phone calls in the last two days from people who want to know why I've decided to play on your team rather than theirs."

"Do you think what I'm doing is bad for the town?"

"No, ma'am. Let me assure you I believe in your integrity and purpose."

For a moment Katie was speechless. Every time she

thought she knew all there was to know about Partonvillers, somebody knocked her socks off. "Thank you, Herb. That was a gratifying statement to hear. Is the purpose of your call to warn me then? If so, let me just say that Arthur Landers covered those bases."

"So you *have* heard, huh?"

"Yes."

"Personally, I think you and me and the mayor ought to get together and maybe come up with a plan for a counterattack."

"Counterattack? Would you go so far as to say my plans are under attack? Serious attack? Or do we just need to ride out the huffing and puffing?"

He chuckled. "Personally, Ms. Durbin, from what I know about you, I'd say it would take a lot more than huffing and puffing to blow your development plans down. But nonetheless, I still think we ought to map out a plan to nip this in the bud."

"All right, Herb. Let's set something up. Why don't you give me a couple times, and I'll give Gladys a call and get back to you."

No sooner had Katie hung up than her cell phone rang again. The Lamp Post Motel. "Jessica! Am I glad to hear from *you*!"

"How did you. . . . Oh, that's right. Caller I.D. One of these days we'll get up to speed around here."

"What's up?"

"Have you talked to anyone around town lately?"

Katie groaned. "Don't tell me they've gotten to you?"

"If you mean Sam Vitner or Cora Davis, yes, they have."

Katie sighed. "So give me your honest take on this. Do you think I have a problem here?"

"Oh, Katie. I'm not a good person to ask."

"Too late."

"I think that people will take to the idea of a mini mall once they understand your plans. Sadly, though, fear has set people's imaginations to working overtime. Cora said by the time you were done creating Durbinville . . ."

"*Durbinville?*" So Arthur was right.

Jessica's face went beet red. She felt like a traitor to her best friend having just uttered the ridiculous word. "*I* don't think like that, but Cora . . . well, she is being Cora. She went so far as to say that by the time your Durbinville plans were complete, they would undoubtedly include a Hampton Inn if not a Hilton, and that pretty soon our little motel would again be boarded up, just the way it was when we bought it."

Katie couldn't help but chuckle. "Well, now. I am even more powerful than I might have imagined!" Silence. "Jessica, *you* don't believe that nonsense, do you?" Silence. "Jessica!"

"No, of course not. But you know, she carried on long enough I have to admit that she did unnerve me a little. I just needed to hear your reassuring voice, Katie."

"Jessica, I promise you that I have no plans for creating a *Durbin*ville. All I'm trying to do is to help save Partonville, bring you *more* business."

"I know. I know. Actually, I guess it's a good thing I did have that moment of doubt since it helps me understand what's probably really going on around town."

"Which is?"

"Fear."

"Fear?"

"Fear."

Katie processed the thought for a moment. Then it all

became clear. "BINGO! *Thank you*, Jessica, for pushing just the right button in my brain." Josh's recent late-night arrival from Chicago zinged right into her mind. When she was afraid something had happened to her son, her imagination conjured up squad car lights in her driveway, police officers with sorrowful eyes. Fear *was* a terrible thing, something she'd had to keep fighting herself lately, realizing how much she needed to depend on the people of Partonville to make this all work, and now here they were rallying against her. "Jessica, you are a genius." Of *course* people in town were afraid; they'd lived here all their lives. It was one thing for them to worry about Hethrow swallowing them alive, but now they feared their demise had become an *inside* job. "How to *fight* fear," she said, including her own in the statement, knowing full well she had risked pretty much all she had. "Now *that* is the question."

"You might want to give Dorothy a call," Jessica finally said, a hint of sheepishness lacing her voice. She knew what she had to tell Katie next would make her even crazier.

"Jessica! Don't tell me Dorothy has bought into any of this!"

"No. *No!* She knows you better than that, Katie. But her name has gotten caught up in the gossip. People think she's ... colliding ... no, in concoctions ... no ... They think she's ... What *is* the word Cora used. ... "

"Collusion? They think she's in *collusion* with me?"

"That's it!"

Katie heaved a great, loud sigh. "Thank you again, Jessica. I'll give Dorothy a call before I phone Gladys. I hope Dorothy hasn't had to endure any *personal* attacks."

"I'm glad you're gonna call her, Katie. Dorothy always knows what to do."

⚜ ⚜ ⚜

"I'll tell you, Katie, I don't have a clue what to do about this other than to maybe start knocking a few heads together," Dorothy said. As much as she loved her town and its people, sometimes some of them could just make her nuts.

"Dorothy!" Katie said, a surprised laugh bubbling out of her. "I don't think I've ever heard you say something like *that* before."

"And shame on me for saying it. Besides, if I did set out to knock heads together, I'm sure I'd do myself in; my heart couldn't take all that knocking!" When their burst of laughter died down, Dorothy knew it was time to call in the Big Gun.

"Lord, thanks for the gift of laughter that often shakes some sense into us! Yes, we both know we shouldn't knock Your children's heads together—although honestly, sometimes I can't help but believe that thought must occasionally flicker through Your mind when we're acting plumb fools!" Chuckles. "Truth is, Lord, everybody's probably just afraid of the unknown." Katie's breath hitched. How did she know? "I ask You right now, God, to help direct our hearts and find the words to help settle everyone down. You know *I've* been through my share of changes the last year, and I remember how hard it was when fear gripped my throat." How quickly, how clearly and perfectly Dorothy got right to the crux of the matter and took it to God, Katie thought, hoping for the day she'd be able to do that. "But You brought me through. And so You will continue to help all of us. Keep us from getting caught up in the frenzy, Lord. Help us see one face at a time and to look for You in it. I *know*, Lord, that You are rootin' for Katie Durbin here.

You're rootin' for her to not only help make us a better town, but for her to grow through this, too. Help us to see this conflict as just a little . . . fertilizer." Another group chuckle. "Amen."

⁂

"Amen." With his prayer behind him, Edward Showalter gingerly picked up the kittens one at a time and placed them back into their cardboard home. He'd left the twelve cans of cat food, the four cat toys, a new litter box, a giant bag of litter and the super-dooper-pooper-scooper in his van. "Come on, Kornflake. We've got us a delivery to make. You'll have to wait in the van, though. If you hear me yellin' from the top of Nellie Ruth's stairway, start the engine. We'll be running for our lives!"

22

Nellie Ruth just had to get over being nervous about Edward Showalter visiting her home. After all, he was going to come paint her kitchen and living room in two days! But how could she help but be nervous? He said he was bringing her a surprise to beat all surprises and he sure hoped she liked it. Something to match her new paint color, she bet. Maybe a bouquet of flowers. Yes, she bet that's what it was. She scurried to her kitchen to prepare something to put them in—just in case. She had that cheap vase somewhere she'd bought at Now and Again Resale for the gladiolas Bernice often picked from her garden. But it wasn't very pretty. She had a cut glass pitcher she thought might work. She dragged a kitchen chair over in front of her sink to reach the high shelf in the cabinet above it, got it down and washed it. Yes, this would do nicely. She set it on the table, and pushed the chair back in exactly its proper place.

But what if it wasn't flowers? She didn't want to seem presumptuous. Well then, she'd say she had the pitcher out since she thought he might like a pitcher of. . . . She searched her fridge. Yup, thankfully she had just enough lemons and one orange—all from the "bruised and reduced" shelf—to make a pitcher of lemonade. Not too seasonal, but then that would be the surprise of it.

Her thoughts were interrupted by a quiet rap on her

door. She peeked through her curtains and there he was, a *box* in his hands. She unlatched her door and let him in, a cold gust surging in behind him. What had she been thinking assuming flowers and dreaming up lemonade? she wondered. She wished she could hide the pitcher.

"Wow!" she exclaimed a little too loudly, her nerves spewing. She pulled her sweater tight around her neck. "I can't believe how the temperature has dropped!" she said as she closed the door behind him.

"Lots of surprises in the air today, huh?" he said, standing with the box in his hands like a frozen soldier, his heart beating so hard he wondered if she could hear it. He looked around at her immaculately kept home, wondering what on earth he'd been thinking just showing up with a box full of kittens.

"Here, let me take that so you can remove your . . ."

"NO!" he said, clutching it closer to his chest. Nellie Ruth was clearly stunned by his reaction. He'd never before even slightly raised his voice with her. "I mean, not yet!" he said with a perky smile. "It's the surprise! How about we go into your living room so I can set this down on the floor maybe?"

"Okay," she said, a hesitance in her voice, the surprise of his volume sticking with her.

Together they made their way to her living room just off the kitchen. He sat down on the couch and set the box on her coffee table, on top of her perfectly aligned magazines, causing him to fret all the more about what could surely be considered a chaotic gift. Maybe he should just pick up the box and . . . Just then something thunked in the box causing Nellie Ruth to jump back and scream *"OH!"* like she'd been electrocuted. No turning back.

"I'm sorry, Nellie Ruth. They didn't mean to scare you."

"They?" she squeaked.

"I know this might be hard for you right now, but how about you close your eyes and hold your hands out. You'll just have to trust me, okay?"

Trust Edward Showalter. Wasn't that what she kept praying for the strength to do? If he told her she had nothing to fear, why should she think otherwise? With a huge leap of faith she did what she was told. Edward Showalter opened the box and reached in to pick up . . . which one? White? Black? White? Black? She had her hands cupped together in front of her. Maybe he should ask her to separate them so he could put one in each hand. But he knew if the kittens were separated they might not stay put until she even opened her eyes. So he closed *his* eyes and just reached in, his fingers landing on the white one. He put his palm under Nellie Ruth's cupped hands to steady them, then he set the kitten in her cradle. "Okay," he said quietly. "Open up."

Nellie Ruth had barely fixed her gaze with that of the little white cherub—there was no other way she could think about the soft silky bundle—before a tiny mew vibrated out of the box. "Oh, my," she said, leaning forward to get a better look at the black kitty who now had her front paws up on the edge of the box obviously looking for her sibling.

"ES, wherever did you get yourself such beautiful kittens?!"

"Well, actually they . . ."

"Why didn't you tell me you'd expanded your family beyond Kornflake? Who I also cannot wait to meet. But OH! these wonderful *kitties!*"

"You see, Nellie Ruth, they are for . . ."

"They are just beautiful, ES!" She picked up the black

one with her empty hand and tried to nestle the two of them together in her lap. They were a squirming ball of activity— it was all she could do to contain them. She was aglow with immediate fondness for them, which Edward Showalter hoped boded well. He couldn't take his eyes off her.

"What I'm trying to say, Nellie Ruth, is that I got them . . ."

"Hey, you little monkey, get back here!" The black one had tumbled off her lap onto the couch and was making her way toward Edward Showalter. "Got her!" ES said, scooping the kitten into his lap. Her white brother, on the other hand, had stretched out on Nellie Ruth's lap and started to purr while Nellie Ruth stroked his sweet back. "How does Kornflake get along with his new playmates—or doesn't he?"

"To tell you the truth, he doesn't seem to mind them one bit. But then it doesn't really matter because . . ."

"Just listen to her purr, ES."

"Him."

"Just listen to him purr," she repeated as she picked him up and cuddled the little muffin under her chin. "He is just so sweet, so beautiful," she said, raising him away from her far enough to look into his green eyes.

Edward Showalter scooted closer to Nellie Ruth, close enough that his thigh accidentally grazed hers, sending a zing through his body. He quickly drew his legs in tighter and leaned his upper body toward her so he could observe the purr she'd beckoned him to hear. "Here, lean a little closer," she said, "or can you hear him from there?" Whether he could hear the purring or not, he certainly was willing to lean in a little closer, close enough his chin was nearly against Nellie Ruth's. "Hear him?" she asked, turning her head his way for the briefest of questions, placing her lips just a smidgen away from his, his lips suddenly giving hers the quickest of kisses neither of them saw coming.

Edward Showalter backed away just enough to see Nellie Ruth's eyes opening. They stared at each other for a moment, hearts beating. "Thank you," she whispered, drawing herself back and once again cradling the kitten close up under her beet-red face.

"For the kittens?"

"No, silly. They're *your* kittens. I mean for the kiss." Her neck was so red it looked to be on fire. The blush continued to grow, then tears filled her eyes. She could hardly believe the words came out of her mouth and yet she could do nothing but say them, so grateful was she to, for the first time in her life, have been properly, tenderly and sweetly kissed.

"I assure you, it was my pleasure, Nellie Ruth," he said, his eyes twinkling. Although he certainly wanted to kiss her again, he knew better. This was enough for today. Oh, aside from telling her about the kittens. "And by the way, Nellie Ruth, you can thank me for the kittens, too, since they are yours. That is, if you want them." Her eyebrows flew up.

"But Bernice might . . ."

"I've already talked to Bernice. She said the way you took to her cats, she'd always wondered why you hadn't gotten some of your own."

"But I don't have any food or litter for them."

"Kornflake is standing guard over them in my camyvan." She smiled. "Got you everything you need. But Nellie Ruth, if you really don't *want* these kittens, or you decide after a day or two they are just not for you, please let me know and they'll be gone in a jiffy. I realize this gift was a little bold on my part."

"Don't you dare think about taking them away from me, ES, especially not now that we've . . . well, sealed the deal with a kiss," she said with a shy smile.

⚜ ⚜ ⚜

Jacob looked at his desk clock. 9:20 P.M. Most of the people in his high-rise office building were long gone for the night, save the custodians and a couple other workaholic diehards like himself who often burned the late-night oil. He was exhausted but determined to finish the task at hand before heading out. Yes, he could have worked at home, but he felt jittery or something, unsettled. Like he was forgetting something important and had to wait here until he remembered it. That niggling feeling that made him nuts, and it seemed to nag at him constantly since his return from Partonville.

He looked at the blinking cursor on his laptop, something else he'd have to cram in his briefcase when he packed up for the night. He noticed he'd stopped typing mid-sentence, having been distracted by . . . what? The memory of his mother licking that frosting off her little finger. Yes, she was sadly slowing down, he thought, but she was still as feisty as ever. He recalled Helen's tears when she handed over Rick's office keys. He pictured Caroline's glass bird ornament nestled near the top of his mom's tree, and laughed picturing his mother hammering a three-penny nail through a bedpan in the middle of the night. He wished he had a piece of May Belle's custard pie and somebody to share it with. His only consolation was that he'd be going back again in less than a week if all went well on Friday. Funny how a week and a half near family reminded him there was more to life than work and made him long for his roots, his hometown, what suddenly felt to be his own lost soul.

No wonder I work so late every night.

The alert on his computer let him know he'd just received an e-mail, so he clicked to his inbox. Something from Joshmeister, which made him smile. What a great kid, he thought. The subject line said "Wheels report." All the e-mail said, however, was "None yet. Just thought your inquiring mind would want to know. Test tomorrow so that's it for now. JM." *JM? Must be for Joshmeister. He must really have to study.* Jacob wondered if Josh had even looked at any other cars yet, if he was still giving it a full-court press with his mom, and how Katie's project was coming along. Maybe he should call her and find out. As he reached for his phone, his e-mail alert came on again. His partner took her work home and knew he'd still be sitting at his desk. She had one quick question about Friday's case.

Back to work.

⏚ ⏚ ⏚

Josh got off the bus on Friday and started his long walk up the drive. What a pathetic week, he thought. His mom told him to stop whining about a car or guaranteed him he wouldn't get one. Alex had sent an e-mail every day asking about it, which only fueled Josh's frustration. Even Dorothy said it was always good to know when to leave well enough alone and trust the process. *Whatever.* She's the one who'd gotten Arthur Landers involved, and that had slammed the brakes to the whole process. He adored Dorothy, but this time she'd stepped into his life a little too far.

By the time he got to the end of the lane he noticed a Ford pickup truck parked next to the SUV, and wondered who was visiting. He'd seen that truck before. . . . *Oh, Charlie Carter, the guy who leases some of our land. I suppose Mom's trying to finagle him out of more per acre, now that she's all about her projects.* A couple kids at school had chided him this week about Partonville becoming Durbinville. It was the first time he was glad he didn't share his mother's last name. Joshua Matthew Kinney suited him just fine.

He started to open the door to the back porch but decided to go to the barn first to shoot a couple hoops and stare out at the open fields. He didn't feel like chatting with Challie, and he felt even less like talking to his mom. He'd met Challie at Rick's funeral dinner, and a couple times before when he'd stopped by to give his mom a check. Nice enough, just not as interesting a guy as say, his Uncle Delbert, who could at least preach a whale of a sermon, as Dorothy said, or Jacob, who could do almost everything. Yup, he'd hang out in the barn till the old guy was gone.

But after an hour's stalling the truck was still there and Josh was cold and starving. Might as well just go on in, say his hello, grab a snack and head to his room, he decided. He entered the back porch and cruised up the stairs into the kitchen, surprised not to find his mom and Challie sitting at the kitchen table, which is where most visitors plunked themselves. He poked his head into the living room but nobody was there either. Odd. Maybe his mom and Challie had walked out toward the fields? But he'd have seen them from that upper barn door. Then he heard footsteps upstairs.

"*Mom?*" he yelled up the stairway.

"Josh! You startled me! Where have you been?" she said from the top of the stairway. "Why didn't you call and tell me you were going to be late?"

"I've been home for an hour. I was just out in the barn," he said as she huffed past him toward the kitchen, clearly upset with him. But then what was new? "Where's Mr. Carter?"

"Mr. Carter?"

"Yeah. That's his truck out back, isn't it?"

They were now in the kitchen, Josh having followed behind her. She stopped near the refrigerator, whirled and leaned back against the counter, folding her arms across her chest. "Not exactly," she said.

"What's that supposed to mean? Who's truck is it then?"

"It *was* his truck," she said.

"Mom, speak English here. I don't have a clue what you're talking about."

"This isn't the happy moment I was hoping we'd share after a week of cranking around." She looked oddly disappointed about something.

"*What* happy moment?"

She walked to the window and pulled back the curtains until her SUV and the truck were in view. "Come here and look at this," she said. Josh sidled up behind her and looked over her shoulder. She turned to face him, shocked to realize he'd grown another inch or so. *How does that happen?* she wondered, but she snapped her mind back to the business at hand.

"What am I looking at here, Mom?"

"The truck."

"I see it."

"Merry Christmas, Josh."

It took a few seconds to sink in. "You're not telling me that old truck is my new wheels, are you?" He sounded disgusted rather than grateful.

She rested her palm on his chest and gently pushed him back out of her way so she could get past him to sit down at the table and collect herself before she spewed a lecture on gratitude. She laced her fingers in front of her on the table and stared at him. Yes, he had grown. It was even more obvious as he stood next to the refrigerator. She'd been told by many in Partonville what a handsome son she had, what a "nice boy" he was. She stared at him as though she'd never seen him before. He was nearly the spitting image of his father, who, when she'd called him to ask what he thought about a car for Josh, wondered what had taken her so long. "Of course the boy needs transportation, Kate." She hated when he called her that. "You've moved him out into the middle of nowhere." She shook her head, erasing Bruce's voice from her mind. This child . . . this growing man standing before her, was *not* his father. He was his own person, struggling to find his way—just like his mother. *Patience, Katie, patience.*

"I *am* telling you that truck is your new transportation, Joshua. Arthur phoned me yesterday and said he'd heard Challie was going to sell his truck. Arthur's personally worked on that truck, Josh. It only has about thirty-two thousand miles on it, and to be honest, Josh, I do think that truck has an element of the 'cool factor' you're looking for." Josh rolled his eyes. "No, it's not a racing car with leather seats, but Arthur said it has an engine big enough to get you in trouble." She stopped here, hoping this would elicit a smile from Josh, which it did not. "It's only eight years old, and it's big enough to seat two passengers in the front with you. And there's a bed liner and. . . ."

"Mom. It's a pickup truck," Josh said as though that was that.

Katie pursed her lips. This was not going the way she'd pictured it. "Yes, but it is *your* pickup truck, Joshua Matthew Kinney, which you have done nothing to deserve, and I am now beginning to think it was a huge mistake." She stood up from the table and turned her back on him. "Perhaps I should have made you get a job and save your *own* money to buy a car," she said, turning back to face him.

They stood staring at one another, her words filling the space between them. It would probably take Josh years to save up enough for a semi-cool car, let alone a cool one.

"So," he said reluctantly, "you've already paid for it. This isn't just a check-it-out scenario, right?"

"Yes. I have already paid for it." She retrieved her hand-bag and rifled through it until she found the keys. She'd made a special trip to Hethrow to find Josh a unique key-chain, something to present him with for her fun surprise. Right. She tossed the set of keys onto the table. "If you don't *want* the truck, Josh, I'll just go ahead and use it for the mini mall. It'll be perfect for hauling *whatever* around, since I'm sure I'll need to be doing some of that anyway."

"So *that's* why you bought me a truck instead of a car? So you can use it for your precious mini mall?"

To be honest, it was a half-truth. When Arthur first called about the truck, Katie said she didn't think Josh would be interested in a pickup. But the more Arthur car-ried on about it, the more she began to reconsider. Arthur assured her it was safe, Josh could use it for transportation, and she *and* Edward Showalter could use it should they need to haul more than his van could hold. "I bought it for you, Josh. True, it might serve an occasional double duty, but I was not shopping for me, I bought it for *you*. As your parent, my first priority is to make sure it could safely and reliably get you from here to there.

"Here's the deal, Josh. You can either take it or leave it. You can either take what I bought for you or find a job and start saving up."

Josh's eyes flashed to the keys on the table. They splayed out so he could see the fob, a miniature Illinois license plate. He leaned in ever so slightly to see what it said. JOSH-MEISTER. He looked up at his mom, who appeared both angry and wounded. She'd gone to an engraver! A surge of guilt ran through him. He hated when that happened, so he tried to swallow it down—at least for the most part. He picked up the keys and couldn't help but give his mom a halfhearted grin. "Okay," he said reluctantly. "I accept. And thanks, Mom," he added, giving her a quick hug. He shuffled his feet, looked at the keys, then out the window. "Wanna go for a ride?"

Katie audibly exhaled. Parenting was hard, hard, hard. "I'll tell you what, I've got some work to do, but I can't think of anything I'd rather do right now. How about you just run me up and down the road where nobody in town can see you schlepping your mom around, then you can drop me off and go take Shelby for a spin. After all, it's Friday night, date night." She smiled a genuine smile, a surprise tear actually pooling in the corner of her eye. "But don't think for a moment we're not going to be talking about gas and insurance money tomorrow," she said, making it clear that with the truck came responsibility.

Her baby was growing up, and so, she hoped, was she.

23

⁂

The Piece was jam-packed. Edward Showalter had invited Nellie Ruth to "The Great Unveiling of the NYC Dish," as it had come to be known around these parts, so they could officially celebrate her beautiful Splendid Rose living room, which, between bouts of corralling, sequestering and playing with Morning and Midnight, he'd finished painting just in time to get home, clean up and zing back around to pick her up. He promised Nellie Ruth he'd bring her by his house on their way home so she could meet Kornflake, Morning and Midnight's cousin. "And by golly, you surely did give those kittens the perfect names!" he'd told her.

Mary Mathis had seated herself at Edward Showalter and Nellie Ruth's table, anxious to get to know the "Vision Herself" as Johnny kept referring to Nellie Ruth. Thus far, Mary hadn't managed to learn much about Nellie Ruth since all she could talk about was Morning and Midnight and the "sunbeam of a man" who had given them to her. Josh's new truck—which he'd decided was *way* cooler than he'd first thought—was parked out front. He and Shelby shared a corner booth, both taking note that Deb Arnold had just arrived with her new flame Kirk Webster from the debate team. Even Jessica, Paul and Sarah Sue had made the journey, as well as Pastor Delbert's family, all of whom were looking for Challie Carter when they walked in since they'd seen his truck outside. Josh had learned from his first trip out with his new wheels that this was going to happen about a gabillion times before the minds of the townspeople grasped that Challie's old truck had become Josh's. He and his Uncle Delbert had a good laugh speculating how long it would take people to recognize Challie's *new* truck lest they start wondering whatever happened to *him*.

All in all, the restaurant was buzzing with excitement, filled with local-locals, as they were referred to, from Partonville and Yorkville. Yes, it was a packed house. Johnny told ES to spread the word that he would serve the now infamous New York City Dish free as a side dish to anyone who was in the place at 12:30 eating at least one paid-for lunch per table. A week ago he'd also posted notice of the same on his front door and added one-sheet flyers in the menus. He was no dummy: word of free food had spread like wildfire and he hadn't even had to buy an ad in the *Partonville Press*. And now at long last the moment had arrived. He'd asked ES to pay attention to his wristwatch and at the crack of 12:30 to stand and make a "booming announcement" that the New York City Dish was about to be unveiled. In his best and deepest voice and at precisely 12:30, Edward Showalter stood and let it be known that all eyes should turn toward the kitchen. Johnny was standing behind the door, a giant tray loaded with the NYC Dish samplers balanced on his right hand, wrist cocked back shoulder high, just waiting for the cue. He was positively beaming, he was so proud of his Diversity Stew that boldly encapsulated the entire "ethnic flavor" of New York City.

As soon as his best buddy ES sat down, Johnny kicked the swinging door open to clear his way. He was so excited that he'd given the kick-open a bit more gusto than he intended, and the door flew back so fast that before he could stretch his left arm out far enough to stop it, the door crashed into the edge of the tray, sending it first toppling (eliciting a collective gasp), then crashing to the floor behind his back, pieces of kosher sausage, smears of fried onions, green and banana and jalapeño peppers, sauerkraut, pasta and black-eyed peas spewing this way and that. Mouth agape, Johnny stood frozen in the middle of the mess staring at what was around and on him, his wife now standing just outside the circle of food on the floor afraid she'd slip and fall if she moved a step closer to help. Thankfully he'd used Styrofoam cups to pass out the samplers, the amount of people who showed up far outnumbering his bowls.

Nobody knew what to do or say, they felt so aghast and sorry for him. The place was bone silent. Suddenly Father O'Sullivan, priest at Partonville's St. Augustine church, stood up and in his wonderful, grace-filled jovial way said, "Johnny Mathis! I baptize you not only in the name of the Father, the Son and the Holy Spirit, but with the sauerkraut, the sausage and the . . . ," his eyes searched through the mess, "green peppers *and* in the name of the entire of New York City. Believe you me, we shall never, *ever,* forget the grand unveiling of your New York City Dish. AMEN!"

Edward Showalter stood and started clapping. One by one, everyone followed suit until the place became a cacophony of merriment, despite the fact that the New York City Dish of Diversity Stew was, for now, still to remain a mystery to their palates.

⚞ ⚞ ⚞

Right after Edward Showalter closed Nellie Ruth's door, and after he apologized for the dog hair on her seat, his new cell phone rang. (He made a mental note to put a blanket on that front seat when Kornflake was riding shotgun.) Nobody but Nellie Ruth and Katie Durbin had his number, so he knew who it had to be before he even looked at the caller I.D. "Excuse me, Nellie Ruth," he said as he unclipped the phone from his belt. "My new boss is calling."

"Howdy," he said into the receiver. "Yes. I was just taking Nellie Ruth by my . . . Yup. Well, I guess I can. Sure thing. Be there as soon as I can." He walked around the front of the van and got behind the wheel, hoping it hadn't been a mistake to get a cell phone. "I hate to have to tell you this, Nellie Ruth, but I'm going to have to postpone your meeting with Mr. Kornflake. Seems Ms. Durbin, the mayor, Herb Morgan and me need to hold us an emergency meeting." The tone in his voice made him sound very important to be cavorting with such influential people, Nellie Ruth thought. How did she ever get so lucky? she wondered.

Of course, that was before she arrived home to discover what all can happen between Morning and Midnight.

🌲 🌲 🌲

Katie had decided there were a number of reasons to hold the meeting at her house rather than in the Taninger building or Gladys's office, not the least of which being they didn't need to add fuel to the already blazing rumor mill by sitting around her makeshift table within eyeballing distance, as Arthur would say, of everyone on the square. She also didn't want Gladys to be on her home turf, the implication being that she would then be in control. At first Katie wasn't going to invite Edward Showalter, but she'd made the decision to make him her right-hand man in all things involving the mini mall, so what other choice did she have? Risky, yes, but unavoidable, she decided. She'd really wanted to invite Dorothy, too, but decided to keep her away from the gossip as much as she could. Now here they all were gathered around her kitchen table. She'd made a pot of coffee for Gladys and Herb, whose giant thermal plastic mug went with him everywhere, water with lemon for herself, and she'd stocked a twelve-pack of Coca-Cola for Edward Showalter who pounded them down one after another. They were all served and readied—laptop, notebook, index cards and/or legal pads in front of them—for this emergency brainstorming meeting.

"Thank you for coming. As I'm sure you all know, the word around town," Katie said, getting straight to the point, "is that rather than trying to breathe new life back into this town, we are trying to put many hardworking people out of business." She stopped to shake her head. "You already know my intention, *our* intention, is to continue building on the fine work of our Acting Mayor Gladys McKern and her Centennial Plus Thirty when she helped us stand up and be counted." Gladys opened her mouth to speak but Katie kept talking in order to hold the floor. "Herb, it also has not escaped my attention that for years you have single-handedly served the progress of this town through your involvement with its people and their land. I only wish Rick Lawson were here to receive his kudos, since he looked out for the legal interests of nearly *all* involved in those acquisitions and turnovers." Herb tapped his mug with his finger and nodded in agreement, then cast his eyes toward Edward Showalter, as did Gladys, since Katie was obviously working her way around the table. Although Katie hadn't prepared any back-pats for him, the first thing that came to her mind was his recent clock and billboard installation on the town hall in the middle of the square, so she extended a brief kudo for his handiwork and his commitment to helping her oversee the mini mall.

"Praise is all well and good, Ms. Durbin," Herb said, "but it would help us, well at least me, to have a solid answer to the verbal attacks."

Katie raised her eyebrows at the tone of his voice when he used the word "attacks." This was indeed serious business. She opened the lid to her green file box and rifled through the folders until she came to the one marked "Publicity." "What an excellent point, Herb. Perhaps one of the most important things we can accomplish at this meeting is to come up with a mission statement that describes our intent. Here are some of the words, phrases, *strengths* I've observed about Partonville. Attributes that I believe will, under our direction, help sell our vision to the townsfolk, visitors and perhaps even nationwide travelers one day." Gladys cleared her throat. "Of course, some of these are things I've heard Gladys say." Gladys repositioned her blazer and sat up a tad straighter. There, Katie thought, all settled.

"Partonville is cozy and comfortable." She stopped speaking for a moment when she noticed them all starting to write things down. "Safe." Pause. *"Vibrant."* She made eye contact with each of them in order to drive this last point home. "Vintage. And I mean that in the best ways. Partonville *cares*. And I think this might point toward a slogan or mission statement. What sets us apart is that we are not more of the *same* old, as in just another bunch of chain stores you can find everywhere. We are striving to become the *new* old by accenting what is best about us, infusing new stores with our heritage and the town's quaint, circle-the-square feel."

"That was just beautiful," Edward Showalter said with sincerity, looking like he might tear up.

"You are exactly right, Katie," Gladys added. "I have in-*deed* referred to our town as vibrant—such a good strong word—and cozy," she said looking at her notes. "You've done a fine job of capturing Partonville's essence." *Capturing Partonville's essence,* Gladys wrote on her notes. Yes, she liked the way that rolled off her tongue.

"Herb, what do you think?" Katie asked, noticing Herb had not looked up from the table in some time.

"I think we're on to something, I'm just not sure it's what we need right now. I mean, if Sam Vitner came storming into my office taking issue with the rehab and land acquisitions, I'm not sure spewing words like *cozy* and *comfortable* would stop his ranting. I'm not sure," he said, running his finger down his notes, "saying to him, 'But Sam, Partonville cares,' is going to calm him down. Know what I mean? I mean these are good words and phrases to use in advertising, but will they convince folks who've lived here their whole lives and are worried we're *changing* things? I don't think so."

"Now, Herb," Gladys chided, "no need to be such a naysayer. Katie has come up with wonderful ideas!"

Katie waited a moment to respond. "You know, Gladys," Katie said thoughtfully, "Herb is exactly right. I *have* been thinking in terms of advertising. This is not how we're going to quell a riot."

"Quell?" Edward Showalter asked. "Quell," he said this time without the question mark, as though repeating the strange word would bring it into focus, make it comprehendible, understandable.

Katie nearly moaned out loud. This was her right-hand man? She was doomed.

⁂

Joshmeister,

Congrats on the wheels! I told you Arthur knows his stuff. And you're right: anyone can own a car but not many teen boys I know these days (which admittedly isn't many) own a pickup with a V-8. However, your attorney is hereby advising you to never tell him in an e-mail how fast you can do zero to sixty, since it will leave what used to be known as a paper trail, one you wouldn't want your mother to find. (As my mom would say, HA!)

Thanks for asking about my case. It went well. We won and the rich got richer. However, I didn't save a town like your mom is trying to do. Now *that* is honorable. Sounds like she's got her hands more than full, though. Mom says she's really up against it.

I'll be back in town Thursday in time for the Hookers' (such talk) Christmas party on Saturday. Can't wait to see your new ride. Stay out of trouble with it.

Jacob

⁂

"Thanks for the call, sweetie," Dorothy said into her receiver as she sipped a cup of tea and continued her chat with Katie. Eight o'clock and Dorothy already had her robe and slippers on, an uncommon state of affairs but one that just seemed warranted this chilly, tired evening. "I think you're all on the right trail. If you'd invited me to your meeting I probably would have declined anyway. I can tell you this, walking around being mad makes a body tired! I decided to cozy in today and just calm myself down. Aside from walking over to church this afternoon to set up the altar for tomorrow, I haven't done a thing today but rest. And answer my crazy ringing phone."

"Oh, Dorothy, don't tell me you're being tormented by people for consorting with the enemy."

Dorothy laughed. "Well, first off, I am, as Jacob says, a tough old bird. Don't you worry about me, I can hold my own. But no, that's not what the calls were about. I'm not sure if you'll think this is good news or bad news, but your Durbinville plans have momentarily taken a back seat to the exciting events at The Piece."

"Oh? Josh and Shelby went there for the great unveiling but he wasn't home long enough afterwards to talk with me. He picked up a warmer coat and off they went again. What happened?"

"Oh, honey, I'll let him tell you since he actually saw it. Must have really been something. I can hardly wait to hear his version myself."

"I'll make sure I'm in the kitchen when he gets home since we need to talk about his truck anyway. He's already had to ask for more gas money and I told him that was the last handout, that he was going to have to start thinking about conservation and responsibility, maybe even a part-time job. Actually, now that I think about it, I could use some advice on something else. I have an idea that might not only help Josh learn a little more responsibility and earn some gas money, but I believe it has the potential to help a couple other people as well. I'd like to fly it by you, see what you think."

"I'm all ears."

24

🌲 🌲 🌲

Nellie Ruth scurried up her back steps, wind whipping at her heels, key in hand. She chuckled every time she recalled Father O'Sullivan's prayer. Honestly, if she wasn't such a happy Methodist, she'd join the Catholic church just to hear that man preach. Wait, she thought, priests don't preach, they give homilies, right? But were those the same as sermons? *They must be.* And it's not that she didn't enjoy and learn from Pastor Delbert's Sunday morning messages, but that Father O'Sullivan was such a card! "Baptizing with sauerkraut and the whole of New York City," indeed, she mumbled while laughing and putting her key into the slot. Then a strange thought occurred to her. *OH! You* know *he was just being* funny, *right, Lord? That he was just kidding around and not making fun of a holy sacrament? Of* course *You do! What's the matter with me! You created him! Nellie Ruth McGregor, get over yourself! Sometimes you take things entirely too seriously.*

"I'm home!" she shouted to Morning and Midnight as she closed the door behind her, marveling at the way her new Splendid Rose paint made her whole house seem warmer and brighter. Since this was her first "new look" at the place since ES had finished the job this morning, if it hadn't been so cold outside she'd have gone out and come in again just to experience the utter joy in the rediscovery.

The smell of the fresh paint reminded her of him, the way he'd been so careful to cover her furniture, the absolutely straight line where the Splendid Rose on the walls met the cream color of her ceiling, the cream color having been his *perfect* idea. "I'll tell you what, Nellie Ruth," he'd said when she'd marveled over his steady hand, "that line wouldn't have looked straight like that when I was drinking! It woulda looked more like waves in a pink ocean splashing up onto the shores of the ceiling." She adored his humor, his turn of a poetic phrase.

And in three short days she'd grown to utterly adore her kitties and become a little more relaxed about parenting them. It was wonderful to come home and have someone waiting for her arrival, happy to see her, she thought. Just wonderful. She'd sounded nothing short of a proud mama when she'd invited Bernice up on Thursday to meet her babies. "Oh, I can hardly *wait*," Bernice had said. "It seems like years ago mine were just little munchkins. Your Edward Showalter was such a gentleman when he called to ask me about you having pets. It was all I could do not to follow him up the stairs when I saw him getting out of his van with that box. Such a wonderful surprise!" Bernice had adored Morning and Midnight, just like Nellie Ruth knew she would. She'd brought them a toy she'd packaged in one of those gift bags with tissue paper stuffed in the top. She'd even added a card from "Your Meowing Friends Downstairs." "Nellie Ruth, if you ever need me to look after them, just give me a call. Or maybe we should set up a . . . what do the moms call that now? Oh, a *play* date. Maybe we should set up a *play* date for all our felines to meet each other." The ladies had laughed, but in truth, they each thought it was a marvelous idea. Already, Nellie Ruth could barely remember her life without her new beauties. But it was the sounds of *"your* Edward Showalter" that kept vibrating in Nellie Ruth's heart long after Bernice had left. Yes, her life was now beautiful, full and exploding with joy.

And then she went to open her bathroom door, which she thought she'd closed but which was slightly ajar. Much to her shock, the kitties' box was empty and they were nowhere in the bathroom to be seen.

"Morning! Midnight! Here kitty-kitty!" she called as she moved back into her kitchen, on into her living room, then to her bedroom, looking under her dust ruffle, behind couches, plant stands and curtains. Then back to the bathroom to draw back her shower curtain and check her bathtub—just in case, then back into her kitchen. Maybe they were curled up on the kitchen chair seats which were tucked under the table. Nope. "Here kitty-kitty! Morning! Midnight! *Here* kitty-kitty!" She'd heard cats could disappear for hours when they wanted to, but she'd never really believed it. And kittens? Truth was, their little bodies could probably sneak into all *kinds* of places, *dangerous* places like next to electrical cords and outlets, a thought that caused her heart to skip a beat.

There was now only one place she hadn't looked: her music and craft room. She remembered she'd gone in there after ES had left to clean himself up for their venture to The Piece. She'd hauled her plastic bin of Christmas decorations down and scattered the items around the room, picturing which of her many treasures might best compliment her new paint color. Before she'd left she'd also taken a look in her plastic yarn bin, thought she might crochet ES a granny-square Christmas stocking because he didn't have a stocking and Nellie Ruth said that would simply *never* do, especially since she was looking forward to filling it. Just when she had the perfect yarn colors picked out and was retrieving the right sized crochet hook, he'd knocked at the door and off they'd rushed so as not to be tardy for the unveiling of the NYC Dish.

Running out of places to look, she entered her music and craft room and gasped. Her eyes scanned the room in disbelief: there were Midnight and Morning knee deep in tangled yarn, the pine comb Christmas wreath she'd made last year was batted to pieces, the cotton balls on Santa's beard were hither and yon, his bare Styrofoam chin looking like someone had just shaved him. But the worst was yet to come. While scanning the chaos, she set her eyes on her precious hooked rug which she'd made herself when the Happy Hookers actually hooked, the very rug she still snuggled her bare toes into when she practiced her saxophone. Precisely in the middle was a pile of kitty poop.

🌲🌲🌲

Nellie Ruth looked at her bedside clock. It was nearly 10 P.M. For hours she had fussed with the chaotic mess, gagging, wondering if her hooked rug should be dry cleaned, fumigated or thrown away, praying about trying to get over having *had* the mess. The whole incident was so upsetting she found herself wondering whether or not she was cut out to even *be* a pet owner. Her utter frustration with her vulnerable little kittens singed her with guilt like a hot poker straight to her moral center.

She bolted out of bed and scurried to the bathroom to look in the kittens' box, just to make sure Midnight and Morning were where they were supposed to be. "Just look at you two," she said, "all rolled up, sleeping in a sweet little ball, looking so innocent." Her heart melted. How could she even think about getting rid of them? This must be how parents felt, she thought, when they looked at their sleeping children at the end of a frustrating day. "But if you can get into this much trouble when you're this small," she whispered to them, "what's going to happen when you're full-grown? How can I even put my Christmas decorations up with you two? What will happen to my *tree*? I'm just not sure I'm equipped to handle it."

But then, the deal had been sealed with a *kiss*. She'd said so herself. Out loud. To ES.

Back to praying she went. By 11 P.M. it occurred to her that maybe God was going to use these kittens to at long last help her get over her fretting, neurotically tidy and serious self.

Maybe.

🌲 🌲 🌲

Wednesday afternoon delivered a miracle: Jacob left his office at 2 P.M. He had Christmas shopping to do before his early-morning trip to Partonville tomorrow and he wanted to be thoughtful about the gifts. Yes, he could finish his shopping after he got to Illinois—it was only December 17—but he had a few more gifts than usual to buy this year. He'd already ordered a couple items online for his brother and nephews to be delivered directly to Colorado after receiving the hard news they wouldn't be coming to Partonville for Christmas. Vinnie had ended up with the boys for Thanksgiving and his ex said she now needed them home for Christmas because she and her boyfriend were hosting a party to announce their engagement. Jacob already had his mom's gift but he wanted to get her a little something more. He'd never exchanged gifts with May Belle and Earl before and didn't want them to think he was starting a gift exchange this year either. But he wanted to get them each something special for being such good new neighbors to his mother. Maybe, he thought, he should give May Belle a handwritten gift certificate to discuss legal options regarding Earl. His mom said since Rick died, May Belle had been distraught she'd never put anything in place. Perhaps he could help relieve her. Then there was Josh. How could he not get him a cool truck accessory or two? He needed time today to leisurely cruise through that giant auto store and do some scouting. And then he needed a housewarming gift to take to Katie for the Hookers' party, then maybe a little something extra, just because she was working so hard. Just because.

⚜ ⚜ ⚜

When Jacob arrived back in his Philadelphia home, shopping bags in tow, he noticed the message light on his answering machine was flashing. It was Roscoe. "*Nobody's* stepped forward to handle Rick's clients, Jacob. Mom and I are beside ourselves, not to mention poor *Helen*. I hate to bother you again after all you've already done for us, and I know it's probably a crazy thing to even ask since you live in Pennsylvania, but we wondered if you might by chance know of *someone*, or a referral service, or. . . ." He'd exhausted any leads he'd been given and didn't know where to turn next. "Anyway, give me a call if you can, Jacob."

Jacob took off his coat, tossed it across the back of a chair, poured himself a glass of merlot and sat down on his couch. That awful antsy feeling was back, the one that made him think he was forgetting something.

Perhaps, he thought as he took his third sip of wine and looked at the bags full of gifts he'd plunked down in his entryway, he'd just heard the right questions to help him finally recognize the stunning answer to his unrest.

🌲🌲🌲

Katie handed Jessica a tissue, then reseated herself at the kitchen table. "Here. You need to stop crying right now before you set me off," she said with a smile. "It's bad enough I've already had two hot flashes this morning. More often than not lately I feel utterly hijacked by my own hormones."

"Welcome to my world," Jessica said through her sniffles before she gave her nose a good blow. "I think that's one of the worst things about pregnancy."

"At least we'll both come out the other end of this—I certainly hope!"

"I can't imagine being pregnant much longer." Jessica slumped down in her kitchen chair.

"Hopefully the word menopause actually means it *is* only a pause."

"Like 'We interrupt this program for the following announcement' kind of pause, right?"

"Like we interrupt your *life* for the current menopausal meltdown!" Katie said, sending Jessica from crying to laughing. "And honestly, I never thought my offer to have Josh work for you would cause you to cry. I thought you'd be jumping for joy that help was on the way."

"I *am* happy, Katie. It's one of the nicest things anyone's ever done for me. And I know you told me not to feel guilty, but it just doesn't seem fair you're the one who'll be paying him."

"What's not fair about it? Just figure it's a roundabout

trade, okay?—which is exactly the way Dorothy put it. I'm trading use of your decorating talents for the Hookers' Christmas party tomorrow—as well as mini-mall counseling, of course—for cleaning help at your motel, only Josh and Earl are the ones who will actually do the cleaning. I'm trading Josh his cleaning services—which you're getting to use—for gasoline money, and May Belle said if you and Josh take it slow with Earl, after he gets the hang of it he can help Josh out when he has too much homework or needs a hand. And I'm trading May Belle baked goods for the party for an advance against Earl's payment for his labors at the Lamp Post. *Voila!*" Katie said, throwing her hands in the air. "Oh, my gosh! I just morphed into Maggie Malone!"

Jessica laughed so hard she snorted. When they settled down she said, "The only way this can even possibly be close to a fair trade—and like I said, I need to check with Paul about this before I can *officially* accept, and after I hear Josh *himself* say he agrees to this and that his mother is not just farming him out for slave labor," she laughed again, "is if I begin right now to pay out my end of the deal and it's already ten-thirty. Sarah Sue and I need to be back at the Lamp Post no later than one since I expect the first of my check-ins around two."

"Deal."

"Oh, Katie, I can't tell you how much of a relief it is to know I'll have help over the holidays!"

"Good. Now where should we start for tomorrow's party?" Katie asked, whirling on her heels, already heading for the living room.

"Since you've got the tree done—and OH!" she exclaimed getting her first look at it. "It looks beautiful!" She nodded her head, cast her eyes around the room while she squinted, her decorating genius at work. "Let's start by rearranging your fresh garlands. It's not that you've done a bad job with those, it's just that it could be better."

"Thanks, I think."

"This is going to be so much fun," Jessica said, a small wave of nausea rippling through her. But even her morning sickness was settling down a little. Maybe there *was* light at the end of the tunnel, help for the weary, hope for the soon-to-be mother of two babies in diapers.

25

♣ ♣ ♣

Katie hustled to her ringing phone. It was 9:30 A.M. already. The Christmas party guests would be arriving at 2. The hands on the clock seemed to be flying. "Hello," she said somewhat breathlessly.

"Katie, Jacob Wetstra. Catch you in the middle of something?"

"Funny." She assumed he was joking. He knew darn well the party was starting in a few hours. "I guess you made it back into town then. You *are* calling from your mom's, right?" Katie didn't admit she'd seen him entering the street-level entryway to Rick Lawson's office early yesterday morning when she'd stopped by the Taninger building before Jessica came over. She'd watched to see if Rick's office light came on, which it did not long after he entered the building. She wondered what Jacob was doing back there, knowing his volunteer job for the Lawsons was over. What she didn't know was that he'd caught a glimpse of her SUV disappearing off the square, sorry to have missed the chance to chat, see how the mini mall and party preparations were coming along. At least now he had an excuse to call.

"Are you ready for the town of Partonville to descend on you? Or are you in a tizzy, as Mom says?"

"Tizzy. One hundred percent tizzy."

"Good. It would have worried me to hear anything else."

"Because?"

"Because that would make you a little too organized to be-lieve." She detected the lilt of teasing in his voice. "Mom said people are chomping at the bit to party, especially after Rick's death. Oh, and of course they're anxious to snoop around your house," he said, as though it were an afterthought.

Katie sighed. "I hope I'm up for this." She sighed again. Jacob was surprised by her admission since it wasn't like her to show even a smidgen of weakness.

"Mom wondered if you might need me to come over and help with anything."

"No, I think we've got everything under control. You're bringing her over a couple hours early anyway, right?"

"M-hm. About two-and-a-half hours from now. I've also been instructed to stop by May Belle's to pick up whatever so you ladies can get it set up, too."

"Good. I'm glad we're all on the same page. Since your mother and I are co-hosting I want to make sure we're pre-senting a united front and that she feels this is as much her party as it is mine." Jacob wondered if Katie had any idea how hard it was for his mom *not* to be holding *her* usual party out at the farm this year. "There's not too much for her to do when she gets here, but we should get our things organized and make sure we have enough room for every-thing and everybody. I'm glad she can come early and put things where and how she wants them. This must be diffi-cult for her."

"She's doing okay, but yes, I think she'd admit it is diffi-cult. Co-hosting helps though."

"Good. We've gone over the traditional menu several times so I think we have the bases covered."

"You didn't cook a turkey, did you?" he asked, teasing

her about her disastrous first attempt with one for the town's Thanksgiving gathering.

"I did not."

"Good. Then the menu will probably be fine."

"Very funny," she said, trying to sound annoyed. "What I have done, though, is just about run Josh ragged sending him to the store for this and that, setting out dishes, cleaning the bathrooms and the bedrooms, the spare room. I was going to have people just toss their coats on my bed upstairs but then I figured if it got as cold today as they were predicting—which it has—there'd be too many coats to fit, so Josh and I kicked it into high gear this morning and cleaned up the spare bedroom we use for storage."

"I'll have to check it out, see how you transformed my brother's old room into a closet for a party," he said flatly. Silence. "Katie, I'm just kidding." She acknowledged that she'd known that, but he wondered. "If you change your mind about needing help, let me know. Besides, I'm anxious to check out Josh's new wheels. And by the way, Mom told me about your great trading idea. That was very kind of you to offer to help out the Joys and Justices in that way."

"Hey! First of all, the actual *trading* concept was your mom's, and I'm not doing this to help Jessica or Earl or anyone else. I'm doing this to teach Josh some responsibility. Just make sure you remember that when you talk to him, since he has this strange idea you're in his corner." She'd tried to mimic Jacob's dry sense of humor, but she'd done a lousy job and simply sounded snarky.

He got her drift anyway. "Ah, you've got me pegged. But just the same, I'll try not to interfere with your important moral lessons, Ms. Durbin. By the way, has he told you yet how fast that thing can go from zero to sixty?"

"Jacob! Don't tell me he . . ." Jacob laughed. He could really pull her chain. "Listen, I've got too much to do for this kind of torment. I'll see you and your mom shortly. Tell May Belle I said hi and thanks. Hey! How are she and Earl getting here?"

"I told Mom we should just bring them with us when we come but May Belle thinks there'll be enough cooks in the kitchen. I guess they're coming with someone else."

"Try harder to convince May Belle to come with you, okay? I have a feeling she'll be just the calming effect we all need."

"You don't find me calming?"

Such a loaded question, she thought. "Depends."

⁑ ⁑ ⁑

It was just as Dorothy and May Belle had predicted. Cora Davis was the first to arrive, and without her husband. She pulled up the driveway at 1:45. When she entered the house, her eyes casting about so quickly they looked like lights on a pinball machine, she said, "Oh! Am I the first one here? I had no idea I was early!"

"Right," Dorothy whispered into May Belle's ear, causing May Belle to cover her mouth and snicker. But Cora wasn't there long before a snake of vehicles started making its way up the driveway. Josh wondered if he shouldn't leave Shelby to fend for herself while he went outside to try to direct traffic. "Stay with your sweetie," Dorothy said, smiling at Shelby, who looked stunning in her green blouse and slacks, a beautiful Christmas barrette in her hair—no doubt purchased by her Grannie M. "They'll all figure out the parking, they always do. Also, you better stay near your mom while people are arriving in case she needs you to do something."

"Don't worry," Jacob said, "we're both on high alert in case either of our mothers needs *any*thing, like a rescue squad should the troops become restless and decide to put an end to Durbinville right here and now."

Josh high-fived Jacob. "Good one!"

"Such good—and devilish—boys we have, Katie," she said, shaking her head. "Jacob Henry, you keep your voice down. Let's don't be stirring up trouble."

"No need to worry," Katie said to Jacob. "With your mom's help we've come up with the perfect plan for a counterattack. We're going to kill them with kindness, assurance and hopefully Doc's special eggnog." May Belle and Dorothy busted out laughing, as did Jacob.

As if on cue, Doc walked up behind Katie. "Well, Katie Durbin," he said, "I guess you *have* learned everything important about hosting this party! Now, if you will show me to the special punch bowl, I'll get right to it," he said, rattling the bag with the mysterious contents in his hand. Dorothy ushered him over to the punch bowl on the left, its usual placement. Of course, Doc never brought more than a cup or two of his special brew; it was actually more the *idea* of his contribution that made everyone who dared try it extra merry.

‡ ‡ ‡

Katie and Dorothy had their hands full greeting everyone, showing them to the coat room, pointing out food, hooking up folks who were looking for each other, asking Josh and Shelby if they'd mind running some of the coats upstairs for people whose legs weren't what they used to be, dishing up punch and conducting mini tours for those who actually asked rather than just nosed through the house on their own. But in spite of the fact Katie felt an occasional prickle at the obvious gawkers, she was also beginning to understand why Dorothy had loved hosting this party every year. The entire house, which lent itself surprisingly well to large groups, was filled with the sounds of joy and laughter. And Jessica was right: people loved discovering the mistletoe as they entered, even though Katie thought it was hokey and had tried to talk her out of it. Mice aside, the place was suddenly growing on her.

⁂

George Gustafson was one of the last to arrive. He'd argued with himself and his wife, Beulah, whether they should even drop by, but nearly three hours after the party started Beulah finally badgered him into it, chastising him for being ridiculous and announcing that she was going whether he did or not. When she put her coat on he knew she was serious. He also knew—which is just the way Beulah'd played it— that it just wouldn't look right for her to show up without him, so he begrudgingly donned his tie and off they went. Upon arriving Beulah was none too sad to learn they'd just missed the Best of the Hookers' Moments including Maggie's tattooed ankle show-and-tell. Beulah'd always been jealous of Maggie's flirty ways (she'd seen that woman bat her eyes at George) and gorgeous gams, especially since *her* legs had been covered with varicose and spider veins at such an early age.

When George first set eyes on the tree he was happy it seemed small compared to all of Dorothy's past trees. Even if Katie were still here next year, which he sincerely doubted, he'd be danged if he'd cut down that treasure of a tree for the likes of her. Although he had to admit the tree *was* beautifully decorated, and the fresh garlands made the whole house smell so good it gave him a slight twinge of pride to have provided them. Well, provided them for a hefty fee, that is, cutting *her* no bulk discount the way he did most of his regulars. But by golly she could afford it. He strolled around the room snacking on his piled-high plate of food, taking note of every rich-looking, fancy-schmancy thing the City Slicker had on display. Such a showoff, he thought. Then he saw Sam and Cora holding court in a corner of the living room so he sidled up to them, joining their tight little circle just in time to hear the words "Durbinville for *sure!*" George chimed right in. He'd now seen proof of "that woman's lofty ways" with his very own eyes.

Dorothy noticed George congregating with Cora and Sam and knew the perfect opportunity had arrived. She flagged Katie, Gladys and Herb over. (She couldn't catch Edward Showalter's eye. He was glued to Nellie Ruth who was talking nonstop about the wonders of Morning and Midnight.) Dorothy discreetly nodded her chin toward the smoldering corner clique. "Now's the time, folks," she said in a low voice. When Katie asked her if *she* was ready, she bowed out saying, "You three need to stand alone. You're the *real* movers and shakers, and I'd say this is your perfect opportunity. I'll just stay right here and pray." The trio took a collective deep breath before readying to infiltrate the group and tackle things head on, "play offensive ball," as Herb had put it. Just as they were taking their first steps across the room, Dorothy added, "And remember, we're *all*–every single one of us in this room–Partonvillers and *for* Partonville!"

⁂

Jacob and Pastor Delbert sat in the front seat of Josh's new truck, Josh behind the wheel. "Wish I could take you for a spin," Josh said, clearly pouting about the circumstances. "If I'd have been thinking ahead I would have parked down at the end of the lane." Party attendees' cars and trucks were not only blocking him in but they were scattered throughout the yard and halfway down the lane.

"That's alright, sport," Delbert said. "We've got plenty of time to catch a ride with you some time. I have a feeling I'll be seeing a lot of this truck circling the square, cruising from here to there, especially since you're going to be working part-time for the Joys. You can knock on the church door any time and kidnap me. You know what they say, 'Pastor writing sermon. Please interrupt.'"

"So you've already heard about the job thing, huh?" Josh said, his voice sinking.

"Yes. It's one of the hot topics at the party. But I don't know why you sound so glum about it," Delbert said. Out of habit he put his pointer finger to the bridge of his nose to push up his glasses, but once again ended up feeling foolish since he kept forgetting he was wearing contact lenses. (If he'd have known how easy soft contacts would be to get used to, he'd have made the leap years ago.) "Do you have any idea how many prayers have been swimming around for those two to be able to manage their business and finances through this pregnancy and the birth of a new mouth to feed? And May Belle is nearly popping her buttons, she's so proud to be announcing Earl's new job. She's beyond grateful to you, Josh." Delbert opened the glove compartment and took a peek. "Lots of room here. Nice."

"Not to mention you'll need the bucks to keep this gas guzzler's tank topped off," Jacob added while scanning his eyes around to make sure Josh didn't already have an ice scraper with an extendable handle, sunshield with a cool graphic or roadside safety kit including flares. He didn't see anything but a short-handled scraper with an antifreeze advertisement on it, which made him feel very good about his shopping efforts.

Josh had his right hand on the steering wheel while mindlessly zipping and unzipping his jacket with his left hand, finally stopping mid-zip to take a deep breath. "I guess you're both right." It was nice to have the full attention of the two men even if he didn't particularly like what they were saying. "It's just that between school, homework and now a part-time job, I'll hardly have time to enjoy this thing let alone spend time with Shelby."

"Somehow I have the distinct feeling you'll be able to manage just fine, especially with the Shelby part," Jacob said, giving Josh a playful elbow.

"I ditto that. When a man has it as bad for a woman as you do for Shelby, we find time, believe you me. I haven't been married so long I've forgotten that!" Delbert laughed, recalling his own sleepless nights, single longings, the sudden thought of his wife in a new black nightgown popping into his head which he fought hard to dismiss.

"And even though I've never been married," Jacob said, leaning forward in the middle-seat position to rest his forearms on his knees and lace his fingers together, his long legs starting to feel a little cramped, "I guarantee you throughout the ages men—yes, including me—have always found time for both women and their cars, so chin up. We know what we're talking about here. I remember when I got my first car. I saved up money from detassling corn. Dad chipped in some but he said I had to earn the rest plus enough to keep it in gas. When I finally bought that Chevy my dad wouldn't let me drive it until he made sure I knew how to change a tire, clean the spark plugs, change the oil . . . maintenance things he said no man should be on the road without knowing how to do. I also remember how the car became his parental leverage. The first time I blew my curfew, no car. The first time I mouthed off to him, no car. Just remember, vehicles give parents leverage."

Delbert had opened the glove compartment again and was reading the manual. "This thing's got a V-8?"

"Yup," Josh said, the perk returning to his voice.

"No wonder your mother wants you to earn your own gas money. Man, a V-8. I bet this thing could lay quite the patch of rubber popping off the line."

Josh leaned back so he could look behind Jacob to see his Uncle Delbert's face. "Lay a patch of rubber? Pop off the line? What kind of pastor talk is that?" he asked, grinning.

"It's not. It's guy talk. We're just three guys sitting in a cold truck," he said, swiping at the foggy windows.

"We better get back to the party before people start to talk," Jacob said, laughing. "Let me out of here." Both doors opened at once.

When they were almost to the back door Josh stuck his hand out first to Jacob, then to Delbert. "Thanks, guys," he said, giving them each a hearty shake. "Jacob, how long you gonna be in town this time? I want to make sure I do get to see if my new wheels can pop off the line before you go. After all, you *are* the one who asked me how fast it could do zero to sixty, aren't you?"

"Don't get me in any more trouble with your mom than I already am, sport, okay? As for how long I'll be around, let me get back to you on that."

♣ ♣ ♣

Jacob arrived in the living room just in time to see Katie, Herb and Gladys working their way into a tight-knit group of . . . who was that? "Uh-oh," he said to his mom. "Show-down time?"

"Hang on a minute," she said. "I'm praying."

Jacob watched the shifting gathering. He was used to studying body language in court, which had always served him well. He couldn't help but stare at the smile on Katie's face. Man, he thought, she was certainly turning on her high beams. Cora was nearly salivating. It was clear she knew she had the best seat in the house. Herb looked ner-vous. George spread his feet a little farther apart as if to plant his position. Jacob was sure George'd have crossed his arms over his chest if his hands had been empty. Sam Vit-ner's eyes were slightly squinted as he listened to whatever Katie was saying. Gladys's eyes were focused on Sam. She yanked down on the bottom of her blazer. Jacob had been around Gladys enough to know that could mean anything, but she was most likely readying herself to exercise author-ity if need be. He looked at his mother for a moment. Al-though her eyes were open he could tell she was still praying—her lips were moving.

He saw Sam lean in toward Katie. He must have a slight hearing problem, Jacob thought, and the party was plenty loud. He scanned the room and noticed he wasn't the only one studying the group. A few heads were nodding toward what folks figured was a face-off. George started talking, then Gladys said something. Katie held her hands up in front of her as though she were a crossing guard stopping traffic. She began to nod her head, agreeing with something George was saying. Herb put his hand on Sam's shoulder and Katie smiled at him. Cora's eyebrows flew up in the air at whatever Katie said next. Then . . . Katie extended her hand to Sam and he took it. Sam was actually smiling at the handshake, which astounded Jacob. Katie ought to be an attorney, he mused. Next, for the briefest of moments, she rested her hand on George's upper arm. No handshake, nothing over-done, but George gave his head a quick up-and-down nod. Didn't look like a bond but a guarded agreement. "Amen," he heard his mother say next to him. Herb said something to Cora who pursed her lips.

Katie was the first to excuse herself from the circle. Gladys and Herb stayed on a bit longer, the circle clearly talking about Katie. Cora's husband walked up, said something to her and she waved good-bye to him. Herb left the circle next, then Gladys, leaving George, Sam and Cora alone together again. They said a few words to each other, Sam shrugging his shoulders, then they dispersed into different areas of the party.

"How'd it go?" Dorothy asked Katie who had walked up beside her.

"Brilliant. Dorothy Jean Wetstra, you are a genius."

Jacob snapped his head around at the sound of Katie's voice and raised his eyebrows at his mother. "My mom the genius, huh?"

"Well, I *will* admit to being clever, but really, only the Big Guy can calm these kinds of waters."

"What the heck happened over there?" Jacob asked, clearly in awe.

Katie turned her high-beam smile on him. "I just told Sam that I'm going to need his help learning about an-tiques, how to price them so whatever crossover we might have is compatible." Jacob nodded his head. "I told him we're going to put flyers in the mini mall advertising his business and that I hoped we could send customers back and forth, maybe occasionally even swap out some of our items, help keep each of our offerings fresh. It was clear he was completely shocked and disarmed, but more importantly, he liked the idea."

"How'd it go with Herb and George?" Dorothy asked.

"Herb told George how much the value of his corner station property has no doubt already increased since it's on the main stretch to our soon-to-be revitalized downtown area. Said he ought to be thinking about things like that for when he retires and is ready to sell."

"Okay, I'm impressed," Jacob said.

"But wait until you hear this," Katie said, lowering her voice and checking to make sure nobody else was within earshot, "and this one I thought up myself. I told Cora Davis that a clueless City Slicker such as myself will certainly need to depend on the vast wealth of knowledge she has about this town." Dorothy laughed out loud. "Cora immediately started chomping at the bit to become my best friend."

"Of course," Dorothy said, "since that will glue her right to the horse's mouth."

"Exactly. But honestly, Gladys came up with the most ingenious thing. She told them she's going to make a proclamation at our mini mall's grand opening touting all three of their fine contributions to our town improvement endeavors."

"I must say, it sounds like the plan of action went better than I would have ever expected," Dorothy said. "*Thank You*, Jesus!"

"Sounds like you've certainly covered the bases," Jacob added.

"Oh, but there's more: I've decided I need a break. There will be no moving forward with any of this until after the holidays, which will hopefully also give any negative buzz a chance to die down. I'm not even going to work on the gutting of the Taninger building for now. The beginning of the year we'll grind back into action, hold a town meeting to explain the strategies, gather input and implement a town-wide competition to name the mall. That made a huge dent in gaining a few converts, enough to convince Sam to shake my hand. I think George's verdict is still out, but Sam did seem calmed down, for which I'm grateful."

"Brilliant," Jacob said. "I should have you come to the East Coast to give my closing arguments."

"Oh, no. It's your mom you need to fly to Philadelphia. She's the brilliant one."

"I have a better idea," he said, his eyes twinkling as he put his arm around his mother and drew her close to his side. "How about she stays put in her Vine Street home and I come to her for that kind of action. See if I can do my part to help revitalize Pardon-Me-Ville, say maybe by investing in my own piece of real estate and taking over Rick Lawson's law practice."

Dorothy looked up at her son and did a double take. Katie looked puzzled. Josh, who had walked up with Shelby just prior to Jacob's statement, let out what could only be described as a war-whoop.

"Surely you don't mean to tell us, Jacob Henry Wetstra," Dorothy said, staring at her son, "that you're moving back here, do you?" The hopeful lilt in her voice revealed the sudden depth of her joy at the possibility.

"Not only do I mean to tell you, Mom, but I *am* telling you—with a few reservations, of course. Merry early Christmas," he said, giving her a peck on the cheek.

Josh let out another war-whoop which caught the attention of several people in the room, especially when he high-fived Jacob when Jacob lifted his head from kissing his mom.

"Oh, Jacob!" Dorothy's eyes were tearing up. She wanted to grab a bullhorn and tell the world that her first-born son would be moving back to town! She wanted to let everyone know they could quit worrying about their legal matters since undoubtedly the best attorney in the land (okay, she *was* his mom) would soon be there to help them. She wanted to squeeze him and thank him and. . . . "OH!"

"Now don't get too excited yet, Mom. I have to go back to Pennsylvania right after Christmas and it's uncertain how long it will take for me to handle things with my practice. Preliminary talks with my partner sound encouraging, but we're a long way from a deal."

"Have you talked to the Lawsons about this yet?" Katie asked, her cheeks suddenly reddening, the beginning of a hot flash revving itself up.

"Several times."

"What's all the hooten' and hollerin' about over here?" Doc asked.

"My Jacob is moving back to Partonville and taking over Rick's law practice," Dorothy all but sang.

"Now, Mom, that's just the tentative plan. Let's not get ahead of ourselves."

"Well, now, if that doesn't call for a cup of Christmas cheer from the punch bowl on the left, I don't know what does!" Doc said.

Word about the corner powwow, including the mini-mall naming competition, had already been circulating. But now Jacob's return spread through the party like wildfire. One of their own who had made good was coming back home!

Suddenly the sounds of Arthur Landers's Hohner harmonica could be heard playing "Happy Days Are Here Again," which he immediately followed with "Jingle Bells" to start everyone singing. It was the beginning of the annual songfest, one that would go on for the next forty minutes. Katie, whose body had cranked itself into a full-fledged hot flash by now, enjoyed the music but needed a breath of cool air. The house was warm with all these bodies, especially since they'd gathered close to sing. She wormed her way through the crowd, made her way to the front door and cracked it open. She stuck her head out and started taking deep, long breaths. As it turned out, she'd mindlessly moved herself right under the mistletoe. Jessica saw her there, she and Paul having visited the mistletoe twice already, Sarah Sue squished between them as they puckered up. "Look who's under the mistletoe," she said to Paul. Jacob overheard the comment and checked to see for himself.

Katie Durbin, under the mistletoe. Now there was something worth teasing her about. He looked around the room to see if anyone else had noticed other than Jessica, who had since become distracted by Sarah Sue's onslaught of crankiness. He overheard the Joys say they needed to get going before Sarah Sue let loose with a wail and intruded on the singing, and off they went upstairs to retrieve their coats. The rest of the crowd was gathered around Arthur, too busy singing and making merry to notice Katie's whereabouts.

Katie was unaware Jacob had stepped up behind her since she still had her head stuck outside. When she backed up to close the door, she stumbled right into him. She gasped, and he caught her by the arms, where he held her a moment before looking up, which caused her to do the same. "Mistletoe," he said, noticing her cheeks were flushed.

"Jessica's idea. She thought it would be fun."

"Hmm. What do you think?" he asked, releasing her arms.

"Honestly?"

"Honestly."

"Hokey. But I guess people have enjoyed it," she said, quickly sidestepping around Jacob to get out from under the awkward predicament.

Jacob turned to see where she was off to in such a hurry. She pressed her way through the songsters and disappeared into the kitchen. Then he caught his mother's eye. She'd obviously witnessed the encounter. She was wearing that mischievous twinkly-eyed look on her face, the one that said she knew something. She winked, then gestured for him to stay where he was as she quick-footed in his direction.

"What are you grinning at?" he asked when she arrived.

"Look who's under the mistletoe," she said, looking up, then giving him a smooch on the cheek. "Welcome back to Pardon-*Me*-Ville, son," she said with a merry laugh. "I have absolutely no doubt it's right where you belong."

THE END

A Note from the Author

♣ ♣ ♣

Writing this book was an ongoing adventure in serendipity. Never has the veil been thinner between fiction and Real Life. Never has the breath of transcendence blown me more freely and wholly into "the other"—or "the same," depending upon how you want to look at it. (Or, am I leading a parallel life with myself? Ah, a topic for a *different* kind of series, huh?)

Call this synergy between Real Life and Partonville what you like, but I call it blessing and wonder. What's a girl writer to do other than simply allow herself to get caught up in it and enjoy the ride?! (Swirl-swirl-swirl. Type-type-type.) To my ongoing amazement, it seemed like every time I was about to tackle a scene, something in my Real Life would "just happen" to feed straight into it.

For instance, one day I was writing away, eyes on the monitor, and when I looked out my window, a new dusting of snow blanketed the ground. YIKES! I was just about to write that! (Or *had* I typed it and *then* it snowed?) Or I'd be reading my local newspapers (la-la-la) and . . . OH! I can't believe it! I just wrote about this in Partonville yesterday!

I'm currently enjoying reading the "ride" of another author, but I'm also finding that some of her plotline is freaking me out! In her story, someone's odd aunt dies, an event that brings the protagonist to a small town. The attorney in this small town is a character and his office is on the second floor of a brick building. WAIT! That all happened in Partonville in 1999 when I was writing my first draft of *Dearest Dorothy, Are We There Yet?* Is there really only one story in Imaginationland? And do all the authors tap into it? Or, is it just that there are so many attorneys, who also happen to be characters, who handle cases in small towns where odd aunts die that we can't help but write about it? Or, are authors, by the very nature of their imaginations, *offing odd aunties*?

WHOA! It just occurred to me I *am* an odd auntie.

So . . . let's imagine *these* things in Partonville, Charlene: a young mother gets pregnant. Grief is hard. Mistletoe is enchanting. Memories bind us together. Friendships are grace in action. Vision and hope—along with a fair amount of bucks—drive progress. Love lurks and endures. Pets are a wonderful thing.

And so it goes in Real Life, too. Amen.

Charlene Ann Baumbich

www.welcometopartonville.com

charlene@welcometopartonville.com